BOY AT THE WINDOW

Visit us at www.boldstrokesbooks.com

BOY AT THE WINDOW

by

Lauren Melissa Ellzey

2022

ISBN 13: 978-1-63679-092-3

This Trade Paperback Original Is Published By
Bold Strokes Books, Inc.
P.O. Box 249
Valley Falls, NY 12185

First Edition: February 2022

Credits
Editors: Jenny Harmon and Cindy Cresap
Production Design: Susan Ramundo
Cover Design By Inkspiral Design

Acknowledgments

I would like to express my deepest and sincerest gratitude to all those who have guided and supported me along this journey. To Shanté and Lisa, I will never forget how the two of you read the first draft with such kindness and encouragement. To Patrick, for imparting all your cross-country wisdom. To my father, for his penchant for details and honest criticism of Chapter One. And last but not least, thank you to my partner, Bridget, for supporting me, every chapter along the way, always ready to listen, and ceaselessly asking me for an update on the story. *Boy at the Window* would never have existed without you.

"There could not have been a lovelier sight; but there was none to see it except a little boy who was staring in at the window. He had ecstasies innumerable that other children can never know; but he was looking through the window at the one joy from which he must be for ever barred."

—J. M. Barrie, *Peter Pan*

CHAPTER ONE

The door clicks open. Light spills from the hallway and across the bed. Daniel closes his eyes at the blinding intrusion. Even though his shoulder aches beneath his weight, he can't bring himself to uncurl from a fetal position. Midnight approaches, yet he hasn't slept a single minute. He loves the nighttime, when the clinic is finally quiet and his daydreams whirl for hours on end.

"Having trouble falling asleep tonight, Daniel?" asks the nurse in a sweet tone meant for six-year-olds, not sixteen-year-olds. "It must be hard to rest when you've only got two more nights here."

Daniel blinks. Rickety wheels squeak toward him. The shadowy shape of a portable vitals monitor settles beside the bed. As his eyes adjust to the new light, he makes out Mrs. Chaney's salt-and-pepper ponytail and wispy arms. Her scrubs brush together as she approaches. She kneels until their eyes meet, but Daniel widens his focus like a camera lens blurring a landscape.

"Sweetie, why don't you take a sleeping pill," she states without a hint of question. She leaves, only to return moments later with a small plastic cup of water and an even smaller paper cup that rattles.

"Sit up now," she says, but her arm already supports him up from the waist. She shakes the paper cup next to his hand. Daniel places the capsule on his tongue. She passes him the water cup. He swallows the pill. He doesn't need any help resuming his fetal position, his light brown hair brushing against the coarse hospital pillow.

"Good night, Daniel," she whispers as she wraps a blood pressure cuff around his forearm even though he's reclining. The familiar whir of pressurized air hums as Daniel shuts his eyes. Mrs. Chaney smells like ammonia, and he considers whether that might be the scent of fear. He pretends to be asleep for the nurse's benefit, but he isn't anywhere near tired. His daydreams call him to a world even better than sleep. He'll stay awake and go to Neverland.

As Mrs. Chaney's loafers pad out the door, Daniel's footfalls pound into the earth like ripened apples cast from heavy trees. He wishes he could lighten his steps, but he can't manage to run swiftly and softly at the same time. The cacophony of his comrades' retreat echoes through the forest. Neither bird nor squirrel makes a sound. All of nature keeps a sage silence. If the Lost Boys are fleeing, nothing good can be in pursuit.

Daniel spies a hollow trunk and takes shelter. He needs to catch his breath and conjure up a plan. This mission marks his third failed attempt to reclaim the Lost Boys' stolen treasure. Sure, the Lost Boys themselves had not-so-chivalrously nabbed the chest of golden sea stars from the merfolk, but Daniel always intended to return the gold. The people of the sea would much prefer it if the Lost Boys borrowed their treasure for a few weeks, over whatever the wicked pirates have planned. Pirates never return anything, except an eye for an eye.

"I can smell the rotten stench of your fear, boys!" shouts none other than the most deranged pirate of them all: Captain James Hook. The callous timbre of his sea-faring accent rekindles a sharp pain in Daniel's shoulder. A bloody crust stains the green fabric of his tunic where the captain's hook-for-a-hand grasped him just as he'd leapt from the pirate ship. While the pirate managed to tear through his skin, he failed to pull Daniel back aboard. Daniel can only hope that all his boys have been as fortunate.

"Come out, you cowardly rascal," Hook howls from a safe distance.

Daniel's ego sparks, then roars. Cowardly is the complete opposite of his character. He hates the word almost as much as *bedtime* or *boredom*.

Proudly, he exits the hollow and cups his mouth with his hand. "Chicka-chicka-roo!" he crows, calling the Lost Boys into position. From the trees, they will wage war. If Hook wants a fight, he'll have to pay the price.

❖

When the door opens again, sunshine peeks from the edges of the drawn curtains. Daniel struggles to open his eyes. At some point in the night, the sleeping pill must have overpowered him. He summons up the last remnants of his daydream before he fell into unconsciousness. The Lost Boys were rounding up for a doomed battle against the pirates.

"Good morning, Daniel," Mrs. Chaney says, but she might as well be talking to the walls. "Believe it or not, I'm still here. Ms. McKinley is running a bit late, so my shift has gone longer than expected."

After she reaches to secure the blood pressure cuff, she casually checks Daniel's blemishless wrists. The same wrists that Captain Hook has bound twice-over with rope. A storm brews in the blackening clouds as the pirates lug the captured Lost Boys back to their ship. Once aboard, Daniel and the Lost Boys are left on deck, exposed to the brutal pelt of frigid rain. While his comrades have lost all hope, Daniel slips his trusty sword from his waistband. The sharp blade slices through his binds.

"Captain James Hook!" he shouts tauntingly.

When Hook bursts onto the deck, Daniel lets out a mocking peal of laughter. In no time, he and the pirate captain are tangled hook-to-sword. All the while, the storm rages about them. The pirate ship takes on too much water, old wooden boards groaning as the vessel careens wildly. Lightning flashes, illuminating Hook's toothy scowl, but Daniel glimpses Tinker Bell above the pirate's shoulder. A mischievous grin flickers on her incandescent features, signaling to Daniel that all is not lost.

Mrs. Chaney moves toward the door, but then turns back toward Daniel. "Are you still tired, sweetie?" she asks.

The sleeping pill maintains a firm grip on Daniel's limbs. From his bed, he watches as Mrs. Chaney heads to the window. She pulls the curtains back, unleashing a glorious waterfall of Southern California sunlight into the room. So, the thunderstorm has passed. Captain Hook and Daniel gaze in awe as a rainbow embraces the sky. Tinker Bell takes advantage of the distraction to tie Hook's boot laces together. Daniel never misses a beat, though, and he reinitiates the duel. When Hook lunges forward to parry Daniel's sword, he loses his balance and plummets to the ship's deck. Both Daniel and Tink erupt in triumphant laughter. From behind a mast, the Lost Boys cry out in victory before charging the captain's quarters.

"The golden sea stars are ours once more!" Daniel tries to shout, but his voice cracks and withers, laced with sleeping medication.

After a sigh, Mrs. Chaney continues, "Breakfast is ready in fifteen. Wash up and change, and then why don't you come meet us in the cafeteria?"

In the three weeks since he arrived at Mercy Mental Health Hospital, Daniel has learned to recognize the orders concealed within the nurses' questions. Or has it been four weeks? Or two months? How many adventures has he undertaken with the Lost Boys?

When Mrs. Chaney withdraws behind his closed door, Daniel begins the struggle to rise. His arms are weary from swordplay, but he knows that an unwashed face smacks of barbaric hygiene. His legs tremble under his weight. Still, he drags his feet against the cold tile of the tiny bathroom. Cheap hospital soap and warm water dry out his skin, so he rubs a sheen of lotion on his chin and cheeks. The supposedly scent-free cream wafts into his nose with the sting of disinfectant.

After swiping a toothbrush across his teeth and tongue, he stumbles to the dresser. Trading plain blue pajamas for a plain gray T-shirt and sweatpants feels tediously unnecessary, but the hospital attendants frown upon pajamas in the cafeteria. As he fits his feet into slippers, he realizes that he's forgotten to fix his hair. A second visit to the bathroom has him combing his fingers through the messy brown waves that fall doggishly to his eyebrows. He catches his own reflected gaze. The world seems to slow around him.

There, in the mirror, a boy stares back at him, and even though Daniel knows that it's his own reflection, he barely recognizes the pale, lifeless figure. Daniel cautiously lifts a hand to knock on the glass, and the boy in the mirror follows. He and his reflection lower their fists in tandem. As a cold sweat breaks out across Daniel's forehead and palms, his throat pulses in time with his thrashing heart. He takes a step back. The reflection reciprocates. Daniel ducks under the cover of the sink, burying his head in his knees.

"That's not me," he whispers, because as much as he recognized himself in the mirror, he is sure that who he saw there is an imposter. Carefully, he crawls out of the bathroom and into the bedroom. He can hear voices calling to one another in the hallway. Someone walks by, their shadow filling the crack between the door and hardwood floor, muttering, "If it's pancakes or cereal again, I'm gonna be a problem."

Daniel sucks in a breath. It's time for breakfast. He has to stand up and press on through the hallway to the cafeteria. There is little choice in the matter. After all, breakfast is synonymous with morning medications. The one time he skipped his meds, his brain haloed into a cyclone of nausea and jitters. His hand finds the doorknob, and he intentionally avoids the distorted reflection in its shiny brass.

Somehow, the corridor seems bare even with its warm coffee walls and uniformly hung paintings of plants. He tarries in the hall in front of a watercolor of a white, long-stemmed daisy. Images of neon lilies and glowing tulips flash through Daniel's mind. Tink could sprinkle the daisy's plain petals with fairy dust and make the whole flower gold.

The savory aroma of sizzling sausage refocuses Daniel. When he finally enters the cafeteria, the rumble and motion of a dozen chattering bodies engulfs him. The buzz of the coffee machine tempts him, but whatever medicine he's been ingesting has killed all the positive effects of caffeine, so he heads straight to the food counter.

"Well, hello there, Mr. Daniel Kim!" says an elderly man who knows his name despite the fact that Daniel can't place his face. "What'll it be today? We got sausage and biscuits or veggie omelets the size of watermelons."

Neither sounds appetizing. He points to the fluffy yellow omelet, which is served to him on a tray alongside a sickly-sweet lump of fruit cocktail. After filling a reusable plastic cup with orange juice from concentrate, he assesses the seating situation. Most of the other teenage patients sit in groups of three, and even though the tables fit four, Daniel chooses a spot by himself. It's quieter alone, the empty chairs leaving no space for questions.

"Catch!" shouts a burly boy that looks about Daniel's age, although he's half Daniel's height and twice his girth. Daniel has seen his face for some days now but never learned his name.

A wadded-up paper napkin flies through the air and into the hand of a preteen with an undercut. "Yuck!" she yelps and tosses the paper ball to a lanky Goth boy, who throws it to another boy, who is no longer just a normal teen in plain clothes but suited up in a Lost Boy's raccoon skin. The raccoon boy laughs madly and passes a priceless Neverland sea star to a Lost Girl in fox furs.

"Go long!" she yells, her fox tail wagging as the star sails toward Daniel. He jumps to attention, deftly catching the prize in his right hand. Surveying his comrades, he weighs whether to aim the star at a new, lemur-clad recruit or his favorite pal, Tootles.

A whistle pierces their ears, effectively halting the game. Ms. McKinley looms in the doorway, two fingers against her lips. "This is breakfast," she scolds them, "not daily exercise. Settle down. It's time for meds."

As though released by her punitive proclamation, two more sure-footed nurses enter the cafeteria, holding red trays lined with paper cups. Daniel sinks into his chair. The napkin still rests in his fist, but when he opens the crumpled paper, he cringes at the remains of a rumpled spider. Sighing, he drops the napkin on his breakfast tray. He can't help but sympathize with the crumpled pixie. He will need to chide the Lost Boys for their mistreatment of one of Neverland's beloved creatures. Perhaps they should schedule a proper burial.

"Here you are, Daniel." Ms. McKinley sets a paper cup next to his orange juice. "I missed you this morning. How did you sleep?" Daniel shrugs, which seems to satisfy her. He tips the three pills into his palm, casts them onto the back of his tongue, and forces them down with a swig of juice. Ms. McKinley marches to the next patient with only the slightest glance. Daniel doesn't have a reputation for defiance. Close-mouthed and lethargic are his labels, at least outside of Neverland.

Chapter Two

While Daniel can't pinpoint the specific day of the week, he knows therapy sessions typically occur somewhere between Monday and Friday. So, when Ms. McKinley escorts him to Dr. Greene's office, he makes a mental note that he is living through a weekday.

The office is an extension of the hallways, with caramel walls and nature art, but Dr. Greene maintains a well-stocked bookcase of medical and psychiatric texts. His desk is pristine, adorned with even piles of paperwork, crisp manila folders, and a spotless Tiffany lamp. An empty accent table rests beneath the windowpane.

Dr. Greene himself stands at a formidable height and wears a navy jacket-and-pants set beneath a white coat. A strained smile pulls up the deep brown skin along his high cheekbones as he welcomes Daniel to the embroidered armchair by the window. The psychiatrist prefers his swivel desk chair, which he guides away from his desk and toward Daniel.

Once Ms. McKinley shuts the door, Dr. Greene takes out a deck of playing cards from his coat pocket. "What should we play today?" he asks.

Daniel shakes his head. Some days he gives in to the psychiatrist's penchant for games, but not today. He would rather sit quietly through Dr. Greene's examination.

"That's all right," he replies, pocketing the deck. "It's our last inpatient meeting, so we have a lot to discuss anyway. How are you feeling today?"

"Awake," he mutters, because he can't think of another way to express his current state.

The psychiatrist nods. His hands are folded in his lap. Daniel wonders how he keeps track of their sessions without a notebook or clipboard.

"Have you been experiencing any feelings outside of your body today? Or that your surroundings aren't real?" Dr. Greene asks.

Daniel presses his lips together as he considers the question. "I'm still figuring out what's real and what isn't." He stops, already feeling a tug to leave his body. A part of him wants to let go, to set his mind free and watch himself and Dr. Greene from somewhere higher up—maybe tucked on the top of the bookshelf or floating near the air vent.

"That's good," the psychiatrist replies serenely. "When you first arrived here, you weren't sure that this hospital or any of us in it were real. You seem to be balancing that perspective. Am I more real to you now?"

"I know you're real."

After a moment of hesitation, Dr. Greene presses, "What else is real?"

"The nurses, the other patients, the dead spider."

Dr. Greene's mouth quirks. "What spider?"

"The Lost Boys were playing catch with it in the cafeteria, throwing it around in a napkin. I played, too," Daniel adds, a little surprised that he had engaged at all.

"The Lost Boys?"

Daniel sighs. "That's what I call them, but I really just mean the other patients. They were acting like the Lost Boys."

Dr. Greene blinks thoughtfully, clearly considering an appropriate response. "Thank you for explaining, Daniel. Only three weeks ago, you wouldn't speak at all. Your voice is a powerful tool."

Reflexively, Daniel touches his throat. There was a time when he spoke freely, completely unaware of the power of his own voice. His Adam's apple bobs as he swallows. A blurry memory reminds him that words can fail. Daniel shakes his head, dismissing the recollection before it can set in. He focuses on his feet instead, toes buried in his slippers. Still, his legs and arms and shoulders start to slip away. Maybe this office isn't an office at all. He could be anywhere.

"Daniel, where are you right now?" Dr. Greene inquires.

Daniel sucks in a breath. An analog clock ticks on the wall, like a crocodile in patient pursuit. He's in the ocean beside the crocodile, but the beast isn't interested in him. Just yards away, the pirate ship looms on the open sea. A black flag, the Jolly Roger, rises to full mast. Beneath the waving sails, a shadow emerges. Even from this distance, Daniel recognizes the long, lean figure topped with a proud feather. After losing the sea stars, Captain Hook will renew his vow for vengeance. A pirate never relents.

A snap like cracking bones startles Daniel, hoisting him from the waters and onto the office's dry ground. Sweat coats his temples. Dr. Greene's hand still hovers midair, thumb and forefinger at ready.

"I'm at Mercy Hospital," Daniel mumbles.

"Yes, that's right, and where were you just now?"

"The cafeteria," he says.

Dr. Greene drums his fingers against the armrest of his chair, then opens his mouth, but holds back, withdrawing a question left unvoiced.

"And now, here you are with me," he finally says. "But tomorrow will be different. Do you remember why?" When Daniel shrugs, the doctor continues, "Your parents believe you're ready to return home. While my opinion may differ somewhat, you have been here for three weeks, and we can't keep you any longer without your parents' permission. Your third year of high school starts soon, so your parents want you to readjust at home for a week before going back to school life. Perhaps returning to familiar settings will help keep you grounded."

Daniel absorbs the information, half-certain he has heard it all before. A warm longing hugs his chest at the thought of sleeping in his ordinary bed beside his everyday view of the sweetgum tree outside the bay window in the room he's known since birth.

"I am very concerned for you, though," Dr. Greene admits with the casualness of someone accustomed to sharing and hearing bad news. "You seem to still be feeling depressed and anxious, and disconnected from those around you, and these feelings are perhaps what is causing your persistent daydreaming. While we've been able to talk some here, the nurses have told me that you keep mostly to yourself and haven't talked much with either your peers or the staff. And also, Daniel, we still haven't spoken much about the event that led you to our hospital, or at least, you haven't felt able to open up to me about it."

The man leans forward despite the insurmountable distance between them. "So, Daniel, I have to ask, are you still contemplating taking your own life?"

Daniel recalls the scratching roof shingles beneath his bare feet, the midnight breeze that tousled his hair, the sky bright with stars and a crescent smile. His family's cerulean pool glowed like a nightlight beside the expansive porch and trimmed shrubberies. Daniel spread his arms like wings. What qualified as a happy thought? He conjured the blissful image of Neverland. *"To die will be an awfully big adventure,"* he recited to an invisible audience.

"I don't want to die," Daniel tells Dr. Greene. I want to fly, he doesn't say.

The psychiatrist nods solemnly. "Are you considering hurting yourself?"

"I don't want to hurt myself."

Dr. Greene's armrest drumming resumes, matching the clock's cadence. "That's good, Daniel. All the same, we'll keep the SSRI and the mood stabilizer. I'll be sure to leave instructions for your family."

Daniel readies himself to leave, but the psychiatrist continues, "But, Daniel, I'm worried that it will be challenging and frightening for you to return home and confront the memories of the event that brought you to the hospital. We'll continue to meet twice a week, and hopefully your parents will begin family therapy. We need to talk more about this and make plans for how you will deal with your feelings about your parents, the events that led to your suicide attempt, and your concerns as you return to school. Your parents told me that you'll be going to a new high school. While a change like this can be a lot, it's also an opportunity. A chance at a fresh start. You can make healthy friends, and build upon this foundation we've laid as you grow into the courageous young man we both know you already are and can continue to be. The past affects us all, but the future is our choice."

Daniel watches as the boy in the armchair listens to the psychiatrist's advice. From his safe place atop the bookcase, he thinks, *what a sorry-looking kid.*

❖

Fraternizing in the common room after dinner is strongly encouraged by Mercy's staff. So even on his final night in the hospital, Daniel whiles away a few hours at an isolated table as far from the TV as he can manage. Some patients stretch their legs from the couch to the rickety coffee table, while others cram into recliners and around board games.

The TV flickers from cutscenes to commercials, stabbing Daniel's tired eyes. He lazily presses his cheek against the cool, empty table as an advertisement for sugary cereal plays on the screen: a toddler unsuccessfully spoons milky flakes into her mouth before she accidentally flips her entire bowl onto both the floor and the family dog. A laughing mother enters, serving another full bowl for the little girl, whose teary expression is immediately replaced with a gap-toothed grin.

Daniel sighs, wondering if there are boxes of granola at home. He thumbs through his memories of the countless bowls he Hoovered as a child, but he can't recall a time when his mother prepared his breakfast.

The pitter-patter of nurse's loafers enters the common room. Mrs. Chaney, back for her night shift, carries a red tray in her spindly arms. Daniel averts his eyes. After his evening pills at dinner, he isn't required to take any additional nighttime medication, excluding the occasional sleeping pill. So, Mrs. Chaney delivers a set of paper cups and water to the others but then stops by Daniel's table.

"Since it's Daniel's last day with us," she announces, "it's his turn to pick tonight's movie."

"Mr. Catatonic is going home?" another patient asks. "Let me guess, he's gonna pick *Peter Pan*. He picked that on his last turn, and the turn before that, too."

Muffled laughter tugs at Daniel's ears. He shuts his eyes, just as Tinker Bell alights upon his shoulder. Her giggles are sweet, a little prankish, but not at all unkind. Daniel treks toward Hangman's Tree, eager to rest after his eerie encounter with Hook and the pirate flag. He will check on the Lost Boys, bind any cuts or bruises, then crawl into his favorite hammock for a well-earned respite.

"That's enough, all of you," Ms. Chaney says with a voice like crushed ice. "Need I remind you that the common room is a privilege. You can accept Daniel's movie choice or spend the evening alone in your room."

That effectively halts the complaints. With the arrival of silence, Daniel finally speaks up. "I want to watch *Peter Pan*," he tells the nurse, who shoots a scowl at the other patients, promising a fair trade of hellfire for any misbehavior.

As everyone settles into their seats, Mrs. Chaney retrieves the film from the entertainment shelf and sets it into the disc player. The lamps dim, leaving just enough light to monitor for foul play.

The exhilarating strings of the opening theme beckon Daniel from the table. The couches and chairs surrounding the TV are at full capacity, but he doesn't mind. He arranges himself on the floor and squeezes his knees to his chest, attention firmly fixed to the melodic opening credits.

A tingling anticipation curls his fingers around his knees—his body solid, his mind clear. With a smile, he repeats the familiar first line of the beloved story, *"All children, except one, grow up."*

CHAPTER THREE

The car smells of cinnamon, leather, and his father's cigarettes, but for now both of Sung-Min's hands brace the steering wheel. Monica glances at Daniel repeatedly through the rearview mirror. Her dark blond hair falls resplendently past her shoulders, her frozen features betraying neither age nor emotion. All is quiet during the drive. Daniel silently wishes Nana could have signed his release forms.

Thankfully, his neighborhood comes into view. Two- and three-story brick stone residences punctuate a winding road. Expansive yards and automated gates separate the elegant structures, competing against each other for best-landscaped lawn or most ornate fencing. No children grace the sidewalks, all preferring the secret paradises of their backyards. Daniel has visited a few of these monolithic homesteads for elementary birthday celebrations or farewell parties. The embellished staircases and manicured gardens cultivated the children's vivid imaginations until puberty struck. Suddenly, they gave up hide-and-seek and stick fights for hamburger joints or surreptitious sips from wine bottles—stolen from their parents' cellars—in the back seats of the older teens' BMWs.

Once Sung-Min reaches for the remote to the household gate, Daniel accepts the reality that he has come home. Three stories of slate stone rest beneath a slightly sloping attic, all peeking from behind an expertly planted plot of pine and sweetgum trees. The gray garage door rises, and the sun gives way to artificially lit darkness.

"Come along, Daniel," Monica says as the car doors open and close. He follows his parents up the double steps that lead inside. Shoes slide off and are stacked neatly upon a rack.

Nothing has changed. The marble floor greets Daniel's socked feet with an unwelcome chill. His slippers are nowhere in sight, perhaps tucked away in his closet upstairs. It would be just like Sung-Min to make sure that unneeded items are put out of sight.

As they proceed into the pristine kitchen, Nana bustles in, wiping damp hands on her apron. Nana is a good head taller than Daniel's decent height. The smells of organic glass cleaner and citrus detergent swirl about her.

"There he is!" Her blue eyes crumple with a wide smile as she blankets Daniel in her muscular arms. "Welcome home. How I've missed you!"

Her wiry brown hair tickles Daniel's neck. Instead of replying, he simply melts into his nanny's warmth. As Daniel has grown, her role has switched from childcare to housekeeper, but no one denies that the sturdy woman was the one to teach Daniel to tie his shoes and say, "Please," and "Thank you."

Monica waves a rattling paper bag toward Nana. "There are instructions inside," she explains. "If you could make sure he takes everything as prescribed—"

Nana releases Daniel, and the cold returns to his toes. "Of course," she says.

"Thank you, and, Daniel, why don't you unpack your duffel bag? Your father and I have a few things to discuss in the parlor."

One at a time, his parents gently touch his shoulder before departing. Once they're out of sight, he dumps the black bag at his feet. Nana busies herself with the medicines, chatting the whole time.

"This house has been too quiet without you. You know how your parents are—always at their head office or working upstairs on their projects—if they're not traveling to some exotic location for another marketing opportunity. Sometimes, I even found myself making breakfast for you instead of just myself. These rooms are much brighter with you in them."

Daniel takes a seat at the bar, observing the orange translucent containers that Nana lines up along the counter. Four vessels in total. One SSRI, one mood stabilizer. The third might be sleeping pills, but Daniel can't discern the writing on the fourth.

"What's that?" he asks, pointing to the bottle that holds a dozen perfect, tiny circles.

Nana lifts the container to her squinted eyes. "Take one tablet by mouth as needed," she reads before shuffling through the leaflet of printed instructions. "Lorazepam is the name. Says here that you might take it for anxiety or panic attacks, but only if it's an all-of-a sudden kind of thing. I suspect it can calm you down really fast, so you don't do anything irrational that you might regret later on, like hurting yourself."

Like jumping off the roof, Daniel thinks, or as Dr. Greene stated so eloquently, "Taking your own life."

"I don't have to take the Lorazepam every day?" he asks.

"No, just when you feel extra anxious. This other one you take when you can't sleep. These other two—"

"Two pills twice daily, one pill twice daily."

Nana nods, her brown hair flopping like dog ears. She stores the containers in a cabinet full of diet supplements and over-the-counter anti-inflammatories. From an adjacent cabinet, she unearths a packet of dried mango. Pressing the packet into Daniel's palm, she dusts the crown of his head with a kiss.

"I hid the last one from your father last night, so it'd be here when you got back. Now, you can eat this while watching me make lunch, or you can listen to your mother and unpack your luggage."

He crinkles the mango, weighing his options. The promise of his window-view lures him to mind Monica. As he collects his duffel bag, he pauses, turning once more to Nana.

"Thank you for the mango," he says and heads toward the hall.

"Hold on, Daniel." Nana paws purposefully into a drawer of organized food storage containers. After fetching a tiny glass cylinder, she twists the lid off his newest medicine and taps out a single white tablet. She seals the pill tight and hands it to Daniel like a vial of priceless pixie dust.

"Better put this in your nightstand. You never know when the teeny thing could come in handy."

The rustle and clinks of cooking follow Daniel into the foyer. Fresh-cut flowers spill from vases on tables and vases on the floor. The scent of living water follows him past the closed double doors of the parlor. He skirts around the sun-drenched living room, heading to the staircase. The banister winds around a lengthy art deco chandelier. He scans the second floor, reserved for his parents' separate bedrooms and offices. Climbing to the third landing, he passes beneath the attic's ceiling entrance and pointedly avoids the secured entryway to Nana's private quarters.

The sight of her closed door reminds him that as early as his feet could whisk him into mischief, Daniel's parents had admonished him for knocking on Nana's door. If her door was open, he could pad inside, but knocking was strictly prohibited. This arrangement would have gone as planned if not for childhood nightmares. The bad dreams occurred rarely, but whenever an especially frightening nightmare interrupted his sleep, he wailed. Too confused to call for Nana or venture downstairs and choose between Monica and Sung-Min, he paced the hall. Eventually, Nana started leaving the door cracked, so he could scramble past the threshold and into her bed. Even then, if Nana ever caught a cold or endured an especially troublesome day, Daniel found himself friendless in the night. As he grew older and learned to handle nightmares on his own, her quarters became permanently off-limits.

Daniel understands why Nana needs her privacy. Sometimes, the Lost Boys drive him crazy with their needs and demands. Even as the most rambunctious member of this unruly gang, he often seeks the solitude of forest strolls. Even now, the Twins are shoving each other, and Tootles shouts, "Who ate my jerky! I'd saved that for later!"

Daniel steals away like a reticent deer, up the tunnel leading away from Hangman's Tree. He breaks the surface, breathing in fresh, open air. Hurrying into the woods, he relishes their quiet shade.

The sweetgum tree outside Daniel's bedroom window waves a breeze-filled hello. Daniel deposits his bag on his mattress, then returns the tree's gesture. He has to stifle the urge to clamber onto the slanted rooftop—his mother's office beneath—and over to the rustling leaves. Lunch is due soon.

By the time he's unpacked the few clothes his parents had delivered to Mercy, he's rallied downstairs by Sung-Min's distant call: "Food is ready, Daniel!"

The dining table seats eight, so Daniel and his parents crowd into the half nearer the window. The crystal blue pool winks at them from the backyard. Plates of salad, grilled chicken, and tender rice steam gently before them. The family artfully spread cloth napkins into their laps and cut into their first bites.

"All this time you've been gone," Sung-Min begins after stalling a spoonful of rice above his plate, "your mother and I have been out as well. We're very close to securing a partnership with a Singaporean firm that admires our graphic design. We could be building their online platform, as well as several advertising templates. It is imperative that we make one more lasting impression on them to seal the deal."

He pauses to take a long draft of water. Monica seizes the opportunity to add, "You'll be busy this week anyway, Daniel. What with readjusting and preparing for your first year at Cranbrook Preparatory, you'll have so much to do that you'll hardly notice we're gone."

Daniel spears a tomato with his fork. The juice sprays across the lettuce, gushing seeds and pulp. Piecing together his parents' vague conversation, he realizes a family trip to Singapore is on the horizon—minus their only son. He traveled to Singapore once, when he was in elementary school, with a suitcase full of summer shorts and sunscreen. Apparently, Singapore is very hot and humid. All he recalls is the flat-screen TV in the hotel suite.

"Cranbrook Prep is an exemplary school, basically just down the street," Sung-Min explains as though facing an inquiring press conference. "We would have sent you there before if not for our connections with Cambry's board of trustees. Some of the families in this neighborhood choose Cranbrook over Cambry."

"A fresh start is what you need. We don't want a repeat of last semester."

"Especially after the accident with the pool."

"Yes." Monica pauses thoughtfully, her flushed lips pursed with careful words. "While we're gone, we expect you to behave less recklessly. Jumping into the pool from the roof might seem like a fun thing to brag about to your friends, Daniel, but you truly gave everyone, especially Nana, a real scare. And the note you wrote displayed a clear lack of maturity. Jokes about flying away to Neverland right before you acted so irrationally. The way the doctors perceived your actions was so embarrassing, and then we were all forced to go along with the psychiatrists' recommendations."

Monica's excuses settle uncomfortably in Daniel's ears. Risky teen behavior probably sat better with nosy neighbors than attempted suicide.

Sung-Min slices his chicken breast in half. "Besides, Dr. Greene is among the best in his field in Orange County. He seems to have taken all the appropriate precautionary measures. All of your bruises and that nasty gash on your cheek have healed. No damage done."

Daniel touches the sensitive skin on his left cheekbone. A pocked scar dips inward. The pool seemed like a painless way to land his final fall. Too painless in the end. The water cushioned gravity enough to save his life, even if he almost drowned after losing consciousness from the impact. Daniel had hoped to fly to Neverland. Instead, Nana fished him from the deep end in an adrenaline-fueled frenzy and delivered CPR, all while the ambulance sped to the night-struck neighborhood.

"We'll only be a phone call or an email away," Monica coos over her wine glass, "and you're old enough now that you don't really need your parents to hold your hand on your first day."

Running water fills the silence as Nana washes up the pots and pans. Monica and Sung-Min stare at Daniel, eagerly awaiting a vindicating response.

"I'll be fine," he says before crushing another slice of tomato between his teeth.

CHAPTER FOUR

A gentle knock pulls Daniel out of a restless slumber. Out of habit, he lifts his arm for a blood pressure cuff, but then he takes in his green and brown patterned comforter, the old white lamp on the plain nightstand, the soft white walls. Sunlight streams in from the bay window, casting starry shadows from the sweetgum leaves outside. He needs to take a trip to Mermaid's Lagoon and return the sea stars soon, but each day in Neverland is so exciting that he can hardly remember to finish an adventure before heading out on the next one.

The knock persists. "Come in," Daniel calls, but he has to say it twice before the frog in his throat clears.

Nana creeps in, holding a small saucer and glass of water. A real glass—no plastic or paper—but he immediately understands what's to come. Raising himself against the headboard, he takes three pills at once, barely sipping any water to push them into his system.

Nana sits on the edge of his mattress and pats his shins like she might coax a testy cat. "How did you sleep? Did you wind up getting any sleep medicine?"

Daniel shakes his head. About three hours into insomnia, he considered climbing down the three flights to the kitchen but decided not to bother. Instead, he spent quality time with the Lost Boys, hunting sparrows for a celebratory feast. They roasted the birds over an open fire, bellies growling, but he must have fallen asleep before the actual meal, just as Slightly started boasting about his memories of his life before Neverland.

"I've still got it all up here." Slightly tapped his skull for emphasis. "Give me a few days, and I bet if I cared to try hard enough, I could remember my own mother's face."

"Where's Mrs. Darling?" Daniel says aloud, mind caught between roast sparrows and flights to Singapore.

Nana straightens her apron. "I take it you mean your mom, and not the mother in *Peter Pan*. She and your dad left before the sun came up. Their plane boarded around five a.m."

Daniel tries to imagine other families in his neighborhood. The mothers who drive SUVs instead of two-door cars. The fathers tossing footballs from the front porch to their sons headed to practice. Based on the stories his old friends shared about helicopter parents and vacations to Italy, he guesses that a business trip the day after his discharge is not typical. He sighs and runs a hand through his tangled hair. Comparing his home life from before and after Mercy Hospital, it seems the only difference is an increase in medicine bottles.

What did he expect, that Monica and Sung-Min would cancel all their priorities to sit all together on the living room couch, snacking on popcorn and watching cable TV?

In fact, Daniel hadn't expected to still be alive.

"I've got rice porridge simmering on the stove," Nana murmurs with a smile that doesn't reach her eyes. Porridge is sick food. Sad food.

"Actually, Nana, I've really missed your smoothies and eggs on toast."

"Is that so?" She chuckles, clearly pleased. "Then, I'll save the porridge for later. Maybe we can dress it up for lunch. Well now, I need to peel the fruit, and I can even get out the juicer for a fresh smoothie base. I bet those mangoes are ripe, too."

"Sounds good, Nana," Daniel says in earnest.

Nana stands toward the doorway, hands on her hips in determination. Despite her age, her arms are strong from years of housework. Daniel was unconscious when she rescued him from the pool, and just thinking about her effort stings his sinuses with the threat of tears. So, he breathes deeply, like Dr. Greene taught him, even though he's unsure if deep breathing is supposed to be used in this kind of situation.

By the time Nana looks back at Daniel, he's gotten himself under control.

"Go on and get dressed. Even better, why don't you go for a promenade around the neighborhood?" Daniel smiles at her use of words like *promenade*. "Your doctor left instructions that you get some light exercise every day. Breakfast will be ready by the time you get back."

When she leaves, Daniel swings his legs over the side of the bed. He isn't thrilled at the idea of an early outing, but the fresh air can't hurt him. He was accustomed to the nurses' heavily suggested walks in Mercy's tiny quadrangle that passed for a courtyard. Besides, his joints feel knotted from tossing and turning all night. A trip around the block might loosen him up.

After switching his white pajamas for black sweats and a T-shirt, he digs a pair of gray sneakers from his shoe rack. In a flash, he unlatches the front door, slides his feet into the shoes, and exits the lawn from the pedestrian gate. The winding street is empty. Kids sleep in. Parents have already left for work. Daniel hits the sidewalk to nowhere in particular.

The vacancy of the road presses into his skin. A golden sun spills from thick clouds, reflecting off solar panels and streetlamps. Daniel can sense his soul escaping, hanging in the clouds, scrutinizing the boy that walks alone. He ambles forward, perhaps the only one in the world. He wonders how the boy can know he's really alive. A pulse, a thought, a working pair of lungs? What's the difference between this boy and the Lost Boys? If this boy is alive, how about the Lost Boys? Or Captain Hook?

The pirate appears from behind a pine tree, interrupting the gang's sparrow dinner. "You're surrounded," he declares as his vicious crew takes formation throughout the woods. Daniel should have anticipated an ambush and prepared the boys. Now, all he can do is shout, "Run!"

Daniel's feet pound into the earth. His body knows this action well—a choreography rehearsed for years. He races down the sidewalk, Hook's fevered pants in hot pursuit. Daniel steps easily into practiced inhales through the nose, exhales from the mouth. His limbs glide beneath him. Running is the closest thing to flying on two feet. He rounds a corner, bending through a cul-de-sac, and flees toward home. As endorphins flood his veins, he laughs. Freedom buzzes from his fingers to his toes. This euphoria, forgotten in the hospital, abandoned in his last semester of school, saturates every muscle. The overwhelming bliss harkens back to years of cross-country and track training, to a time when he reveled in team sports and camaraderie.

In an instant, the chase concludes at the safety of his homestead. Daniel catches his breath at the gate, then stumbles into the yard. His legs wobble, yet his mind begs for another lap. Still, breakfast is probably ready, so he settles for a brisk cool down around the front lawn. On the porch, he eases into a few simple stretches. Sweat gathers in the dips of his collarbones. His heartbeat slows, and he shakes out his damp hair.

For a moment, everything faded away—no more hospitals or pills, no more airplanes. Even Captain Hook disappeared. Now, he readies himself for closed doors and marble floors. Nana waits for him with a full plate of eggs and toast. He isn't hungry, but he'll eat, and she might even join him at the table. That's something, right? That's better than no one, or nothing.

CHAPTER FIVE

L unch on the first day of school is supposed to be a time of chatter and jokes and swapping summer vacation stories, but Daniel finds himself in a secluded office, facing a middle-aged man with a few nicks on his shaven jaw.

"Thank you for coming, Daniel," he says. His desk is littered with paper-clipped documents, jars full of pens, miniature staplers, and Post-its. In the center of the chaos rests an orange folder with *Daniel Kim* printed on the cover.

"Don't worry. I won't take up your entire lunch period. We just need to go over the particulars of your accommodations. I assume your parents told you about today's 504 Plan briefing."

Daniel nods, which is a lie. He never received accommodations at Cambry. That he suddenly requires some sort of special education is news to him, but he dry swallows and tries to appear collected. He doesn't enjoy being surprised by important details of his life.

The man extends a chapped hand, which Daniel accepts weakly, and mutters something about his role at Cranbrook. He flashes the folder in front of Daniel's eyes before adding, "This folder contains your copy of the 504 Plan. Usually, I give it to parents, but since yours aren't able to be here today, I trust you'll make sure it gets to them."

He cracks open the file and pulls out a paper that reads, "Section 504: Individual Accommodation Plan (IAP)." Daniel sees his name, date of birth, and grade level. Checkboxes and subsections cram the rest of the sheet.

"As indicated by your doctor, this IAP is for medical reasons only. In fact, I saw your transcripts from Cambry and your junior high. Up until last year, you were a straight A student. I'm sure with these accommodations, we can meet your medical needs and get your GPA back up."

Daniel breezed through middle school and freshman year. After all, his parents had always set high standards for his academic and extracurricular activities. When sophomore year came around though, he stopped focusing. Class lessons, homework, sports—everything dissolved like color into bleach. The summer between his first two years of high school delivered him to the isle of Neverland, away from stress and peer pressure and a flowery bedsheet left forgotten millions of stars away.

"Sorry I'm late!" A tall man in his late twenties bursts into the office. His dark brown hair parts perfectly at the top of a symmetrical face, which is flushed with haste and embarrassment. "There was a disaster with one of the printers. I didn't know that a paper jam could get that bad."

The man merely laughs at some apparent inside joke. "We're just about to go over the details of Daniel's plan."

The tall man throws himself in the chair beside Daniel and flashes him a warmhearted smile. "I'm Mr. Bartel, the school librarian. We'll be seeing a lot of each other, I expect."

"Nice to meet you," Daniel says politely. Mr. Bartel doesn't look anything like the quintessential librarian. With his perfectly straight teeth and clean-cut attire, he could have rushed here from a catalog shoot as opposed to a library. Daniel can't figure out why the librarian needs to attend a meeting about his academic supports.

The other man redirects their attention to the orange folder. He points to various clumps of text and checkmarks, rambling words like diagnosis and medications, photocopied class notes, and provisional class breaks. When he mentions extended testing time, Mr. Bartel perks up.

"That's where I come in," the librarian explains. "There are some semi-soundproofed rooms in the library. Students use them for a variety of reasons, but they'll always be available to you for test taking, and if you need a break, you're more than welcome in the library. I always try to introduce myself to the students with accommodations before their first visit. It helps take the edge off the new routine."

"Thank you," Daniel mutters, because no other phrase seems appropriate. The two men are obviously skilled in friendliness. Even so, a wave of nausea swirls in Daniel's gut. The amount of information thrown at him feels overwhelming. He just wants to go to classes like any other student, take tests, and complete class work.

The man with the orange folder scratches at the cuts on his chin. "All in all, this should really give you the support to bring those grades up and prepare you for college applications next year. Of course, if you have any questions or concerns, just come find me in my office."

He hands the folder to Daniel. "Now, enough of this boring stuff! Why don't you grab some lunch?"

"See you later," Mr. Bartel says cheerily as Daniel excuses himself from the office and into the open air of the outdoor hallway.

When Daniel glances at his phone to check the time, he realizes that he has no idea when the lunch bell will ring. He checks his schedule in his binder, which tells him that there are only ten minutes remaining. He isn't hungry anyway. A hot wind hits his back as he walks toward his locker to deposit his things. PE will be next, then English Literature. After that, day one ends.

Thinking ahead to gym class, he manages to scarf down a few bites of Nana's gimbap before the bell pierces the air. The corridors hum with clanging lockers and farewell shouts. Students with designer T-shirts and jewelry glinting in the sun file toward their assigned classrooms. Daniel grabs his sports bag full of gym clothes, sneakers, and an extra combination lock before heading in the direction of what might be the gymnasium. Verdant trees and bushes line the path. Several statues of historic donors stand at each corner. An impressive royal blue banner cascades down the side of the gymnasium, declaring, "Go Sentinels! Since 1908!"

He spies a stream of boys heading down a dimly lit passageway, and sure enough, he's found the locker room. The students' raucous laughter bounces off the linoleum floors. Boys shove each other as they blindly peel off polos and sweatshirts. Daniel's nerves scurry along his skin as he chooses a locker in the far corner. Only a few awkward teens occupy the space, but Daniel's hands still tremble as he ducks out of his clothes. He isn't ashamed of his body, which still holds on to the lean muscle of his cross-country days, but he can't shake the discomfort of disrobing in front of so many unfamiliar pairs of eyes.

His gaze downcast, he tosses his clothes into the locker. Then, he unbuckles his mind from his body and slides it in beside the clothes. Hunched atop the cold locker shelf, he peers into the room. There is his body, alone, shuffling into loose shorts and an oversized tee. His hand shuts the locker, where it's dark and quieter and conversations echo about him like underwater messages.

The students make their way into the gymnasium, but Daniel wants to stay behind. Everyone else can go run and jump and roughhouse. Instead, Daniel sends a shell of himself with them, but his thoughts remain in the safety of the locker, tucked between his sports bag and jeans like a pixie hiding between flower petals.

A whistle blows, and the medley of boys and girls meet a towering man at the center of the gym.

"Welcome to the first day of PE. For those of you that don't already know me, I'm Coach Rasmussen. Normally, I focus my efforts after school with team sports, but right now, my job is to make sure all of you don't melt into puddles in front of your phones and computers."

The coach crosses his lanky arms around a fit chest. A few girls whisper in each other's ears, thinly veiled flirtations thrown in the man's direction. Coach Rasmussen deliberately ignores them.

"Since it's the first week," he continues sternly, "I'll take pity on you all and save our first mile for Friday. Today, we'll focus on getting your records for sit-ups, push-ups, and pull-ups."

The whispers stop, and several students groan with blatant annoyance. Unfazed by the complaints, the coach adds, "Hopefully you did more than sit on couches all summer. Pair up."

As the class moves toward an array of blue mats, Daniel stifles a flicker of disappointment. Even though his calves are sore from his newly reinstated neighborhood jogs, he hoped to get a little more running into his school day. Sit-ups are a cheap substitute.

When Daniel's back meets the mat, a stranger's face pops up over his. "Need a partner?" a naturally tan boy asks, his honey-colored eyes a little anxious. "I'm kind of new here."

"Sure."

The boy smiles, filling a good third of his face with orthodontically straight teeth. "Cool. The name's Jayden. I went here as a freshman, but my family moved to England last year. I don't know anyone in this class."

Daniel nods and prepares his knees and arms for sit-ups. Jayden holds down his feet. A few seconds of silence stretch between them until Jayden speaks up again, "So what's your name?"

"Daniel." For some reason, getting the words out requires too much effort. A wave of fatigue suddenly crashes into his limbs. Daniel closes his eyes, blocking out the overhead lights. His back sinks heavily into the mat. He's felt this before, whenever he threw himself into Neverland's tall grasses after a particularly drawn-out day at the hospital. Right after taking his evening pills.

The 504 Plan mentioned the possibility of class breaks on account of his medicines. Could this be the reason why? Or perhaps his body simply can't move anymore with his brain still holed up in the locker room. Somewhere far away, a whistle sounds, or maybe it's a Never bird call.

"Hey! It's time to start." Jayden shakes Daniel's legs, but his torso sinks deeper into the mat. "Hey, Coach! I think my partner's asleep!"

Prankish laughter fills the gym, effectively knocking Daniel out of his daydream. When he opens his eyes, he stares directly into Coach Rasmussen's glare.

"Everything all right, kid?" he asks, his tone caught between irritation and concern.

"Yeah."

"What's your name?" he asks, brows furrowed.

"Daniel Kim."

The wrinkles in his forehead deepen. "You sure you're okay?" he repeats, and Daniel wonders if the coach has already been informed of his medical history.

"Yeah, I'm fine," he replies quickly. "Just zoned out is all."

The coach stares a moment longer before accepting the response. He claps his hands and rounds up the students to begin again. Jayden reassumes his position at Daniel's feet.

"That's a weird game you played there," he remarks with a tense chuckle. "Don't give Coach Rasmussen too much of a hard time. He's strict, but he's a good guy."

"Note taken," Daniel says, relieved to find his body responsive once more. He's glad to have the episode written off as a bad joke and plans to make up for the ordeal with a strong sit-up count. When the whistle blows, he pushes past the fatigue with each curl forward, hitting a satisfying score of sixty-one sit-ups before the minute ends.

CHAPTER SIX

Friday rolls around, and as Daniel approaches a spare desk in Algebra II, he is stopped by Mrs. Yasment. "The review test is today," she says discreetly, a few exam papers in hand. "You and Amber should head to the library, correct? To minimize any distractions."

A girl with golden highlights and heavy makeup joins the tête-à-tête. Smacking a piece of gum in her red mouth, she sizes up Daniel with a mix of curiosity and admiration, but when she speaks, she aims her words toward the teacher: "Ready to go, calculator and all. Should we take our bags?"

Mrs. Yasment fiddles with her glasses. "Yes, I believe you'll need the whole period to finish. If you can't complete it, just leave the exam with the librarian, and you can get extra time at lunch or after school."

Amber snatches the tests from the teacher and passes one to Daniel. "I know the drill," she says casually, flipping her hair and already making her way to the door.

Daniel follows, envying the classmates who take their seats as the bell kickstarts their normal, non-accommodated test period. Shouldering his backpack with a sigh, he hurries to the girl who has already managed to make it halfway down the hall.

"So, what's your deal?" she asks once he catches up. When Daniel doesn't respond right away, she offers him a square of gum as a sign of peace. "I've got the four-letter curse: ADHD."

With her confident flair and coy mannerisms, Daniel finds it hard to imagine her as the recipient of an IAP. He accepts the gum anyway, figuring a refusal would be an unnecessary affront. "I told you mine, so you tell me yours," she croons, wagging her eyebrows. Daniel's palms perspire. "I take these meds that make me tired." He avoids the bigger, more intimidating label. Besides, she more than likely has never heard of depersonalization-derealization disorder, and he would rather not waste his breath trying to explain a diagnosis that feels less than real to him.

"That's even more boring than mine," she snickers, but her playfulness quickly evaporates as they enter the hushed library. Half a dozen students and teachers occupy the black wood tables and desktop computers, attentively hammering out essays or lesson plans. The circulation desk is inconveniently vacant. Unperturbed, Amber dives into the aisles of ebony book stacks. Sure enough, the librarian thumbs through an astonishingly large book collection on a portable shelf in the fiction section. A bleached-blond Asian boy accompanies him, his pouty mouth set in clear disinterest.

"You can start off by reshelving these in alphabetical order by author's last name," Mr. Bartel tells the boy before noticing them standing nearby. "Oh, Amber and Daniel!" he chirps, hesitating briefly on Daniel's name. Honestly, Daniel is impressed that the librarian remembers him at all, given their single interaction almost a full week ago. Even more, Daniel is surprised that he remembers the librarian's name.

"Go ahead and try it out, Jiwon," he says to the short blond boy. "Let me know if you have any questions." Then, he motions for Daniel and Amber to follow him back to the circulation desk.

Daniel throws a guilty glance toward Jiwon, hoping the interruption isn't bothersome. To his surprise, the boy's brown eyes meet his with a curious expression. At this point in his life, Daniel is used to long stares—people of all ethnicities trying to pinpoint his ambiguous race. He knows his hazel eyes, light brown hair, and strong jaw attract attention. Jiwon also has a striking appearance—androgynous, each edge slightly softened like morning fog clinging to a distant ship. Fortunately, their uncomfortable encounter cuts off as soon as Daniel exits the shelves.

"Test today?" Mr. Bartel asks without waiting for an answer. "You can leave your bags behind the circulation desk. What's the subject?"

"Math," Amber says nonchalantly.

"Then feel free to grab your pencils and calculators. Oh, and I'll be needing your phones," he adds as an afterthought.

Amber pops her gum as she reaches into her skirt pocket and hands over her phone. Daniel follows suit—not that he has anyone to text for test answers. Mr. Bartel walks them to a row of plexiglass-enclosed, adjoining rooms, large enough for a few students at a time. He and Amber choose neighboring rooms.

"Good luck." Mr. Bartel beams as Daniel slides the plexiglass door shut.

The test is supposed to act as a refresher of previously learned algebra and geometry concepts. Hazy memories of last semester's math classes scratch at Daniel's brain, but the only coherent image that emerges is a wall of posters filled with meaningless theorems and formulas. He had a clear view of that wall from his desk in the back corner of his old math class. The numbers and symbols fused into the dotted lines of treasure maps. The questions added up to intangible matter that produced nothing but thin air. How could he have relied on insubstantial ideas to anchor him in a class full of people who might as well have been ghosts? For all he knew, he was the only real person in a box of shadows.

Now, as Daniel stares at three pages of countless numbers, the temptation to aimlessly circle multiple-choice responses almost wins him over. A small part of him wants to try. School used to be a place in which he excelled. He sucks in a dry breath, taking his best shot at plotting X and Y.

A quarter of the way through, his wrists start to ache. His elbows sag over the side of the table, and his tired head droops toward a question about square roots. He drops his pencil, setting his cheek against the cool tabletop. The same cheek with the pale scar that traced half the underlying bone. Somewhere in that LED-lit pool, he scraped his skin until it bled, but can't recall anything after the jump. *You just think lovely wonderful thoughts, and they lift you up into the air!* Daniel smiles. He can climb the tallest tree in Neverland and sit with the birds and the pixies from sunrise to sunset, basking in the most wonderful world that ever was.

Long fingers curl around his shoulder, and he jumps in his chair, shocked by the unexpectedly solid touch. Mr. Bartel recoils, as startled as Daniel.

"Sorry," the librarian blurts out, embarrassment written into his tense posture. "I thought you'd fallen asleep during your test. There's only a few more minutes before the end of the period."

Blood rushes from Daniel's brain, spiraling through his veins. Dizziness clouds his vision, stirred up from the abrupt intrusion. He shakes his head a few times to regain control.

"I'm fine," Daniel states more to himself than Mr. Bartel. "I just took a short break." His test is still only a quarter complete.

"Take your time. Would you like to get a drink of water?"

"I'm fine," Daniel repeats.

"I'll be right outside if you need anything." The librarian takes cautious steps out of the cubicle, obviously unconvinced by Daniel's assessment of his condition. A few paces from the glass door, Jiwon watches from beside the book cart. When their eyes meet again, the blond boy turns away, feigning interest in shelving several large volumes.

Hot shame pierces Daniel's vision. An entire hour has passed, and he could only manage to answer a few questions—probably incorrectly. He grips his pencil tightly, buckling down to do his best, but when the bell sounds, he's only stumbled through three more problems.

He and Amber withdraw from their rooms and hand their tests to Mr. Bartel. Amber's test is entirely filled out.

"If you'd like some extra time," Mr. Bartel says gently, "I'll be here during lunch and after school."

They head toward the hallway. Once outside, Amber stretches her arms lazily overhead, baring a sliver of abdomen. "Easiest test of my life."

Flashing a devilish grin, she shows Daniel the inside cover of her calculator. Numerous equations and graphs are scrawled on the surface.

"A gift from a friend who has first period Algebra II. You want?"

Daniel doesn't know whether to be impressed or disappointed. The offer is appealing, but he hasn't reached a point yet where cheating feels like his only option.

"No thanks."

Amber throws her hands on her hips before looking him down head-to-toe. "You're a good boy, aren't you?" she says flatly. "Just don't snitch."

"You don't have to worry."

She sighs but appears satisfied with his reply. With a huff and a cheery "Ciao," she scurries to the girls' restroom. Daniel double-checks his schedule, which he can't seem to keep straight, and joins a crowd of students rushing to their next class.

The hours pass by uneventfully. When lunch finally arrives, he opts to sit in relative solitude in front of his locker. He considers looking for Amber but decides not to. The only bright spot of the day is the upcoming mile in PE. That is exactly what Daniel needs now: a moment to fly, to leave Cranbrook and teachers and tests far behind.

With his food eaten, he ventures to the locker room a few minutes early. In the absence of horseplay and banging metal, the corridors emit the discomfiting hauntedness of an abandoned warehouse. Still, Daniel feels more at ease as he dresses down by himself. He makes a mental note to get changed early every day.

The rest of the class comes barreling in just as Daniel makes his way toward the exit. Jayden catches his elbow with a boisterous shout: "Hey, man! See you on the track!"

Circling an expansive football field, the track separates the turf from the high-rise bleachers. Without the shade of trees, the late summer sun beats mercilessly upon the red tarmac. Daniel can already feel his feet pushing off the ground, hurtling him forward, lifting him into the sky. Gone.

The crunch of footfalls announces Coach Rasmussen's arrival. His shadow bridges the space between them. "Nice to see someone can make it to the field on time."

Daniel shrugs. Coach Rasmussen stands a formidable height, but his build is long and lean, more like a marathoner than a football player. His sandy brown hair is slicked back, but a cowlick has pried loose and hangs in the center of his forehead.

"You like running, Kim?" the man asks gruffly.

"A bit."

"Well, show me what you're made of out there.'

A whirl of pride flutters in Daniel's chest. The coach must have noticed his high scores throughout the week's fitness examinations. He'll be watching him out there, to see if sit-ups, pull-ups, long jumps, and forearm hangs measure up to any real talent. Like a key flaring a cold engine to life, Daniel's motivation to run shifts. Perhaps he can prove to one teacher today that he isn't a total failure.

Once everyone settles on the field, they kick off the class with a series of stretches and warm-ups. Daniel takes the slow start in stride, itching to get to the starting line. Eventually, the coach directs them to the track. While most of the students drag their feet, Daniel all but jogs to the white and red stripes. To his surprise, Jayden is right beside him, his curly hair pushed back with a sweatband.

"Let's get this party started." He throws him an exuberant thumbs up before taking on a practiced runner's form—not a showy starting position, but an evident posture that is ready to pounce.

The whistle shrieks, and Daniel forgets about Jayden and all the other students. The math test falls away, lost in the wind whirring in his ears. The 504 Plan, the medicine, and the swimming pool dissolve in his wake. All that persists is the clash of his sneakers against the terrain, the rhythm of his controlled breathing, and the curve of the track's white lines.

This is real, Daniel thinks. This is right now.

Suddenly, Coach Rasmussen's authoritative figure appears only a few meters ahead. His arms are waving wildly, his whistle in his mouth. The sharp trills slide through Daniel's focus, and he slows to a halt. He gasps for oxygen, his lungs alarmed by the sudden switch to stillness.

"Are you crazy?" Coach Rasmussen shouts, but the grin planted on his face contradicts any anger. "We're running a mile not a 3K, you crazy fast son of a—" He stops his sentences short with a bout of laughter.

Jayden sprints over, slinging an arm around Daniel's neck. "You killed me!" he whoops excitedly. "I've been trying to get my mile under 4:30 all summer, and you just kept going at nearly the same speed for two more laps! Coach, we gotta get him on the team. I bet he's faster than Jiwon!"

"If your endurance can really hold out at that high speed..." The coach trails off in thought. "Have you run cross-country before?"

Daniel stands up straighter, his limbs tingling from both the run and their reactions. He has longed for this. The moment when no one sees him as dazed and hazardous. He's just a boy, a boy who can fly.

"Yeah, I have. For Cambry and in middle school."

Coach Rasmussen smiles. "I thought your name sounded familiar. Daniel Kim, Cranbrook is lucky to have you. You're a little late, but we haven't had any meets yet anyway. How about joining us for practice on Monday?"

"I'd like that."

Jayden jumps triumphantly into the air. "Are you hiding wings or something?" he laughs before clapping Daniel hard on the shoulder.

CHAPTER SEVEN

In many ways, a weekend at home feels depressingly similar to the days Daniel spent at Mercy Hospital. Since Dr. Greene specializes in teen psychiatry, he keeps his office open on weekends, meaning that Daniel's Saturday afternoons are reserved for therapy. So, Daniel finds himself sprawled on the linen sofa in the living room, drifting between a mid-morning nap and daydreams, while he waits for the unavoidable appointment.

Nana's footsteps patter on the marble floor. "Can I get you anything?" she asks, softly brushing his hair aside to place a cool palm on his forehead. "You've been on the couch for a while now."

"I'm just waiting."

"Waiting for what?" Nana cocks her head to the side like an inquisitive spaniel.

"Dr. Greene."

"Is there something you're looking forward to telling him?"

Daniel has never looked forward to telling Dr. Greene anything, but the psychiatrist gave solid pointers on grounding techniques. Daniel considers asking for advice on managing his schoolwork, unsure if high school grades are even an appropriate topic to bring up with a therapist. Dr. Greene is almost certainly more invested in monitoring his prescribed milligrams than chatting over math tests.

"Not really. I'm just waiting."

"How about you go for a run?" Nana suggests.

Daniel sits up. The invitation to join the cross-country team burns out the fog in his brain.

"Nana, what do you think about me starting up cross-country again?"

She takes a seat beside him. "That sounds like an excellent idea to me. I still remember cheering you on when you won your first relay race all those years ago."

"That was track and field." Daniel chuckles softly, recalling how Nana had proudly hugged him after he received the gold medal around his neck. That was before he learned to be embarrassed by having a nanny cheer him on instead of his parents. By seventh grade, Nana stopped attending meets, at his request.

"Whatever it was, you had a real knack for it. Think of all your medals and trophies on display in the parlor."

Daniel rarely visits the parlor—the modern room where his parents often disappear in order to talk. They always reappeared with bad news.

"That was a long time ago," says Daniel, referring to his accolades.

Nana lets out a kind-hearted laugh. "I suppose when you're sixteen, half a year feels like a long absence, but maybe you should consider it an extended vacation."

Daniel nods. "Are the Darlings coming home soon?" he asks absentmindedly.

Nana sighs and straightens her apron, as is her habit whenever her nerves jangle. "Your parents should be back next weekend."

When Daniel's eyes start to glass over, she quickly adds, "How about that run?"

"Maybe after the appointment."

With a motherly air of decision, Nana abruptly hops to her feet. "Well, I can't have you wasting an entire Saturday," she says teasingly. "Why don't you start on some homework." She wags a finger in front of his nose. Knowing Nana well, Daniel understands he has little choice in the matter. He taps a foot in mock defiance but heads to his room nonetheless.

While Daniel prefers his home to the hospital, his affection for his bedroom feels just as disconnected. The white walls are nearly bare, except for a few professional sketches that were preselected by an interior decorator. His personal touches are limited to the clothes hanging in the closet and his precious collection hidden within the dresser.

He opens the top drawer. Inside rests a hodgepodge of antique boxes, housing years of collected treasures: pouches of fairy dust purchased at specialty stores; children's collectible figurines molded into Peter, Wendy, Tinker Bell, and company; actors on dainty chains and thimbles in various sizes. He pulls another drawer handle and admires the numerous Peter Pan posters, postcards, and illustrated volumes scrounged from boutiques and theaters.

The third drawer harbors every Peter Pan adaptation that he could find online. He runs his fingertips over the spines of countless plays, musicals, animated features, and live-action renditions. He pries a documentary on J. M. Barrie from the overstuffed stockpile. He's only watched it a few times. Maybe he can watch it later. Setting the film case on his desk, he settles into his desk chair and unzips his backpack. First, he needs to make a dent in a short-answer assignment on the First World War.

A few hours later, Nana drops Daniel off in front of Mercy Hospital's mental health clinic. The contemporary, multilevel building overlooks an extensive, close-cropped lawn and semicircle driveway. Rose bushes line the geometric exterior, crawling up floor-to-ceiling tinted windows. Cicadas bawl from the distant thicket of trees meant to provide a sense of privacy to the grounds. Several cars occupy the hushed parking lot, but nothing moves. Except Daniel, everything sits still as death.

"I'll be back in an hour," Nana calls from the car window. "Those groceries won't shop for themselves."

Daniel waves, and the car speeds away as he passes through the clinic's automatic doors. Even though Daniel visited the clinic only last Tuesday, he can't remember Dr. Greene's floor. Luckily, the lobby receptionist confirms his appointment and directs him to the third level. Another receptionist tells him to wait for his name to be called, so he collapses into a vinyl guest chair. He only has a moment before an unfamiliar nurse arrives and leads him down the coffee-colored hallway to Dr. Greene's office.

"Ah, Daniel," the psychiatrist says, standing up from behind his pristine desk. "Please, take a seat."

Same armchair, same bookcase, same ticking clock—Daniel can already feel his mind slipping from his body. He grips the armrest, trying to stay present.

Dr. Greene notices right away and takes out his trusty deck of cards. "What should we play today? How about crazy eights?"

When Daniel nods, the psychiatrist pulls an accent table between them. As he deals out the cards, he asks, "How has your day been so far?"

"I'm here," he replies.

"Is that a good thing or a bad thing?"

Daniel takes up his hand. He's drawn an eight of clubs. "It's supposed to be good."

"Is it?" Dr. Greene lays a five of diamonds, matching the suit.

Daniel tries to focus on his next play. "Yes, it's good."

"What makes this visit something positive?"

Daniel reflects on the question, losing track of his turn. "I don't know if this is positive, but I could use your help."

Dr. Greene tilts his head in repressed surprise. "What can I help you with?"

"With school. I can't study without completely spacing out. Tests are the worst. I don't want to flunk out of high school or cheat my way to graduation." He punctuates his sentence by playing a four of diamonds.

"Thank you for explaining. It's nice to hear your voice, Daniel. By the sound of it, getting back into your schoolwork might be causing you to depersonalize. Have you tried any grounding techniques?"

"They don't work."

Dr. Greene nods slowly. "Are you saying you haven't tried or that you tried but didn't have any success?"

"I tried breathing, but my breath just flies out of me to somewhere else," he says, then adds, "It's your turn."

Dr. Greene puts down an eight of hearts. "I'll change the suit to spades." Daniel doesn't have any spades. "I can tell this is important to you. I can share a few more techniques with you if you'd like?"

With no other option, Daniel plays his eight of clubs. "Switch to hearts."

"Do you want to learn some new mindfulness skills?" Dr. Greene presses.

Daniel folds his hand, placing it on the table. "If it helps."

"I believe it will," Dr. Greene replies before dropping his own cards. "One technique will be to refocus you physically. The other can help you to mentally reorient yourself.

"To reconnect with your body, you could start bringing a water bottle with you to class. Every time you start to feel distracted, take a sip of water and pay attention to how it feels in your mouth, on your tongue, and as it trickles down your throat."

It almost sounds too easy, but Daniel thinks he could give it a try.

"For your mind, you can try to keep track of the time. Concentrate on the seconds as they go by for about a minute. This simple practice might be all it takes to lasso your thoughts."

The clock on the office wall ticks out its measured beat. So, then, the crocodile would be chasing Daniel out of Neverland. He leans against the armchair, suddenly exhausted by the conversation. Deep breathing, water bottles, keeping time—all for what?

"Do you think you could try these techniques?" Dr. Greene questions delicately, but Daniel's bones feel like sea glass. He could break underneath the heel of any callous pirate's boot.

"It's easier to just give up," he mumbles.

"Is that what you want?"

"I want…" His voice fails him. The clock ticks patiently, but Daniel can't bring himself to look at the shifting second hand.

After a long silence, Dr. Greene asks, as he does at some point during every session, "Do you want to give up on life, Daniel?"

"I don't want to die." Daniel says, wishing he were anywhere but in Dr. Greene's office right now. If he could go anyplace else, he would hide under a blanket in his hammock in Hangman's Tree, but Daniel isn't supposed to retreat into Neverland. Flying has gotten him nowhere.

So then, the racetrack is the only other place for him—the warm sun at his back, the power in his legs as he forces one foot to follow the other, ears deafened by the adrenaline and his cheering teammates. He'll go faster and faster until he crosses the finish line.

"I want to run," he says.

"From what?"

Daniel turns to the clock. The second hand sails swiftly past the numbers, carrying the whole world on its thoughtless journey onward.

"From nothing. I just want to run."

CHAPTER EIGHT

E veryone, welcome Daniel Kim to the team."
The ten runners gathered in the gymnasium clap obediently at Coach Rasmussen's announcement. Daniel doesn't recognize any of them except Jayden and the blond boy from the library. Jiwon.

"He ran for Cambry's cross-country team for two years and also has extensive track and field experience. He'll make a strong addition to the team, so be sure to include him in your activities."

Jayden can't hold in his excitement. "He's ridiculously fast, you guys! I watched him throw down a 4:28 mile like it was nothing."

The team sizes him up, some with friendlier expressions than others. Jiwon's gaze is impassive, betraying neither warmth nor disapproval. Daniel blanches beneath their obvious critical evaluation.

"Speed is speed," pipes up a thin runner with especially sharp eyes and a jersey that reads Kevin Lee. "How's your endurance, Daniel? What's your PR?"

Daniel nervously tugs at the sleeves of his black tee. He never enjoys comparing personal records, preferring to just get on with a run. Maybe there was once a time when individual times mattered most to him, but now he only wants to merge with the wind, in his own space and dimension.

Still, he can't ignore the question. "Last year I hit 15:47 in the 10K."

A brown-haired White boy with a constantly tapping foot whistles loudly in Jiwon's direction. "There you have it, Jiwon. A whole three seconds faster."

Jiwon shrugs languidly. "I don't know what you're getting at, Owen, but it sounds like good news for the team." Despite his casual tone, Jiwon avoids glancing in Daniel's direction.

"I'm out of shape, though," Daniel admits hurriedly. "My summer training was pretty much nonexistent."

Coach Rasmussen throws up his arms. "Enough chitchat. Time for practice. Let's head to the park."

Adequately chastised, the team leaves the gymnasium, water bottles in hand, and saunter off school grounds toward the multiacre park that neighbors Cranbrook. Their trainers light up the grassy field with bright colors, hinting at their individual personalities. Scarlet red sneakers contrast the green earth, as well as neon orange and reflective silver. Owen's shoes shine with highlighter yellow beside the deep gray of the boy with sharp eyes and Jiwon's sky blue. A pair of carefree white trainers tentatively approach Daniel's black-encased feet.

"Sorry if I put you on the spot over there," Jayden says sheepishly.

Daniel shrugs. "It's okay." Even though his gut clenches from the team's interrogation, he doesn't want to put down the only runner who seems to like him.

Coach Rasmussen draws the team to a halt at a well-maintained playground. A few children scream down plastic slides into sand, while parents push toddlers in saddled swings.

"We'll be practicing a 5K today, followed by some strength training back at the gym. Let's warm up."

After a series of squats, walking lunges, and leg swings, the team rallies behind the coach's outstretched arm. A handful of runners execute a few last-minute stretches, pulling at tight quads or rounding sore shoulders. Jiwon bends to nimbly touch his toes. Daniel gawks at his flexibility, rolling his ankles one way and then the other.

"Three laps around the park's perimeter," the coach announces, then raises his arm above his head. "Start!"

Everyone lunges forward, light on their feet but holding back so as to conserve their energy. Being unfamiliar with the course, Daniel settles for a fast jog, taking on a comfortable pace in the center of the team. The path appears flat enough, but he doesn't want to come across as overconfident at the front of the pack only to be surprised by a set of unexpected hills. The steady run is dissatisfying, though. His mind is too distractible, thoughts fluttering to the trees and decorative ponds. What kind of fish live in the shallow water? Could merfolk lie imprisoned beneath the surface, captured by pirates, forced to live behind muddy bars?

Relief blossoms in his chest once the playground zooms into view. The course is as flat as the back of his hand, so he immediately launches into a more gratifying speed. A few meters into his second lap, he passes another runner.

He hates how his brain keeps focusing on the team members ahead of him. Yet, Daniel isn't motivated to beat out the racing figures in front of him. He simply wants to fly with nothing between him and the landscape, and solitude his only companion besides the breeze, the sun, and the racecourse.

Two-thirds into the second lap, he catches up to Jayden and Kevin. Neither runner so much as glances at Daniel as he meets and then progresses beyond them, and Daniel refrains from looking over his shoulder. Why look back when the whole park unfolds before him?

Once he reaches the halfway point of his third lap, he recognizes Owen up ahead. Owen's yellow trainers leap like Tinker Bell, hopping from one blade of grass to the next. Daniel closes the distance between them. Neck-and-neck, they sail. The ponds flash by, mirrors reflecting the harsh sun. Sweat streams between Daniel's shoulder blades. His breath snags in his lungs. Both legs shriek in resistance, the lactic acid building to an unbearable threshold. Yet, even as Daniel teeters at the limit of his aerobic capacity, he glides.

Owen casts him a weary grin as his tempo slackens. Approximately four hundred meters separates Daniel from the playground finish line. Coach Rasmussen stands still as bronze, inviting the runners to the end of their labor.

And there just ahead, crossing paths with the coach, soars Jiwon. His form is flawless. An air of gracefulness marks his agile finish. He is only meters away, yet completely out of reach. Sixteen seconds later, Daniel tumbles past the Coach.

"16:21!"

Daniel nearly collapses onto the grass but refuses to surrender to the exhaustion. He knows he overdid it. Each muscle screams, but his body needs to cool down, so his heart can ease into its regular rhythm. With leaden limbs, he jogs around the playground. Jiwon does the same, several yards ahead. The other runner seems nowhere near as fatigued as Daniel, showing the results of dedicated summer training.

The majority of the team arrives at the playground and circles the sandlot in an almost ritualistic fashion. Daniel's lungs eventually regain their natural flow. He succumbs to the weariness, taking an undignified seat in the grass beside the coach.

"Nice work, Kim," Coach Rasmussen says, his eyes pinned to the last straggling runner. "Take a breather. No need to knock yourself out."

Jiwon quietly sits beside him and hands him his water bottle. Daniel takes a few cautious sips, worried about possible cramps. Sweat shimmers on Jiwon's brow, but his soft features are smooth on his placid face. They drink in silence, watching the other runners cool down. Daniel wonders if this is Jiwon's way of gloating, or of extending friendship.

The practice wraps up with a leisurely walk to the gym and relatively straightforward sequence of strength training exercises. Muted by tiredness, the team breaks up, driving each other home or climbing into their parents' cars. Daniel throws on a thin hoodie and waits in a secluded corner near the parking lot for Nana to pick him up. Jayden and Owen wave good-bye to him before driving off in the latter's Lexus.

A few crickets serenade each other as the sun starts to shift from yellow to dusty orange. In the dusky haze of eventide, Daniel cannot shuck the sensation of otherworldliness. It's as though the cross-country team never really existed. The practice might as well have been a daydream.

The hushed tap of tentative footsteps approaches. "Can I sit?" Jiwon asks, gesturing toward the empty space beside him. Daniel shrugs, which Jiwon correctly interprets as, "Yes."

"Waiting for a ride?" Jiwon says. When Daniel nods, he continues, "I have a car, but I usually walk to school since I live just over there." He points to the assortment of Dutch Colonials that neighbor Cranbrook.

While Daniel earned his learner's permit in Drivers' Ed during the first semester of sophomore year, he quickly lost interest in driving by the winter. Those cold days drew him deeper into Neverland's infinite summer. Despite Sung-min's stern encouragement, he avoided driving altogether. Now, he wonders if he's even allowed to operate a car under the influence of his current medication regimen.

"I saw you in the library," Jiwon says, pushing an invisible shelving cart for emphasis. "I have to volunteer there during my free periods for senior service hours in order to graduate this spring."

Daniel is surprised to learn that Jiwon is a senior, because honestly, he looks younger than Daniel. The initial shock gives way to the hard realization that Jiwon has seen him getting accommodations. He feels exposed, like the other runner stole an important secret from him without asking.

"I remember you," Daniel replies, hoping Jiwon won't bring up his pathetic attempt at testing.

To his relief, Jiwon changes the subject. "You're gonna be sore tomorrow."

"And you're not?"

Jiwon laughs without any derision, a humble bubbling of a gentle fountain. "You know, maybe I need this—you joining the team out of nowhere. I'm competing for scholarships at some colleges—"

Suddenly, he jumps to his feet and extends an open hand toward Daniel. "Let's push each other to be our best," he says with a genuine smile.

Daniel blinks at the hand, stunned by Jiwon's sincere offer. He slides his fingers into a firm grip that feels nothing like rivalry and everything like respect.

CHAPTER NINE

The campfire licks the cool night air, warming the Lost Boys' bare arms and legs. A tub of soapy water sits beside them. Their animal furs hang to dry from the knobby branches of Hangman's Tree. The occasional bead of water drips onto the grass, as though a raccoon or fox cries from above.

"I hate laundry day," Slightly complains in his threadbare underclothes. "Why do we have to wash our suits?"

One of the Twins huffs, dropping his chin into his fists. "It'll take ages to get all that good dirt back."

Daniel swats the boy's arm. "You want the pirates to smell us from a mile away?"

Just then, an incessant tapping strikes his shoulder. Daniel sucks in a breath. Could it be Hook, his claw digging in as he sets them up for another ambush? But the tapping is too gentle. Soft fingers press into the fabric of his shirt. The Lost Boys don't seem to see, their gazes caught in the fire.

"Hey," a whisper calls out. "Wake up, Daniel. You need to finish your test."

Daniel rips his head from the pillow of his crossed arms. The glass walls of the library quiet room come into focus. His weekly Friday history quiz peeks out from beneath his arms, nearly finished.

"I can't have you flunking your way off the team," says Jiwon, his face a few inches away.

Jiwon's words stir up a whirlwind of anxiety. Daniel had, in fact, flunked out of track and field just last January. The thought that his subpar grades could rob him of cross-country brings about a fresh wave of nausea.

Daniel tries to gauge the remaining minutes before both lunch and his extended testing time end. No clock hangs on the cubicle's walls, and Mr. Bartel has confiscated his phone.

"Is Amber still here?" Daniel asks.

Jiwon eyes him, curiosity piqued by his reference to the girl. "She already finished. She's actually the one who told me to wake you if you didn't get up on your own in a few minutes. She called you a space case, actually."

"I'm fine. I just got distracted."

Jiwon raises an eyebrow, unconvinced. "Well, hurry up," he replies, making his way out of the room. "Maybe we can grab some snacks before the bell rings." He shuts the glass door behind him, then reclaims the shelving cart.

Daniel rubs his temples, willing away the lingering sleepiness. He can't believe that both Amber and Jiwon caught him napping over his test. Remembering Dr. Greene's advice, he takes a deep drink from his water bottle. The liquid fills his dry mouth, bearing down on his tongue like a doctor's compression stick. He swallows, concentrating on its journey from his throat through his chest and to his clamped gut. One deep breath in, a steady exhale out. He summons up his studied knowledge on World War I and cranks out a few more sentences on the effects of trench warfare.

He gives the completed quiz to Mr. Bartel. He glances it over. "How'd it go?" he asks kindly, his perfect teeth exposed in his trademark smile.

"Better than nothing."

Jiwon rolls up to the desk. "I finished putting away all the books," he announces a little over-emphatically. "Can I go, too?"

The librarian's eyes shift from Jiwon to Daniel. "Sure," he acquiesces, smiling at the undoubtedly budding friendship. "Why don't you get yourselves something to eat."

Jiwon parks the cart next to the desk as Daniel reclaims his backpack and phone. They head out into the humid, gloomy afternoon. They make their way to a nearby vending machine. While Jiwon slides a debit card and selects a bag of pretzels, Daniel fishes his homemade lunch from his backpack.

"I'm addicted to these," Jiwon says, shaking the plastic bag with a satisfying rattle. "What did you bring?"

Daniel opens his lunchbox to reveal an appetizing array of Korean side dishes with a full helping of fried rice. Even though Nana has Norwegian roots, she long ago learned to cook up Sung-Min's favorites.

"I'm a little jealous." Jiwon snags a piece of pajeon pancake and offers his pretzels as recompense. "My dad can't cook to save his life. Is your mom Korean then?"

"No, she's White. My dad is Korean, but he doesn't cook either. My…" He pauses, flustered by his childish nickname for Nana. "My housekeeper makes this stuff."

"Do you speak Korean?"

Daniel shakes his head, a little embarrassed even though he's asked the question more often than he can count. "My dad was always away on business, so there wasn't really anyone to teach me. I know basic phrases, but that's it."

They walk aimlessly around the campus, past the commemorative statues and patriotic banners, before settling in front of the gymnasium.

"It's just me and my dad," Jiwon comments casually between crunchy bites of pretzel. "We have a housekeeper that comes by once a week, or else the whole place would be a total pigsty."

"Oh, does your mom travel a lot?" Daniel envisions an airplane flying over the ocean, Jiwon's mother tucked comfortably beneath a first-class blanket.

"Nope, she's underground," he replies in the same offhand manner he applied to talk of housekeepers. "Cancer of the brain, six months ago."

Daniel freezes mid-chew. Despite Jiwon's easygoing tone, he can't conceal the stiffness of his shoulders. The empty bag of pretzels crumples in his fist before he hurls it forcefully into a nearby trash bin.

"So where do you live?" Jiwon's hurried change of subject does little to alleviate the unexpected tension. Daniel thinks of Monica, off securing a deal thousands of miles away. How would his life change if she never returned from Singapore? A shudder vibrates through the base of his skull. Would anything be different at all?

"Vandever Acres."

"I know the place," Jiwon says, a little too eager to move the conversation along. "I've partied there a few times. Owen lived in a nice spot over that way before his family downsized."

Daniel's thoughts flail on missing mothers, unable to settle on the small piece of gossip. He stares blankly at his untouched fried rice. He resists the urge to ask Jiwon, "How much is a dead mom like an absent one?"

The bell rings, releasing them from the uncomfortable atmosphere. "See you at practice," Jiwon says. "All bets on Coach taking it easy on us, what with tomorrow's preseason meet."

Daniel nods faintly. "See you later," he replies, not sure if the unpleasant turning of his insides is the result of Jiwon's home situation or the realization that he'll be dressing down with the entire gym class again.

CHAPTER TEN

For the first time in months, Daniel has something to look forward to on a Saturday. He showers, the steaming water flooding rivers down his neck and back. After toweling dry, he dons his brand-new team uniform. The cloudy mirror reflects the royal blue sprinter top and black endurance shorts, and for a moment, Daniel recognizes himself—a sixteen-year-old boy with damp hair and familiar hazel eyes.

Part of him can't shake the feeling that he's staring into his past. Just a year ago, he wore a similar uniform, only crimson instead of blue. Back when, on an early summer night, James and Francisco passed him a game controller and a handle of vodka at the same time, and everyone laughed, and Brooklyn grabbed the bottle before tipping it over her mouth. Daniel slaps his palm against the mirror, covering his face. He doesn't need to be thinking about last summer. Not now, when his focus should be on today's premeet.

"Daniel! Come on down!" Nana hollers from the first floor. "You don't want to be late!"

After grabbing his spikes and a zip-up hoodie from his closet, he hurries down the stairs and into the kitchen. Nana thrusts a banana and a small Tupperware of peanut butter into the crook of his elbow.

"You can eat in the car," she says with a tsk of impatience. "I couldn't remember if you bring lunches to track meets."

"Cross-country," he corrects her. "And it's okay. Coach Rasmussen will bring some food for us."

"All right then. You have everything? Your shoes? Your phone?" He waves the spikes and points to his pocket. "Did you bring your medicine?" she adds.

"You already gave it to me when you woke me up."

Nana straightens her apron. "Not that medicine, Daniel. Your Lorazepam, just in case."

Daniel remembers the glass container with the small white pill, hidden away in his bedside drawer. "I don't think I'll need it," he says.

"You're supposed to always have that on you. Whatever brought about your...choice this summer, Daniel, we can't have that happening again."

Truth be told, Daniel hasn't packed his take-as-needed prescription a single time for school, but he doesn't tell Nana this. Her concern crackles between them, like an electric fence.

Daniel's irritation, sudden and surprising even for him, tightens his throat. The empowering ache that beckoned him to the roof that night hasn't visited him since. He has obediently followed everyone's orders without complaint. His parents told him to change schools, and he complied. He takes pills every morning and evening and even uses sleep capsules on some nights. Words like mindfulness and grounding have become part of his daily vocabulary. Maybe he doesn't need the Lorazepam. Doesn't he deserve some say in what he carries in his jacket pockets?

"Aren't we almost late?" Daniel asks, trying to bury the rising resentment.

Nana opens the food storage drawer and takes out another miniature container. Wordlessly, she retrieves the Lorazepam bottle, dropping a single tablet in the container. Daniel's hands are full, so she slips the prescription into his hoodie pocket.

"Just take it with you," she pleads softly.

"Fine."

They make their way to Sung-Min's silver Mercedes. As Nana reverses out the garage and gate, Daniel forces down the banana and peanut butter. He tries to take deep breaths between each bite, but the anger smolders in his chest.

As they near the school building, where the white coach bus waits to transport the team to the meet, Nana rubs his shoulder. He yanks himself free, but immediately regrets it when he glimpses Nana's trembling grip on the steering wheel. The anger cools to a simmer.

"I'm sorry," he whispers. Outside the car window, the runners gather around Coach Rasmussen. None of them are toting prescription pills in their pockets. But then again, how would Daniel know?

"It's all right," Nana replies in a voice like melted butter. "You're going through a lot these days. More than you'll probably ever tell me. Still, I want you to have fun today. Good luck out there. Your parents will want to hear all about it when they come home tonight."

She touches his shoulder once more, and Daniel lets her. He forgot that Sung-Min and Monica will return while he is at the meet.

"Go on." She nudges him when he doesn't move to exit the car. "Do well."

"I will," he promises before stepping out with all the energy he can muster. Luckily, he's right on time.

The team greets him with offhand waves. Sleepiness reveals itself in their dark circles and bed head. Only Jiwon smiles widely, his face fresh and bleached hair perfectly combed. "Look good, feel good," Daniel's old coach at Cambry used to tell them. Jiwon seems to be one to follow that kind of advice.

"Where's Jayden?" Coach Rasmussen growls, glancing at his smartwatch. He starts typing feverishly into the screen, probably sending a message to the latecomer. Daniel is grateful that he arrived at eight a.m. on the dot.

"All of you, get on the bus," the coach directs. They comply soundlessly, not wanting to get on his bad side. As Daniel's foot hits the first step, he hears a car squealing into the lot. Jayden jumps out, spikes slung over his shoulder and banging against his back.

"I'm sorry, Coach," he shouts, panic coming off him in waves. "My alarm—"

"You're lucky this is just a practice meet, Phillips," Coach Rasmussen interrupts him. "No excuses. Get your lazy self on that bus."

Tail tucked between his legs, Jayden joins the rest of the team. He climbs into the seat beside Daniel and shakily takes out a granola bar. "Why me?" he moans before cramming half the bar in his mouth. Daniel casts him a sympathetic smile.

A few rows down, Jiwon laughs at something Kevin must have muttered under his breath. Owen beams down at them, peering over the back of his seat, until Coach Rasmussen tells him to sit down. Some members squeeze in fifteen minutes of shut-eye before the bus rolls into the parking lot of an expansive nature reserve. Other teams pour out of their respective buses, dressed in yellow, green, and turquoise.

Everyone heads toward a series of gazebos, setting up jugs of water and boxes of healthy snacks. Daniel sits on the grass and trades his plain sneakers for his spikes. The park spreads out toward the horizon, foretelling a race full of varied terrain.

"Wish the girls' teams were here," Owen complains once the coach is out of earshot. "Wouldn't mind surveying the other schools' selection."

"I don't think your girlfriend would appreciate that," Kevin retorts as he rubs sunscreen onto his cheeks and nose.

"Well, she's not here is she?"

Daniel keeps silent. He wonders where Jiwon has disappeared to, only to gasp audibly when he finds him standing directly behind him.

"Wanna walk the course with me?" he asks with a hint of amusement. "We still have an hour before the 3K."

"Sure."

They fall into a comfortable silence as they stroll past the orange cones that mark the course. The path starts flat, then turns toward a dirt road that winds through a sparse woodland. Once they quit the trees, they come face-to-face with a sparkling lake.

"Nice," Daniel sighs. The sensation that he's been here before, maybe even as recently as last year's season, creeps up his spine. Those races seem like centuries ago.

"I've always liked this park," Jiwon comments as they ascend a hill that borders the lakeshore.

"You've been here before?"

"Plenty of times."

Daniel wonders why Jiwon asked to go for a walk if he was already acquainted with the course. Most runners would have whiled away the extra time, horsing around with their friends.

"We'll probably round the lake and then go through that field back to the gazebos," Jiwon adds, pointing as he speaks. "That'll be the 3K. Twice with a shorter distance through the field for the 5K. Four times for a 10K. You're running the 5K, right?"

"Yeah, Coach said that it's for the best since I didn't do a lot of summer training."

Jiwon nods. "We won't be together then. I'm on the 3 and 10K."

Disappointment snakes through Daniel, although he's not sure why it matters if he runs with Jiwon. In the distance, a bevy of swans swims across the lake. Their slender necks curve into question marks. The scene is serene enough to fit into a perfect day in Neverland. Roused by something Daniel doesn't see, the swans suddenly launch into the sky, beating their wings in spontaneous unison.

"*I'm a little bird that has broken out of the egg,*" Daniel recites without thinking.

Jiwon lifts a confused brow. "What's that?"

"It's just a line from a book," he stammers as heat creeps up his neck and across his face. "From *Peter and Wendy.*"

Jiwon laughs innocently. "You're different," he says in the kindest way possible. "Well, Peter, do you want to jog the rest of the way?"

Daniel's flush burns deeper. Without responding, he picks up his pace. Jiwon matches him, and they ease back into silence as the orange cones lead them to the gazebos.

Jiwon heads toward the others, but Daniel steers clear and settles into a series of gentle stretches on the lawn. Not long after, the 3K begins. Runners from all four teams crowd around the starting line, Jiwon, Kevin, and Owen among them. The starter pistol cracks and their bodies snap into movement. Within three minutes, they all disappear into the woods.

With the race out of sight, the rest of the team busy themselves with wasting time.

"Man, you think Coach was bad this morning, you should've seen my dad," Jayden says to a group gathered by the water jug. "He was yelling at me the whole way to my car. He was still shouting when I pulled out of the driveway!"

Daniel pulls his knees into his chest. From his solitary spot outside the gazebo, he can make out the other runners' jokes and laughter, but he doesn't have the energy to join them. His own parents come to mind. Have they landed by now? He wonders how long they'll stay this time.

"There they are!" Jayden cries out, gesturing toward the silhouettes of the runners headed their way.

Daniel can't help but smile. There is Jiwon, leading the pack and crossing the finish line in a flash. Daniel hasn't been keeping track of the time, but he knows that Jiwon has finished in less than ten minutes. He joins his team in their rowdy applause.

Once the last of the 3K runners complete the lap and turn in their place cards, Daniel hustles to the starting line for the 5K. He half expects Jayden to pitch him another cheery thumbs up, but the usually chirpy expression is wiped from his face, replaced by stern determination. Even though the race is only a practice, everyone takes the outcome seriously.

The pistol bangs. Daniel propels forward, starting at a comfortable third place. He doesn't want to burn out before the hills. Sure enough, once they reach the lakeside, he is able to surpass the other runners and gain second. He flies into the field and past the gazebos. Cheers roar from all four schools, but all Daniel knows is there is one turquoise-clad runner between himself and complete freedom.

Now, he only needs to focus on the thrust of his legs. If he can maintain his speed until the first-place runner slows, he'll overtake him. At the hills, the turquoise jersey loses a little momentum, and Daniel springs ahead, increasing the rate of his steps. Nothing can stop him.

The lake shimmers, welcoming him into this momentary liberation. All the shackles fall, every noose is untied. Daniel charges on, his feet rising with each sharp breath. The swans have returned, and they watch him knowingly. Daniel is not just a runner. He can fly.

But just as swiftly as he captures his independence, he reaches the gazebos. His spikes meet the finish line. He sheds his wings. A place card is shoved into his hands. Embedded onto the thick paper is the bold number 1.

"I knew he could do it!" Owen cheers from the gazebo, but Daniel keeps his eyes on the trees. His body, painfully flooded with adrenaline, carries him to the scorers' table. Faceless men receive his card, but he is still in those trees. He never wants to stop. If he stops, he has to eventually go home. He'll take a seat at the dinner table and listen to his parents talk around him.

"Cool down, Kim!" Coach Rasmussen shouts from the finish line.

More applause erupts as the racers pour in. Daniel jogs off to the side. His legs quiver beneath him. His breath declines until it ceases. All the while, his heart keeps pounding faster and faster. White fuzz feathers his vision.

I'm dying, he thinks. My parents are coming home, but I'll be dead.

But he doesn't want to die. He only wants to run. He collapses to the ground, a good distance from the gazebos. He sees his chest rising and falling and realizes that he's still breathing, which means he's not dying after all. Yet he feels afraid, even though he can't pinpoint the source of the fear.

Then, everything clicks into place like the buckles of airplane seat belts before landing. The Lorazepam is for sudden and severe anxiety, or panic attacks. Nana put the Lorazepam in his hoodie pocket. His hoodie is in the gazebo.

Daniel heads slowly toward his team. Jayden has returned, and Jiwon is gone. The 10K must have already started.

By the time Daniel reaches his jacket, his breathing has quieted. The fear slides off him like wet mud. His fingers touch the glass container, but he hesitates. Coach Rasmussen stands only a few yards away. His teammates are even closer. What if someone sees him take the pill? There are questions he doesn't want to be asked or to answer.

So instead, he fills a plastic cup with water and reclaims his isolated spot on the grass. Racers speed by, people shout. But Daniel can only breathe and nurse his water. His limbs sink deeper into the grass, but that's okay. He's floating above the park anyway. He'll be just like the swans, like a pixie, like a boy that soars in a safer place.

❖

On the bus ride back to school, Daniel sits alone. Despite the team's postmeet fatigue, everyone buzzes with excitement at their sweeping victory. Jiwon took first in the 10K, and when all the runners' scores were tallied, Cranbrook won first overall in the 3K and 10K, second in the 5K. In all, the rankings seem like a good omen for the season.

Even so, Daniel feels like lead.

"Hey there," a soft voice calls. Jiwon slides into the unoccupied seat beside him. "You did great."

Daniel turns to meet Jiwon's mild eyes. "Thanks," he says. "You too."

"You look pretty exhausted."

Daniel shakes his head. "Not really."

"Well, if that's the case," Jiwon replies, and Daniel notices that he is speaking very quietly, like his voice could break something precious. "The team is getting together at Kevin's house for a party later tonight. You should come."

Daniel blinks. Partying is the last thing he expects to find himself doing tonight.

"Give me your number, and I'll text you the address."

And even though Daniel knows that a party means sneaking out on the very same night that his parents have returned, he pulls out his phone and exchanges numbers.

CHAPTER ELEVEN

"Your parents will be so pleased to hear about your big win."
Nana carries a paper sack bulging with groceries. Daniel
lugs a heavier bag full of rice, sweet potatoes, and jars of pickled
vegetables.

"I'll fix up a big dinner," says Nana. "Your mother should be
home by then."

Daniel sets the bag on the counter. "Where is she?"

"Off to a hair appointment. Apparently, the only stylist she
trusts these days is all the way in Costa Mesa."

"What about Dad?"

Nana places a bundle of romaine lettuce in the stainless-steel
refrigerator but hesitates on the tomatoes. She turns toward him, her
words forming carefully, "He's in his office, making some important
phone calls. He's asked not to be interrupted until dinner."

Of course, hair appointments and work calls are higher priorities
than courtesy greetings to their only child after a long trip.

"They asked after you," Nana says. "I told them how you
haven't missed a single day of school and about your meet for…"
She bites the inside of her lip in thought.

"Cross-country," Daniel offers.

"Yes, your cross-country meet, and your father said, *it's good
that he's applying himself again.*"

The backhanded compliment might sting if Daniel weren't so
drained from the meet and the possible panic attack. "Do you want

help with the groceries?" he asks, effectively ending any further discussion of Sung-Min and Monica.

"Oh, not at all. It's just a few things. Why don't you go wash off your run and get ready for dinner?" She waves him off and out the kitchen.

Sure enough, as Daniel ascends the stairs, he can hear Sung-Min speaking privately into the phone from behind a closed door. He wonders if their business in Singapore was successful, but then quickly decides he doesn't actually care. While his parents' graphic design agency lives and breathes in almost every dinner conversation, he can rarely make heads or tails out of their affairs.

Flicking the bathroom light on, he supposes he should be grateful for the roof kept over his head. Then again, what would his world be like in a modest house with no housekeeper and a family that couldn't afford international business partnerships? A low-key life seems as unreachable as the stars blinking light years away. Farther than Neverland.

The shower sears his aching muscles. He feels like melting into the tub, only reemerging to drag himself into bed for a long night's sleep. But then, his phone pings from the sink top—an unfamiliar sound outside of waiting for Nana's usual messages about picking him up from school or Dr. Greene. Daniel remembers that his Saturday therapy sessions have been rescheduled to Sundays in order to accommodate future cross-country meets. Evidently, joining a sports team is a big step along the path of recovery.

Sighing, he twists the water knob to off. Tomorrow promises probing questions, and Daniel weighs whether or not to tell Dr. Greene about his anxiety scare.

Glad for a distraction, he unlocks his phone. A text notification appears on the screen from Jiwon Yoon.

If you have trouble finding Kevin's house, just look for the red brick gate

The party invitation muddles Daniel's thoughts. While it feels good to be included, images of expensive liquor shots and spilled glasses of red wine snag at the contents of Daniel's memory. Just a year ago, he would have been hustling to the house of whichever member on Cambry's cross-country team had out-of-town parents. Sound systems intended for immersive family movie nights blared that month's top music hits. Whether ten or thirty attended, dancing swelled by midnight, James threw up in a spotless bathroom, and a meaningless fight between Karter and Khalil broke out.

Once upon a time, Daniel belonged in those chaotic throngs. Now, he stares at his phone, trying to construct a reply.

Daniel: *Okay, thanks*

Jiwon: *You're coming right?*

Jiwon: *The whole team will be there*

Daniel: *Wouldn't miss it*

Jiwon: *Perfect*

After wrapping himself in a towel, Daniel peers into his closet, overwhelmed by what to wear. Normally, he throws on a loose tee and designer jeans or sweatpants. If his memory serves him right, everyone tries a little harder at weekend revels. At school, Jiwon usually sports crisp polos in pale hues. What will he wear to the party? Maybe a sweater or cardigan. Daniel frowns. Why do Jiwon's clothes even matter?

After selecting a three-quarter-sleeve print T-shirt in black, he decides to layer it over a long-sleeve, white button-up. Dark jeans complete the look. He'll grab his black trainers on his way out the door.

The smell of grilled meat wafts into his room, so he heads back down the stairs and into the dining room. Sung-Min and Monica converse at the table, napkins and silverware arranged impeccably in front of them.

"There he is," Sung-Min says from the head of the table, gesturing to the empty chair to his left. "Take a seat."

Monica smiles primly, but any comments are cut off by Nana's entrance. Steaming plates of bulgogi, rice, and salad pass from her hands to the table. Daniel's stomach growls. Today's competition has stirred his appetite.

Before the meal begins, Nana quietly leaves a tumbler of bourbon near Sun-Min's hand and fills Monica's wine glass with Chardonnay, and then places a saucer with Daniel's evening medication beside his glass of water.

As Daniel swallows the pill, Sung-Min fills the silence. "Business went well. So well in fact that your mother and I have been invited as guests of honor to a four-day design conference in Tokyo. We'll leave next Sunday."

"That gives us a whole week at home," Monica adds.

More like a whole week in your offices, Daniel wants to say, but he shoves down salad instead.

"We heard from Nana that you've joined Cranbrook's cross-country team," says Sung-Min. "You had some sort of race today? How did you make out?"

"It was just a practice meet," Daniel says to his plate. "I got first place in the 5K."

"Didn't you run the 10K at Cambry?" Sung-Min asks.

Daniel nods, aware that his father's remarks are more criticism than curiosity. "I have to work my way up to that. I'm a little out of shape when it comes to endurance."

Monica idly stirs her bulgogi into her rice. "That's very good, Daniel, first place in your practice race. You're taking responsibility again."

As opposed to his irresponsible behavior when he dropped out of track last semester, he thinks, or when he recklessly *played at* jumping off the roof into the swimming pool. Or when he snuck out of the house after dinner to party with a bunch of underage high schoolers. Well, he hasn't done that just yet.

Dinner wraps up with Monica and Sung-Min considering potential real estate in Tokyo. Once their plates are mostly clear, they say good night, even though the clock reads 7:49 p.m.

Monica and Sung-Min excuse themselves to their respective offices, Nana finishes cleaning the kitchen, and Daniel retreats to his room to kill time. He pretends at homework, shuffling between math and literature. About two hours later, he hears Nana shut the door to her quarters and rises back to life.

It's not as though Daniel has never snuck out before, but after a year, he's a little rusty. The backyard is his best bet at a clean exit. Trainers in hand, he tiptoes down the stairs, recalling which steps creak, and beelines to the security system near the front door. As expected, Nana set the alarm before retiring. He punches in the code and creeps to the living room, then opens and shuts the back door as inaudibly as possible. With quiet steps, he rushes past the glowing pool, rounds the house, and scurries through the front lawn and out the pedestrian gate into freedom.

Even though the ocean is a good thirty-minute drive away, the California sea breeze has washed away the afternoon heat. Goose bumps tease Daniel's bare arms, but it's too late to grab a jacket. Kevin's house is a solid two miles off, so he figures a light jog followed by a swift walk will get him there in no time. The stars wink confidentially above him, as though glad to find a companion in the sleepy after hours.

Second to the right and straight on till morning! Peter Pan once said, referring to the starry path to Neverland. Daniel follows the constellation of his phone's GPS to a nearby neighborhood. As directed, he finds a red brick gate and slips through the car access— left partially open. Rambunctious laughter spills from the Italianate villa.

Before Daniel can reach the door, his phone buzzes in his back pocket.

Where are you?

Instead of replying, Daniel lets himself in through the unlocked door. The entryway is unlit, guiding him to a crowded, expansive den. A widescreen TV blasts a music video playlist behind two dozen roughhousing boys and girls in baggy shirts disguised as mini-dresses. Stainless white furniture and minimalist artwork rest beneath a vast skylight.

"You made it!" Jiwon cries out, appearing from the midst of the small gathering. His bleached hair is partially tucked beneath a red beanie, and an overpriced, torn sweater hangs loosely off his shoulders toward black skinny jeans. "I was worried you got lost."

"No way," Daniel replies. A hint of giddiness skips his heart as the music shifts to a fist-bumping beat. "*Second to the right and straight on till morning.*" He kicks himself mentally as soon as the phrase escapes his lips.

Jiwon laughs, a red cup in hand. "Isn't that from *Peter Pan?*"

An arm slings around Jiwon's neck. Owen leans forward, a wide grin plastered beneath his glassy eyes. "That movie is trippy," he slurs. "Like was the screenwriter on drugs or something?"

Jiwon shrugs Owen off. "Don't be stupid."

Owen rolls his eyes, but Jiwon doesn't notice, his attention fixed on Daniel. "Let me get you a drink," he says.

A little fairy on Daniel's shoulder whispers that his medication probably doesn't mix well with booze. He follows Jiwon to the kitchen anyway. The room is brightly lit with a chandelier that glints off granite countertops. Everything looks magazine perfect, except for a poisonous arrangement of liquor bottles, liters of soda, and plastic red cups.

"I'm drinking rum and Coke," Jiwon says. "You feeling the same?"

Daniel shrugs, and Jiwon starts pouring a few shots. He overfills the cola and chuckles helplessly as the fizz spills over the brim. Without bothering to clean the mess, they wander back into the den, where dancing has inevitably picked up.

A raunchy song shakes the furniture with its deep bass. Jiwon saunters into the horde of dancers. Too sober to dance, Daniel plunks himself on the couch. He sips at whatever Jiwon concocted in the kitchen. The strong drink burns his throat.

Jiwon sways to the pulsing music with too much rhythm for the average high school boy. A cute redhead from Daniel's PE class takes notice and grabs at his elbow, but Jiwon spins away, lost in the song and his own body.

"He used to do dance back in middle school," Kevin's voice drawls from beside Daniel. The beer in his hand has softened his typical harshness. "Something modern, but Jiwon said it was too girly."

"No, I didn't!" Jiwon shouts, inexplicably cued into the remark despite the booming music. "You said that, if I'm remembering correctly. It's just hard to focus on dance and running at the same time."

Suddenly, the crunch of shattering glass cuts through the music. Kevin jumps up, anger written into his scrunched brows. Luckily, the damage is nothing more than a broken champagne flute. Yelling ensues.

Daniel eases into the shouting, familiar with the mischief of arguing pirates. The lights seem to lower as he takes another swig from his red cup. The tumult melds into a woozy cacophony. Lost Boys and pirates sway around him. The couch fades into a comfy bed of grass. Everything blurs, a blend of whoops and wild twirls.

"Is he okay?" Jayden's voice floats through the haze. "Is there some smoke I wasn't made aware of?"

Derisive laughter envelops Daniel, but he can't tear himself from the dizziness that pins him to the sofa.

"Leave him alone." Jiwon appears in his line of sight. Daniel has seen the concerned look in Jiwon's eyes before, whenever Jiwon has caught him dozing off in the library. "He's probably just worn out from the meet."

Then, the dimness fades to black. Daniel is flying above the partiers, over the house, beyond his own swimming pool and the sleeping figures of Nana and Sung-Min and Monica. High and higher, nothing between him and the stars.

A rough shake rouses him. The dancers have disappeared. Lips smack near him, and he spots Owen locked in a tight embrace with a girl he hopes is his girlfriend.

Jiwon waves a hand in Daniel's face. His eyes are narrowed and his mouth pressed in worry. Daniel fights the urge to cover that mouth with his hand. He doesn't want anyone on the team worrying about him.

"You okay?" Jiwon whispers. "You've been out for over an hour."

"I'm okay." Daniel tries to sit up, but a strong tide of dizziness sucks him back down.

"C'mon, you should go home."

Daniel lets Jiwon pull him from the couch and lead him past the now more sedate partiers. The music fades behind them as they exit into the night air.

Jiwon whips out his phone. "You live at Vandever Acres, right? I'll walk you home. What's your address?"

"I can walk myself," Daniel mutters even as he stumbles on his tottering feet.

Jiwon hooks an arm across his middle. "You barely finished your drink," he says.

"It's the drugs."

"The what?"

The words tumble off Daniel's uninhibited tongue. "The stupid antidepressants and mood stables."

"Stabilizers?"

"Yeah, that."

Jiwon shakes his head in either disbelief or his own drunken cloudiness. "What's your address?" he repeats.

They tip into the crisp night, warmed by the liquor in their veins. Daniel slips in and out of time, but the stars wink eternally overhead, as real as the arm urging him forward. The streets shift from obscure to familiar, until his gate comes into view.

"Here," Daniel slurs.

"Whoa, for real?" Jiwon breaths, eyes wide at the massive brickstone partially hidden by the yard's trees. "And I thought Owen's old house was impressive."

Jiwon clears his throat, perhaps embarrassed by his outburst. "You good from here?" he asks.

Daniel dips his head in a half-hearted nod before plunging forward with too much gusto. Fortunately, his hands meet the cold bars of the gate. "I'm good," he says, words barely taking shape.

"Get some sleep," Jiwon tells him before unlatching the pedestrian gate. "Tonight was pretty fun, huh?"

Daniel stares for a moment at Jiwon. His oversize sweater curves just beneath his thin collarbones. Somehow, in this mess of a night, Jiwon enjoyed himself. He had fun with Daniel.

Daniel's brain clears just enough for speech, and he manages a jumbled, "It was something."

CHAPTER TWELVE

For Daniel, the only thing worse than taking tests in the library is getting his graded exams back in class. Mrs. Yasment slides each algebra exam onto the students' desks, face-down for confidentiality's sake, but everyone immediately flips them over anyway.

"There are clearly a few concepts that we'll need to review," she says, "but overall, I'm pleased with the scores."

The white backside of Daniel's test taunts him. He turns it over slowly, as if the reduced speed might somehow mitigate the damage. He crammed Sunday and Monday night and powered through all his extended time in the hopes of earning anything higher than sixty-five percent. After last Saturday—winning the 5K and gaining a semblance of acceptance from the team—he's determined to keep his grades up. Failing out of cross-country would be like escaping Captain Hook's clutches only to discover that the pirate had stolen his shadow.

With a sharp exhale, he exposes the exam's front page. Red ink spells out, "81/100, B-, Good Work."

Daniel doublechecks the name on the paper. The test belongs to him. He furrows his brows and takes a long sip of water, because part of him is sure that he has woken to a different world. Yes, he answered every question. Yes, his mindfulness efforts during lectures have been improving. Yes, he followed most of Mrs. Yasment's lessons, especially with her emailed notes, but still, a jump from Ds to Bs is an unexpected gift. Math used to come easy to him, but that was his freshman year. The new and impaired Daniel has to keep time on a clock just to stay grounded in his desk chair.

Amber turns in her seat toward Daniel. Today, her lips are pink instead of her trademark red. She waves her test between them, showing off a B+ that Daniel already knows is the product of duplicity.

"How'd you make out?" she asks, leaning forward to check his grade without his permission. Her hair brushes the back of his hand. He pulls away, shoving his fist into his hoodie pocket.

"Look who finally wised up. Who gave you the answers?" A coy smile plays on the corners of her mouth. "A B minus is a safe start. It's always good to get a few answers wrong, so you don't give yourself away."

"I did this on my own," he says. While he could find Amber's assumption offensive, he doesn't blame her. After all, he's struggling to accept the reality of the high score.

She rolls her eyes. "Yeah, and I just found out that I'm the next National Merit Scholar."

"I'm serious."

She looks him up-and-down, gauging the likelihood of a joke gone on for too long. Eventually, she realizes his sincerity and draws herself a little closer.

"Well, how about that," she says, tucking her hair behind an ear. "Good for you."

She stares at him for a second too long before swiveling back to the board as a new lesson begins. Mrs. Yasment writes out a complex equation, but Amber glances over her shoulder with an admiring grin. Daniel's stomach flips. Somehow, he's managed to impress the unflappable delinquent. Yet, he feels uncomfortable with the attention. Smiles like the one Amber just tossed his way usually contain camouflaged messages, often followed by fingers that linger on his arm and too much eye contact.

Daniel isn't blind. Amber is pretty. Her long legs stretch suggestively from her short skirts, and her features complement each other with an easygoing sort of beauty. She's funny and inviting and overall likeable. Yet, the thought of her wanting more from him than 504 banter sends his brain spinning.

Distracted, Daniel searches out the class clock's second hand. After sixty seconds in the belly of the crocodile, maybe he can focus on the real purpose of math period. His fingers graze the red letters that magically form the words, "Good Work." He won't let this test be a fluke.

After an especially grueling practice, Daniel changes clothes in his dark corner of the locker room, then waits at his usual spot for Nana to drive him to Mercy. Yesterday, Jiwon waited with him, and sure enough, he joins Daniel after waving farewell to the team.

Daniel moves his backpack to give Jiwon space to sit beside him on the sidewalk.

"Coach is a real dictator before official meets," Jiwon small talks, rubbing circles into his sore calves. "How are you holding up?"

"I can keep up," says Daniel.

Jiwon nods and then suddenly reaches out to Daniel's chest. "Or is all the stress causing premature balding?" he says, plucking a strand of Daniel's hair from his sports jacket.

Heart hammering, Daniel manages a breathy laugh. As he tries to piece together all the reasons his nerves are racing, Jiwon's phone vibrates. The playful atmosphere kicks the bucket as whatever flashes on his phone stirs up an obvious irritation.

Jiwon's thumbs furiously type against the touchscreen. "Great," he mutters. "Some kind of technical issue with one of my college applications." He buries himself deeper into his phone, and Daniel is glad to just breathe for a moment.

Nana arrives before Jiwon reaches any kind of conclusion in his email war. They exchange preoccupied good-byes. It isn't as though Daniel can help him with technical errors, and he's got a date with an obstinate psychiatrist anyway.

The receptionist points Daniel to the third floor, where he's eventually led down the coffee-colored hallway to Dr. Greene's office. The setting sun bleeds onto the carpet, and Daniel notices that the psychiatrist looks a little tired behind his horn-rimmed glasses.

Even so, Dr. Greene whips out his deck of cards just like at any other session. They fall into a game of war. After a few turns, Dr. Greene launches into a typical open-ended question, switching up the phrasing a bit this time around, "What's different today from the last time you were here?"

Last Sunday, Daniel could have shared that he had rashly gone out drinking and passed out on a couch in a room full of potential friends, but he had opted to stick to less incriminating topics, like the practice meet and his parents' return home. Since nothing about either of those subjects has changed in the last two days, he settles for discussing his math exam.

"I got a B on my test. Well, a B minus, but that's better than any other grade I've gotten so far."

"Good work, Daniel," says Dr. Greene, unknowingly choosing the exact words as Mrs. Yasment. "That shows a renewed dedication to school."

Daniel claims Dr. Greene's queen of spades with his ace of hearts. "Yeah, well, Amber thought I cheated."

The psychiatrist raises a brow. "Amber? You've never mentioned her before."

"She's just a girl who also gets accommodations. For ADHD. We take tests together in the library a lot and sit next to each other in a few classes."

Dr. Greene overpowers Daniel's jack with another queen. "Would you consider Amber a friend, then?"

Amber's curving mouth and equally curvy body invades his thoughts. "Not really," he replies. "I don't know her intentions."

"Intentions? Do you feel like Amber might have ulterior motives for talking to you?"

Daniel shrugs. "She's kind of a flirt, possibly with everyone."

A war breaks out when Dr. Greene and Daniel both draw sevens. They lay out three face-down cards, then whip out the tie breaker. Daniel wins the lot with another ace.

Since their conversation has stalled, Dr. Greene poses a new question. "Would it be good or bad if Amber flirted with you?" Daniel taps his deck nervously. How has a light mention of his math score evolved into a full-blown interrogation on girls? This is something that Daniel dislikes about Dr. Greene. Nothing is ever simple. Each spoken word spirals into a tornado of questions that he would rather save for later, or never broach in the first place.

"Daniel?" Dr. Greene presses him, which is another of his annoying habits. Silence works with Sung-Min and Monica. Oftentimes with Nana, too, but Dr. Greene seems to take pleasure in forcing Daniel to talk.

"It doesn't matter so long as she doesn't push it," he finally replies after losing a two to a four.

"What does *pushing it* look like?"

Daniel rests a fist on his deck, wishing he could dial back the ticking clock to when he brought up Amber and erase the comment from history. Unless Dr. Greene leads a monastic life, he already knows what *pushing it* means. Unwanted touches, useless gossip, hurt feelings after the slightest rejection. Flirting brings on pressure to appease someone else's desires. Then relationships end with boys like Owen playing the field whenever a girlfriend gets even a little boring. Everyone just wants to have fun and feel wanted, until Daniel winds up on someone's floral bedspread just trying to keep pace and hide his fear.

The whole ordeal reads like a scripted story. If his future is mapped out for him, then Daniel will have to find another place with a different plot line—somewhere outside the predetermined role he's long since failed at acting out. Somewhere in between being the model student and the cross-country star, he found himself faking, and he spent a year terrified that everyone at Cambry would call him out on his facade.

"Daniel," Dr. Greene calls, fracturing the glass walls he's raised around himself. "Your hand."

Daniel's nails dig into his palms. He loosens his grip, revealing throbbing red crescents. He strokes the inflamed skin, trying to rub out the dull ache.

Before Dr. Greene can pry, Daniel starts talking. "Amber is just an acquaintance. She's funny and all, but we don't have anything in common besides accommodations. I'm making other friends on the cross-country team."

Dr. Greene tentatively lays a king of clubs on the table, eyes fixed on Daniel's palm.

"And you don't even have to ask," Daniel adds. "I don't want to kill myself. I have a meet this Saturday."

"That's nice to hear, Daniel. It's good to have goals, to look forward to something."

Like getting out of this office, Daniel thinks.

CHAPTER THIRTEEN

While goals are supposed to help keep Daniel alive, Saturday's meet only manages to drag him down. Placing fourth in the 5K was nowhere near his personal expectations. Sure, he finished first out of his own team, but he can't shake the feeling that he let everyone down, especially after the sullen bus ride back to Cranbrook. The defeat weighs him down even after he arrives home and showers and pins himself to his chair for a lengthy dinner with Sung-Min and Monica.

His parents mostly discuss the ins and outs of packing for their next-day flight to Tokyo. Daniel disappears into a bowl of kimchi jjigae. His cheeks flush from the spicy stew, and he remembers the red that tinged Jiwon's face after he took third in the 10K. Self-deprecation poured from him with beads of sweat. No one was pleased with their overall third place ranking.

Once Monica and Sung-Min retreat to their separate bedrooms to double-check their suitcases one last time, Daniel slinks to the third floor with a strained, "Good night," to Nana. He wants to bury himself in anything unrelated to school and failure. At least until Nana goes to sleep, because evidently, whether they win or lose, the cross-country team always parties after Saturday meets. Even in his defeated funk on the bus ride, Jiwon had taken the initiative to text Daniel the address to Owen's house.

Let's drink our sorrows. Team tradition.
I'll be there.

While he waits for Nana to retire for the night, Daniel retrieves a volume of Peter Pan-inspired paintings from his dresser. He glides his fingers across renderings of the London skyline after twilight. A Monet-style landscape of Mermaid's Lagoon soothes his tired eyes. When he thumbs to his personal favorite, the tension in his spine relaxes. There sit Peter and Wendy upon Marooners' Rock, the rising tide threatening their lives. Daniel knows the story well. Shutting his eyes, he can hear the crashing waves, smell the fear in Wendy's soul, taste Peter's pain when he realizes that the one time he truly must fly, he cannot. Hook has dealt a terrible blow to his arm, and no happy thoughts can lift the boy into the sky.

Then, Wendy's little brother's kite floats to them in a stroke of sweet serendipity. The kite can only bear one of them, and, of course, Wendy should go, leaving Peter to a cruel fate on the rock. The water reaches his feet. He cannot fly, the end approaches.

"To die will be an awfully big adventure," Daniel says, preparing to drown. Then, Dr. Greene appears in a Never bird's nest to rescue him.

"Would it be good or bad to come with me?" Dr. Greene asks.

There is someone else in the nest, clad in powder blue. At first, Daniel thinks Wendy has returned to save him, but when the figure extends a hand, Daniel finds Jiwon on the other side.

"Everybody is already at the party," the boy pouts. "Where are you?"

Daniel's eyes snap open. His ordinary room replaces the sea, the only sound the gentle rap of the wind in the sweetgum tree. His phone reads ten after ten. He'll be later to the party than he would like, but at least he won't be as fatigued as last time. He doesn't want another repeat of passing out on the sofa.

Checking his reflection, he smooths out a few wrinkles from his white tee and khaki shorts. After grabbing a jean jacket, he makes his getaway down the stairs, through the backyard, and out the gate. Once his feet hit the street, he preemptively texts Jiwon.

Daniel: *I'm on my way*
Jiwon: *About time*
Jiwon: *Jayden is already trashed*

Daniel: *That's early*

Jiwon: *He's dancing like a madman*

Jiwon: *I'd send you video evidence, but you'll be here soon,* right?

Daniel: *Fast as I can on my own two feet*

Jiwon: *And here I thought you might fly.*

Switching his phone to the GPS app, he tears down the road. According to Jiwon, Owen's family had once resided in Vandever Acres, but he down-sized recently. The address leads him to the identical Dutch Colonials that border Cranbrook's campus—the same neighborhood in which Jiwon himself lives. While lacking ornamental gates and towering multi-storied architecture, the two-story homes are clearly well-maintained. Yet apparently, Jiwon considers his own stomping grounds a step down the financial ladder.

Several cars line the street outside Owen's place. Daniel follows a walkway lined by path lights to the unlocked front door. Once inside, he meanders through a crowd of well-dressed upperclassmen, seeking out a familiar face. If he can at least locate the dance floor, he'll probably find Jayden.

The living room furniture has been pushed to the walls, leaving ample space for a throng of swaying bodies. In the middle of the swarm, Jayden throws his arms and legs in a feverish freestyle that tempts Daniel to laugh out loud.

Jiwon steps out of the adjacent kitchen. A bottle perspires in his hand. "I told you it was bad," he shouts over the music. "I'm pretty sure this will end up online."

That afternoon, Jayden placed a depressing eighth out of thirteen in the 5K. Clearly, alcohol has been his first choice for coping.

"Should we get him?" Daniel asks.

"Let him dance it off. It's more entertaining this way." Jiwon lifts his beer toward Daniel. "You okay to drink tonight?"

The double meaning behind the skillfully crafted question hurts Daniel's pride. "I took a nap," he replies, hoping the dim lights will obscure the shame of the redness he feels burning his ears.

"So, no passing out tonight?"

"Nope."

Jiwon pushes the cold beer into Daniel's hand. "Then take mine. I just opened it, but I was really wanting something stronger anyway."

When Jiwon draws back into the kitchen, Daniel decides to stay put. The last thing he needs is for Jiwon to see him as a lost puppy who can't hold his own at a party, especially after last Saturday's snafu. He downs a satisfying gulp of beer before trailing a rowdy group toward the garage. Several girls and team members, Owen included, circle a billiard table. The balls smash into each other, sinking into corner pockets.

"Daniel! My man!" Owen cries out. He lifts a shot glass to clink against Daniel's beer. "We'll get them next meet, am I right?"

Daniel takes another drink, the cold liquid fizzing down his throat. "If we put in the work."

A frown flickers across Owen's mouth before he chuckles softly. "You're the serious type to a fault," he says. "You need a girl to loosen you up."

"I'm good."

"You sure? I know at least a handful of girls here that are always willing to cheer a guy up after a loss."

Daniel knows for a fact that a random hookup is the least likely cure for his poor performance. Besides, getting together with someone who has probably slept with another team member sounds like a recipe for drama, and taking advantage of drunk girls would be a poor way to build his reputation.

He swallows more beer instead of answering Owen, focusing on the next pool shot. Luckily, Owen's turn follows. He aims and smacks a solid ball into a nearby pocket.

"Well, try to have some fun," he says after passing the cue to the next player. "Want some vodka? My parents import it from Russia."

Daniel doesn't want to turn him down twice, so he takes one for the team and accepts a double shot. The vodka tastes like rubbing alcohol, but he tries to keep a straight face and wash it down with beer.

"Good stuff, right?" Owen smirks. Fortunately, the billiard table reclaims his attention, and Daniel ducks out of the garage. Wondering if Jayden is still thrashing on the dance floor, or if Jiwon is anywhere nearby, Daniel heads back toward the living room. As he makes his way down the hall, he spies a girl who bears a striking resemblance to Amber. She disappears into the bathroom, and Daniel speeds past the closed door before he winds up in another round of uncomfortable rapport.

The excitement in the living room has reached a new peak as the alcohol starts to thrum in everyone's veins. Jayden has calmed down enough to settle into grinding with a dark-haired girl. Daniel thinks he recognizes her as the only Korean on the girls' cross-country team, but he can't remember her name.

On the sidelines, Kevin bumps his head to the beat. Daniel joins him, figuring the relatively stoic runner won't try to make too much small talk. After they nod their greetings, they fall into an easy silence.

"There he goes again," Kevin mutters, and Daniel follows his gaze to Jiwon dancing among the crowd. His red jersey twists around his waist as he curves from side-to-side. His hips flow into a dip, knees bending just enough to form a perfect S.

"He's been like that since elementary school," Kevin adds, shaking his head at the attention funneling Jiwon's way.

Girls whoop and guys clap as Jiwon smiles at their recognition. There is a distinct element of sensuality in each of Jiwon's movements. One hand grips a red cup, the other runs suggestively down his chest. He laughs as a round of whistles trill through the pack.

Daniel's chest ignites, conjuring up images of the Lorazepam he left in his nightstand, but his instincts tell him that the compression isn't a panic attack. He chalks it up to the vodka shot.

"We couldn't dance like that even if we tried, right, Kim?" says Kevin, but Daniel doesn't have time to script out a response, because Jiwon's gaze has shifted from his admirers straight to them.

Daniel tips his beer over his mouth, thrusting his gaze to the ceiling so he can look anywhere but at Jiwon stepping toward them.

"Are you going to sulk all night long?" Jiwon exclaims, words slurring together slightly. He drops his empty red cup on a nearby accent table.

Kevin scowls. "I never dance. You know that."

"What about at the junior prom after party?"

"We agreed to never bring that up."

Dejected, Jiwon changes tactics and sizes up Daniel. He loses his footing and catches himself on the wall, a mere inch away. "C'mon, Daniel. Don't grow up to be like this jerk."

It's not as if Daniel has never danced before. While his skills pale in comparison to Jiwon, he can keep a beat as well as anyone else. His beer drained, he has no believable excuse.

"Why not?" he says more to himself. Jiwon triumphantly grabs his shoulder and drags him near a speaker before he can back down.

As the music drums into Daniel's bones, he can feel the alcohol flooding his limbs. Dr. Greene's prescriptions have obviously derailed his alcohol tolerance. The dancers swirl around him, dazzling his vision. Jiwon yells something that he can't quite make out. The bass drops, and for a split second, Daniel sails above the crowd, even as his feet remain firmly planted on the ground.

Jayden joins them with the girl from the cross-country team. When Daniel steps back to give them more space, his foot catches on the loudspeaker. There is nothing to brace the fall, and he crashes directly on his elbow. Pain buzzes down his forearm, and his stomach wrenches from the impact.

Jiwon cracks up but reaches out to help him up. "You idiot," he shouts, but he then quickly trips over Daniel's shoes. Without a moment's notice, Jiwon plummets onto Daniel, his head brutally smacking against Daniel's collarbone.

Dizziness envelops Daniel with Jiwon's sudden nearness. The music swallows him, the tumult flashing wildly around him. Somehow, in the midst, Jiwon's laughter vibrates through his chest, and from somewhere nearby, the fragrance of the ocean billows forth. Like the sea on a cloudless Neverland shore. He breathes in deeply, only to realize he must be inhaling the scent of Jiwon's shampoo.

"Are they fighting?" Jayden yells.

A pale hand shoots out, seizing Jiwon and pulling him upright. Kevin turns to Daniel and yanks him up in the same way.

"You two okay?" he asks.

"Never better!" answers Jiwon.

"You're drunk."

A wave of nausea sweeps over Daniel's stomach. One beer and a double shot, he thinks. He can't even keep that down. He prays that he can make it to the bathroom before chunks erupt, but then recalls glimpsing Amber over that way. Too muddled to consider that she has probably long since left the toilet, he stumbles to the sliding glass door that leads to the back porch.

"I need some air," he announces and dashes out without checking to see if the others heard him.

An automatic light flicks on. He treks past a maze of furniture before crawling on hands and knees into a bush. The vomit surges out, hot and acidic. He wretches again and again until nothing comes up but bitter saliva.

A soothing hand strokes his shoulder blades, and Daniel wonders if Mrs. Darling has come to nurse him back to bed, but then he remembers just where he is. On all fours in someone's backyard at an underage party in the middle of the night.

The hand has a voice. "Take it easy," Jiwon murmurs. "Just get it all out."

Daniel should feel humiliated, but in truth, he's relieved to not be alone. He wipes his mouth with his wrists and turns to sit on his haunches.

"I'm okay," he replies hoarsely. "Throwing up made it better."

Jiwon sways a little but the alcoholic mirth has drained from his features. "Yeah, I always feel better after purging it all out of my system."

"I should probably go home."

"Let me walk you."

Daniel shakes his head. "That's all right. Don't you live nearby?"

"It's fine. I want to sober up a bit before bed anyway. A walk will be good for me."

Daniel isn't up for arguing, and the company won't hurt him, so they get to their feet and make their way out the backyard gate. As they stalk the vacant sidewalk, Jiwon points out a dark blue house with a red door.

"That's where I live," he says.

"Sure you don't want to just go in?"

"Positive."

A crescent moon shines its faint light over their journey. They pass the next few blocks without a word, until Jiwon finally speaks up again.

"You can't handle alcohol very well at all." He chuckles softly to take the edge off his next question: "Is it because of your medication?"

Daniel sighs. The topic was bound to come up again sooner or later. "Yeah, I'm taking some stuff that doesn't really mix with anything fun."

"Is that why you fall asleep during tests?"

The statement hangs in the air, heavy and unavoidable. "Yes," Daniel admits. "I'm not sick or anything. It's just some meds that are supposed to cheer me up. They suck."

Jiwon kicks a rock, skittering it across the pavement. "I had to take some antidepressants for a few months after my mom died."

"Really?"

"It was stupid. I just couldn't stop thinking about how there were things I wanted to tell her before she died. I thought I had so much more time."

"*It's impossible to say how time wears on*," Daniel replies.

Jiwon gives him a weak smile. "That's deep. Let me guess. It's from *Peter Pan*?"

"Sort of. The actual line sounds more old-fashioned."

They approach Daniel's gate. Black bars loom over them, marking an end to their night.

"Your place is seriously awesome," Jiwon says, gazing up toward the roof that nearly meets the peaks of the surrounding trees. "I want a tour someday."

Daniel decides not to tell Jiwon how empty his house feels most days. His parents are leaving again in the morning. Just him and Nana in three stories of shadows.

"How about tomorrow?" Daniel suggests.

"I can bring my homework," Jiwon replies, rubbing his arms as a gust kicks up. "Time to head back, I guess."

Daniel peels off his jean jacket and offers it to Jiwon. He slips it on without hesitation.

"You can give it back tomorrow," Daniel says. "Thanks for walking with me."

"Anytime."

As Jiwon heads down the street, Daniel can hardly believe that Jiwon, with his fast times and college applications and effortless friendships, once took pills just like him. Perhaps he should feel sad for him, but in truth, the new information makes him feel better. Daniel might not be an aberration in an otherwise uniform world. Maybe he's just like Jiwon. Someone normal.

CHAPTER FOURTEEN

A few hours after Sung-Min and Monica depart for Tokyo, Daniel receives a text from Jiwon saying that he's parked outside his gate. Daniel rushes down the winding staircase. As he passes the second floor, he shouts a warning to Nana that a guest is coming over.

In the foyer, he punches the gate code onto the security pad, then heads onto the patio to wave Jiwon inside. Nana hurries to Daniel's side, astounded by both an unexpected guest and that Daniel has mentioned a friend. The word feels foreign in their household. Schoolmates haven't crossed their threshold for nearly a year.

When Daniel casts an uncomfortable look in her direction, Nana gets the message: *Please go inside. It's weird for my nanny to greet my new friend at the door.* Thankfully, she disappears back into the foyer. Still, Daniel expects to see her again soon.

He certainly understands her reasons. He, too, is excited, although he tries his best to conceal it behind a mask of appropriate enthusiasm. Jiwon pulls his dark blue Acura into the driveway. He hops out and grabs a hefty bookbag from the back seat before sauntering toward the porch.

"Hey there," he says. "How's it going?"

"A typical Sunday." Daniel doesn't mention that his parents left without a good-bye or that later in the afternoon he'll skirt off to a therapy appointment. Right now, he has a solid four hours to be like any other Cranbrook student on a weekend, studying and horsing around with a friend.

Dark circles shadow Jiwon's otherwise wakeful eyes—the only remnant of last night's debauchery. "So, do I get the grand tour?"

"Come on in."

Jiwon slips off his shoes and steps onto the cool marble floor. Inviting someone to his house suddenly makes Daniel hypercritical of the obvious price tags on every piece of furniture, every picture frame, every drape. Jiwon smiles softly at the overflowing vases of fresh flowers, and Daniel wonders what Jiwon's home looks like on the inside.

"Not bad," Jiwon comments, then halts at the foot of the stairs. He tilts back, eyes following the winding pathway. "Whoa, it's kind of eerie."

"My room's on the third floor."

"Let's see it."

Before they can head up, Nana emerges from the kitchen, straightening her apron. Jiwon steps forward shyly—a reservedness that Daniel has never seen before veiling his usual sprightliness.

Realizing that introductions are in order, Daniel speaks up. "Jiwon, this is Na—my housekeeper," he stammers, embarrassed by the nickname but ashamed to relegate Nana's title to just a housekeeper. After Nana's face falls, he thinks better of it.

"Nana, this is Jiwon," he adds.

Jiwon shakes her hand. "I've heard about you. You're the best cook. Daniel's lunches are too good."

Nana perks up at the compliment. "Thank you. It's nice to meet one of Daniel's friends."

"He's in cross-country with me," says Daniel. "We're going to do some homework."

"Then you'll need some brain food. I'll bring snacks up in a bit."

"Thanks."

"Nice to meet you, Nana," Jiwon says, the name rolling easily off his tongue.

They head up the stairs. As they reach the second landing, Daniel explains that the rooms belong to his parents.

"Are they home?" Jiwon asks innocently.

Daniel keeps climbing, hoping to drop the topic quickly. "They're out on business."

Jiwon takes the hint and refrains from asking any more questions. Once the stairs open onto the third floor, he pauses. "Your house honestly seems taller than this from the outside."

Daniel points to the attic door above them. "That pulls into stairs that lead to a storage space. There's nothing up there, except a few unused paintings and some old boxes." Daniel gestures to the three doors surrounding them. "Bathroom, Nana's apartment, and my room."

Daniel guides Jiwon to his door. Once inside, he feels the coldness of the magazine-like decor. Jiwon drops his backpack to the hardwood floor with a thud and takes in the picture-perfect artwork, crisply made bed, and characterless nightstand. He approaches the bay window, gazing out to the sweetgum tree.

"Nice view."

"We can go out there. My mom's office roof is right beneath us. You can even climb the tree all the way to the yard."

Jiwon turns his back against the glass. "Cool. Maybe after we get some work done," he says. "I have to admit. I thought your room would look different."

"Like what?" Daniel replies defensively.

"My room is definitely messier than this, and I have posters and my ribbons and medals—"

"Those are in the parlor. My mom makes a big deal out of having an interior decorator."

"So where do you put all your stuff? Like your games and movies? Or do you keep that in the parlor, too?"

"I don't really play games, and my movies—" Daniel's eyes shift to the dresser, but he's not sure if he's ready to share his collection with Jiwon. The whole house tour has taken a strange turn. For the first time ever, he wants to take out his textbooks and start on math. But Jiwon doesn't miss Daniel's glance toward the dresser. He kneels to the bottom drawer and pulls it open before Daniel can protest.

The rows and rows of movie cases seem ordinary at first. "Wow, you have a huge selection," Jiwon exclaims, tracing the labels with his index finger. As he soaks up the titles, his eyebrows rise higher and higher. "It's all *Peter Pan*."

When Jiwon swivels back toward him, Daniel wishes he could disappear or fly or even run away to the bathroom. He tries to form a lie, but he can't form a single sentence. He has to say something. "It's just a hobby," would do, or "I don't know why my parents buy me all that junk," or, "I'm normal. I swear I'm just like you," but he chokes on every word.

He doesn't expect Jiwon to give him an affectionate smile, and he certainly doesn't anticipate him pulling the handle to the next drawer. Posters, novelizations, and bound collections of postcards rear their incriminatory heads.

"Shit, there's more."

Impulsively, Daniel slams the drawer shut. Jiwon recoils sharply. Daniel's hands, glued to the dresser, visibly tremble. He waits for what comes next. As he braces himself for the laughter, his mind escapes. How far can he roam before the taunts begin? He slips to the window, transports through the glass, and loses himself in the sweetgum leaves. From there, he'll watch the show. Everyone always laughs, just like at Mercy Hospital, because of what he is. A freak.

"It's not like I'm surprised," Jiwon murmurs. His fingers lightly touch Daniel's flexed wrist. "C'mon, you quote *Peter Pan* all the time."

Daniel peeks out from the tree branches.

"Hey, it's okay. Is there more? I want to see."

"Why?" Daniel observes himself talking.

Jiwon shrugs. "It's kind of cool. It beats Owen's porn collection." When Jiwon laughs, Daniel can hardly breathe. Jiwon isn't making a joke at his expense, but about their team member. He takes a few cautious steps from the roof back to the window.

"I liked Peter Pan a lot as a kid," Jiwon continues. "I always pretended it with all the neighborhood kids. We acted the story out with props and everything. Kevin would even play Captain Hook whenever his family came by."

Daniel passes through the window and sits closer, almost near enough to rejoin his frozen body. "What role did you take on?" he asks tentatively, still worried that the conversation is bound for a cruel conclusion.

"Don't make fun of me, but since I was the smallest, they always made me play Wendy."

Daniel smiles despite his uneasiness. Like he would make fun of Jiwon right now, when his entire reputation is in Jiwon's clutches. The last thing Daniel needs is for the cross-country team to learn about his bizarre obsession.

"You'd make a good Wendy," Daniel says.

Jiwon crosses his arms. "You know that's not a compliment, right?" He stands, tugging Daniel up with him. "So, can I see what's in the top drawer?"

"No way," Daniel wants to say, but his mouth forms the word, "Okay."

Jiwon uncovers the array of antique boxes. He gently lifts one out and finds an assortment of knickknacks inside. Thumbing through acorns and dried flowers and miniature hooks, he settles on a tiny metal cylinder with one sealed end.

"What's this?" he asks. "A fairy cup?"

"A thimble. Wendy uses it when she sews on Peter's shadow."

Jiwon fits the piece onto his index finger. "I don't remember that in the movie."

"It's in the play."

"I've only seen the cartoon," Jiwon admits, rapping the thimble against the box. "Do you own the play, like a made-for-film version?"

"Yeah."

"Let's watch it then."

And just like that, Daniel's soul crashes back in place. "Really?" he asks.

"I don't see why not. I'm getting a glimpse of the inner workings of the stoic Daniel Kim." He drops the thimble into the box and snaps it shut. "We should do some homework first, though."

"Okay."

As they take out their binders and textbooks, Daniel bites the inside of his cheek in disbelief. How has Jiwon managed to transform crazy into normal? They'll knock out their assignments and watch a movie afterward, just like any other high school students on a Sunday. On the floor, Jiwon lays out a set of physics notes, while Daniel starts penning formulas at his desk.

Nana knocks on the cracked door and brings in a tray of crackers and sliced cheeses, then leaves them to their work. Jiwon snags a bite, wiggling his eyebrows in fun.

"Classy," he says. "Beats pretzels."

They eat. They study. Struggling with an especially confusing problem, Daniel starts nibbling at his pencil. Jiwon offers to help and glances over his work.

"You got it all right," he says before tapping a particular equation. "You just forgot the exponent here."

"Oh, thanks." How obvious.

Jiwon grins and gets back to his own assignment. The snack plate empties. Two hours pass by swiftly, with Jiwon scrawling on worksheets and Daniel fumbling his way through math and history. Eventually, Jiwon stretches his arms above him with a dramatic yawn.

"How about that play?" he says.

Daniel shuts his textbook. "You still want to?"

"I thought that was the plan."

Not one to push his luck, Daniel fishes a late twentieth-century reenactment from the bottom drawer, and they creak down the stairs to the living room. Daniel inserts the disc, as Jiwon gets comfortable on the gray linen sofa. The play flickers to life. An orchestra sounds. Michael Darling scurries onto the screen, and Daniel almost relaxes. To his surprise, Jiwon chuckles at the funny parts and clucks his tongue when Mr. Darling locks the beloved nanny dog out of the nursery.

When Wendy promises Peter Pan a kiss but gives him a thimble instead, Jiwon lets out an exaggerated, "Oh, so that's the thimble."

About a quarter of the way through the movie, Nana interrupts by clearing her throat. "Daniel, you have an appointment this afternoon," she says, and Daniel thanks her silently for not specifically mentioning his date with Dr. Greene.

Jiwon hits pause on the remote. "We'll finish it next time." Daniel can't believe there will be a next time.

After grabbing his backpack and retying his sneakers, Jiwon heads out the door. "This was fun," he says, before reaching into his backpack once more. "Oh, and I almost forgot. Here's your jacket."

Daniel takes the rumpled jean jacket. "Thanks for hanging out."

"Thanks for showing me the house." As he makes his way down the porch steps, he gives a mock salute. "See you later, Peter."

About ten minutes later, a text notification pops up on Daniel's phone.

Jiwon: *Don't tell anyone about me playing Wendy as a kid.*

Jiwon: *I think Kevin has finally forgotten about that little piece of history*

Daniel: *I'll consider it if you don't tell the team about my Peter Pan collection*

Jiwon: *Deal.*

Daniel falls back into the couch, feeling weightless.

CHAPTER FIFTEEN

You ready to finish your test?" Mr. Bartel waves the vocabulary quiz from the circulation desk as Daniel approaches. He has only a few questions left, so he's hopeful that he'll finish before an entire lunch period is wasted.

"Ready as I'll ever be," he replies, taking the paper gingerly. Vocabulary is relatively easy, so long as he can harness his attention. As he sheds his backpack and phone, Mr. Bartel continues with his typical motivational speech.

"You got this. It's multiple choice, so all you have to do is use the process of elimination." He glances toward the book stacks. "And your friend showed up to shelve today. Maybe you'll have time to grab some food."

As Daniel heads to the quiet room, he shrugs at the librarian's offhand comment. Apparently, librarians enjoy saying the most awkward, strangely perceptive things. Even so, he peers through the aisles, hoping to spy Jiwon. They haven't spoken since yesterday's text. A spark of anxiety flickers in his gut. Will Jiwon really keep quiet about his unconventional interest?

But he doesn't spot Jiwon, and his test needs taking care of, so he settles at his usual table, swallows a mouthful of water, and starts bubbling in responses. After each answer, he drinks. Water, vocabulary, water, vocabulary—the cycle goes on as he tries to remember the difference between *egregious* and *erroneous*. The technique works. Another quiz conquered.

As fate would have it, Jiwon is chatting with Mr. Bartel at the circulation desk. Two identical books rest on the counter.

"This one goes in reference, and the other belongs with History and Geography," Mr. Bartel explains as Daniel joins them. To Daniel, he says, "Record time."

"I wouldn't know. There's no clock in there," he replies. At the same time, Jiwon murmurs a friendly, "Hey, Daniel."

Daniel's neck burns from his flaring nerves. He averts his eyes, suddenly too invested in the dirt smudge on his trainers.

Mr. Bartel either doesn't notice or completely ignores the interaction. "Well, if you'd like, you can always bring a watch with you. Just be sure it's not a smartwatch. High schoolers are pretty resourceful these days."

Daniel doesn't mention Amber's low-tech cheating skills. He collects his book bag and phone, hoping that Jiwon will still think he's a decent choice for lunch company.

Mr. Bartel quickly dashes those dreams. "Jiwon, I need you to finish putting away what's left on the cart before I can dismiss you. Sorry, Daniel," he adds knowingly. "Service hours can't be fudged."

Jiwon waves a dismissive hand as he wheels the cart to the reference section. Doing his best to feign apathy, Daniel follows close behind toward the exit. Before he can push open the door, someone yanks him back by his backpack.

Jiwon smiles mischievously. "Let's hang out after practice. I've got a surprise for you."

"What kind of surprise?" The image of the entire cross-country team laughing Daniel out of the parking lot invades Daniel's mind. A surprise sounds dangerously close to a prank.

"It's something you'll like," says Jiwon, picking up on Daniel's nervousness. "You said your parents are out of town. Can I come over?"

"Just you?"

"Who else?"

"I don't know," Daniel stammers. Just the whole team with torches and pitchforks and a camera phone set to video. Jiwon looks confused, so Daniel forces himself to stop assuming the worst.

"Sure, let's hang out."

Jiwon beams. "Great! We can walk to my house, and I'll drive us to your place."

Plans finalized, Jiwon rushes back to the shelving cart before Mr. Bartel catches him slacking off. Daniel prepares himself to fend off a slurry of worst-case scenarios for the rest of the school day.

From his pickup spot, Daniel warily watches Jiwon fist-bump their teammates good-bye. He messaged Nana before practice to let her know that he already had a ride. Now, he waits for Jiwon's surprise to unfold. Part of him knows that his fears are irrational, but the hook in his gut churns up every terrible possibility. Daniel focuses on his breathing as Jiwon makes his way over.

The walk through Jiwon's neighborhood takes all of ten minutes. Jiwon's step is light, which means he has to slow down every few paces in order to match Daniel's leaden footfalls. When they reach the red-doored Dutch Colonial, they head to the Acura in the driveway. Jiwon unlocks the doors, and they slip inside. The car is tidier than the average high schooler's, but dirty spikes and random receipts layer the back seat floors.

It takes Daniel a good minute to notice that Jiwon hasn't switched on the ignition. "Are you okay?" Jiwon asks. "Your time was great today. The whole team is improving. There's no way we'll have a repeat of last week's meet this Saturday. I won't be getting third place in the 10K again."

Jiwon seems like his carefree self, but for sports worries. Still, Daniel listens between the lines for any hint of ill intention—a possible sign of what may come.

"You're right," Daniel answers, playing along. When Jiwon smiles, Daniel starts to wonder if his surprise might be harmless. Maybe Jiwon wants to shock him with a new pretzel brand. Or even better, Jiwon has discovered a cure-all for his grades.

"Let's go then," says Daniel.

The drive is swift. Daniel punches in the gate code, and they hop out of the car and inside the brickstone.

Nana greets them in the foyer. "More studying?" she asks. "Let me know if you need anything to eat before dinner."

When Jiwon rubs his belly longingly, Daniel requests some dried mango. They steal away upstairs, snacks in tow. Jiwon flops onto the green and brown comforter, backpack in his lap. Daniel takes the desk chair. They open their snacks, chewing lazily on the gummy fruit.

"Do you have any homework?" says Jiwon as he unzips his bag. "Because I wasn't really planning on studying."

"I don't have anything due tomorrow."

Jiwon digs his hand through his belongings. "All right then. Time for the big reveal."

The hook fillets Daniel's stomach. He grits his teeth, but all that materializes is a clear plastic compartment box. The fading light from the window glints off the contents. Jiwon brings the plastic container to the desk, his expression a little sheepish.

"I found it last night with all my old dance stuff. I told you that I used to practice modern in middle school?"

Daniel nods, not sure where the conversation is going.

Jiwon nervously rakes his fingers through his hair. "I'm better suited for cross-country and track, but back then I had to do a lot of performances. When we watched that play, it kind of stirred up old memories. I thought, I bet Daniel would like this." He rattles the shimmering box for emphasis. Finally, he unlatches the lid.

Tubes of glitter, palettes of creamy hues, clip-on feathers, vials of spirit gum, and loose reflective stars crowd together in individual compartments. "Is this makeup?" Daniel asks, confused more than ever.

Jiwon presses his lips together. "All your little knickknacks made me think of it. These are for costuming. We'd have to layer this stuff on before recitals." He pauses with an insecure exhale. "I thought you liked things like this. The actors in the play wore gobs of makeup."

"What are we supposed to do with all of this?"

Jiwon shuts the box. "Nothing. Never mind."

Before he can whisk the cosmetics away, Daniel flattens his palm against the container. "Did you want to…dress up?"

"That kind of thing is weird, huh?" Shoving his hands into his pockets, Jiwon tries to laugh casually. His voice shakes. "I'm sorry. This was stupid. I thought it might be fun to—I don't know, just turn you into Peter Pan or something, but now, I guess it is kind of ridiculous."

Daniel blinks owlishly. All day, he worried that Jiwon found him freakish or childish. Now, upon seeing Jiwon flustered and regretful, a peculiar flutter spreads across Daniel's chest. The hook releases. Jiwon just wants to deck him out as Peter Pan.

"Let's do it," Daniel says.

"What? Really?"

"Yeah, sure. It's only the two of us."

Jiwon nods energetically. "Exactly. It's just pretend."

So, Daniel ends up cross-legged on the floor beside Jiwon, who selects a few brown and green feathers from the bunch.

"Just like in the story," Jiwon says as he clips the feathers into Daniel's bangs. His brown eyes squint in concentration. Daniel tries to look anywhere but at Jiwon's face. He's sure that at any moment, he'll wake up, nose-first in a test in the library. He taps his nails against the wood floor. Everything is solid and real.

"What about stars?" Jiwon muses, easing into his role. "For fairy dust around your eyes."

"I trust your opinion." Given Jiwon's proximity, he hopes his breath doesn't smell.

The corners of Jiwon's mouth lift a bit. As he paints the microscopic flakes with spirit gum, his brows scrunch slightly. Each movement flows naturally.

"Did you do this with the neighborhood kids?" Daniel wonders aloud.

"Nothing this elaborate, but we wore costumes." He delicately presses the first star onto Daniel's skin with the pad of his finger.

"What did you wear?"

"Well, I was Wendy, so I usually put on a blue shirt." Jiwon adds another star. "You should put on something green when I'm finished."

The thought of getting in costume sends an unexpected thrill through Daniel. "Most of my clothes are black or white. I have a green hoodie."

Jiwon shakes his head as he applies star after star. "That won't do. A hoodie is too bulky."

"I have a green camo shirt."

"Perfect," he says. "All done. Take a look."

Daniel pivots to the full-length mirror hanging on the closet door. A boy with hazel eyes and brown hair stares back, but he's adorned with wispy feathers, and his temples twinkle with fairy magic. Daniel recognizes himself with a startle. Instead of feeling uncomfortable, he's put on a bit of Peter Pan's confidence.

"Get dressed," Jiwon says with a smile.

"You too," he replies boldly.

"What do you mean? All I have is my tracksuit."

Daniel opens the closet and sifts excitedly through his shirts. "I have a blue sweater."

Jiwon laughs. "You want me to be Wendy?"

Daniel picks out a teal turtleneck. "And you should put on some glitter, too."

Jiwon crosses his arms tightly across his chest. The events have quickly spiraled out of his control. Yet, his eyes gleam with curiosity. When Daniel tosses the sweater his way, Jiwon catches it reflexively.

"Okay then," he says softly. "It's just the two of us."

When Jiwon unzips his jacket and peels off his tee, Daniel focuses on finding his own shirt. They have changed in the locker room on multiple occasions, but the urge to give Jiwon privacy overwhelms him. Concealed partly by the closet door, Daniel hurriedly trades shirts.

"This sweater is way too big on me," Jiwon groans in embarrassment. "And I look ridiculous with my gym shorts on."

"You and me both. Don't forget the glitter."

"I feel like you're getting some kind of sick revenge right now. Is this payback for me bringing the makeup?"

"Maybe."

As Jiwon spreads silver glitter on his eyelids, an idea sweeps over Daniel. He riffles through his top drawer and uncovers an acorn on a leather strap.

"You can wear this too," he suggests, dangling the charm between Jiwon's eyes.

"Is that Peter's thimble or kiss or whatever?" When Daniel doesn't respond, Jiwon snatches the acorn with a complacent huff.

"Okay, okay, I guess I brought this on myself," he says, but he can't hide the small smile on his lips as he slips the leather strap over his head.

Their costumes complete, they stand in the center of the room with nowhere to look but at each other. With the glitter and oversize turtleneck, Daniel can't help but think that Jiwon appears almost cute, just like an actor playing Wendy.

Jiwon whips his phone from his shorts pocket and turns on his camera app. "Want me to take a picture of you?"

"No way!" Daniel covers his face with the backs of his hands.

Jiwon laughs. "C'mon, you look great, like the real Peter Pan. If he were real that is."

Despite himself, Daniel blushes. "Not on your phone," he relents, grabbing his own from the desk. "That's blackmail for life."

When Jiwon aims the camera lens, Daniel stands awkwardly, not sure what to do with his arms or his legs. He's too nervous to smile. Jiwon chuckles quietly before counting down from three. After he snaps the photo, he flips the phone screen toward Daniel. While his pose is half-baked, he likes what he sees.

"Your turn," he says, because he'll feel less out of place if Jiwon takes a picture too. Jiwon passes his personal phone to Daniel. Unlike Daniel's camera-shy posture, Jiwon assumes an effortless stance. A wide grin breaks out on his face. The camera flash flares, cascading light across the dazzling glitter.

Jiwon scrutinizes the resulting image, the wheels in his head obviously turning. "Let's take one together. I'll send it to you, so we'll be even, but we have to swear that the picture is top secret."

"I'll take it to my grave."

As they shuffle onto the bed, Daniel can hardly believe he's agreed to do this, but if he's being honest with himself, he is having fun. For the longest time, Peter Pan has been his secret obsession. No one shared Neverland with him. Then, out of nowhere, Jiwon is watching the play with him and dressing up and taking photos like a newfound Lost Boy.

They scoot close so that the camera can capture them both. Daniel can smell Jiwon's shampoo again, and his bleached hair tickles his cheek. Involuntarily, he leans in, closing his eyes for a split second. If this really is a dream and he's about to wake up to a half-finished exam, he wants to savor the adventure—this fleeting moment when he is not completely alone.

The shutter clicks, and Daniel reawakens to his bedroom. Jiwon is still there, viewing the displayed photo.

"Daniel! You blinked!" he complains. "We'll have to retake it."

A knock stops short their conversation. They exchange terrified glances. Nana knocks again. Asking her to wait long enough for them to change and rub off their makeup would be too suspicious. Heart racing, Daniel tells her to enter.

"Is Jiwon staying for dinner?" she says, peeking her head into the room. Her question hovers tensely as she absorbs their costumes. Jiwon stares at his knees.

"We were just playing around," Daniel mutters weakly.

Jiwon jumps to his feet. "Thanks for the offer, Nana, but my dad expects me home for dinner. It's a school night."

Nana nods slowly as Jiwon gathers his clothes and locks himself in the bathroom. The sink faucet running behind the closed door is the only sound as Daniel avoids Nana's gaze. He yanks the feathers from his hair and rubs off sticky stars into his palms. A few minutes later, Jiwon reemerges in his jacket and T-shirt, his face mostly clear of glitter. Wordlessly, the three of them descend the stairs. Daniel sees Jiwon to the door. They say half-hearted good-byes, and Jiwon hustles to his car.

Hands on her hips, Nana examines Daniel, taking in speckles of spirit gum stuck to his temples and his green shirt. "Daniel—"

"It doesn't mean anything," he snaps, amazed by his venomous tone. "He's just my friend. Mind your own business."

He tears away from the foyer and roughly takes a seat at the dining room table, hoping desperately that Nana will leave him to eat by himself.

CHAPTER SIXTEEN

Daniel feels the whole bed quaking, his body tossing like debris caught in a sandstorm. The comforter twists around his sweaty legs. He groans, a dull headache throbbing in his brain, but the shaking won't let up. Desperate, he swats his arms to escape the maelstrom. His skin meets skin.

"Time for school," Nana states forcefully. "Daniel, wake up."

Dawn slices through his split lashes. Morning has arrived too soon. After a night of tossing and turning, Daniel gave in to his sleeping pills, creeping to the kitchen at two a.m., seeking any relief. His brain refused to shut down, bubbling with the surreality of playing Peter Pan and Wendy, but also seething with his harsh words to Nana. How could something so perfect sour so quickly?

"Can't move," Daniel whispers, each limb imprisoned by the bedsheets.

Nana releases him. "What's wrong? Are you sick?"

"Not sick."

Even so, she places a cool hand to his forehead. "You feel fine. What's going on, sweetheart?" she asks, her tone surprisingly kind. Despite last night's temper, she coaxes him gently, sweeping his hair rhythmically. A parasitic beetle of guilt burrows deep into Daniel's drowsiness.

"So tired."

Nana puts two and two together. "Did you take your sleeping pills last night?" When Daniel nods, she asks, "When?"

"Late. After midnight."

"That's not enough sleep for it to wear off. Go back to sleep. I'll wake you in thirty minutes and see if you're any better."

Half an hour later, Daniel manages to sit up and swallow his antidepressants and mood stabilizers. Sluggishness cloaks every action.

"I can call the school," Nana offers. "You could just rest today."

Daniel flings his feet to the floor. He can't miss school, or practice for that matter. His grades depend on his attendance, and his place on the team depends on his grades. "I'll bounce back soon. I can just use the 504 Plan if I can't focus."

He lumbers to his closet and searches for something comfortable to wear. Nana tsks in disagreement, but seeing that his mind is made up, she leaves him to get ready. A plaid black flannel and Cranbrook sweatpants are the most presentable yet most pajama-like outfit he can put together.

He skips a morning shower, thankful to have washed up and washed off all of yesterday's makeup before bed. Brushing his teeth takes longer than necessary. In the hazy bathroom, the pixies giggle at the Lost Boy stuck in a nearly catatonic stupor.

When he trudges into the kitchen, Nana lines up his lunchbox, water bottle, and a breakfast bar. He can barely think, much less eat, so he stuffs everything into his backpack. With one last worried appraisal, Nana grabs the keys, and they climb into the car.

The engine's hum lulls Daniel into another sort of dream. The mixed medications suppress the vivacity of his usual adventures. All he sees is an ocean full of stars. Stranded in a rowboat, the waves toss him farther out to sea. The water sprays over him, carrying the scent of salt and paradise. Yet, instead of serenity, an inexplicable loneliness overwhelms him.

When the car stops in front of Cranbrook, he jolts back to wakefulness. Nana reaches to stroke his forearm, but pulls back. An echo of last night's outburst replays in her eyes. Daniel blinks away the forsaken rowboat and stares hard at his Nana.

"I can turn around," she says, and for the first time, Daniel realizes that she is scared. Scared for him but trying to hide it so he won't be scared for himself. Wendy's voice rings in his ears, *If you knew how great is a mother's love, you would have no fear.*

Daniel sinks his head onto Nana's shoulder. "I'm sorry."

"For what?"

"Yelling at you last night."

With her free arm, Nana nudges him into a warm hug. "I forgive you. I already forgave you. Don't you ever go to bed thinking that I haven't forgiven you."

After a beat, she lifts him off her shoulder. "Now, are we going home or are you going to school?"

The warning bell beeps from the building, corralling the students to their homerooms. "I'll see you after practice," Daniel decides. He drags himself out of the car and slams the door, too fast to hear Nana say she loves him.

Only five minutes into his first class, Daniel excuses himself from Chemistry to take a break in the nurse's office. Being counted present is his only consolation prize. At least absences won't mar his standing on the cross-country team.

The nurse guides him to a cot, draws a blue privacy curtain, and promises to wake him at the end of the period. As soon as he's comfortable, his phone buzzes in his pants pocket. A text from Jiwon.

I almost forgot to send you this

Attached to the message is the photo of the both of them. Daniel traces his fingers along the feathers in his hair. Jiwon smiles happily through the screen, his eyes sparkling beneath the glitter. The memory of Jiwon's hair brushes against his cheek. Neither of them suspected that a moment later, their pretend would meet a mortifying end.

Another text pops up.

Jiwon: *I hope everything went okay with your housekeeper*

Daniel: *I've probably done stranger things around the house*

Jiwon: *Do I even want to know?*

A sleepy laugh rasps the back of Daniel's throat. He tries to thumb a witty reply but gives up halfway. Forty minutes remain before his next class, and he needs sleep now, so he can function and run later. His screen shines in his eyes. The light dims as his vision blurs. Then, a sweet black envelops him.

CHAPTER SEVENTEEN

Four nights later, just twelve hours before Saturday's meet, Daniel receives another text from Jiwon.

Let's run

Daniel's laptop displays a set of digital history flashcards. While Tuesday's essay exam looms over him, he is tempted by Jiwon's uncharacteristic offer. Coach Rasmussen went easy on them during practice, out of consideration for the upcoming meet, but a 3K recovery sprint didn't really get the juices flowing. Still, wisdom tells him that a night run might not be the best way to prepare for tomorrow's competition. Even more, ever since his return from Mercy Hospital, Nana prefers to keep Daniel indoors after dinner. He'll have to sneak out again.

Daniel: *Right now?*

Jiwon: *Yes, I need it*

Daniel doesn't ask any questions. He knows exactly what it's like to itch for a run.

Daniel: *Let's do it*

Jiwon: *I'll drive to you*

Homework he'll save for the weekend. He shuts his laptop and presses an ear to his door in vain. Nana won't hole up in her quarters for at least another hour. With his usual escape route off limits, he has no other choice but to climb down the sweetgum tree. While scaling the tree is a skill he learned in late elementary school, the feat requires as much luck as practice in the dark.

After trading pajamas for compression leggings, shorts, a T-shirt, and trainers, he unlatches the window. As an afterthought, he switches off his lamp. Hopefully, Nana will assume he has gone to bed early and retire without checking on him.

Leaping onto the slanted rooftop, he inhales the crisp air. The promise of a run stirs his adrenaline. Artful strides mark his path to the tree, but he waits a minute for his eyes to adjust to the dimness before diving into the leaves. Once his fingers touch down on a sturdy branch, he swoops toward the trunk. His shoe seeks a solid landing. Finding one, he crouches, switching his foot for his hands. Continuing in this fixed rhythm, he descends. A few minutes later, he reaches the grass, sweat gathered on his brow.

The parlor looks out onto the yard, but fortunately, the windows are unlit. As quietly as possible, he dashes to the pedestrian gate. Streetlamps greet him in the deserted street. In the silence, he seems utterly alone—a boy in a postapocalyptic suburb, so isolated that he could have dreamed up everyone he thinks he knows.

Then, a familiar Acura rounds the corner and parallel parks. Jiwon steps out, clad in similar athletic gear, plus a track jacket. He fiddles with his keys before securing them in a zippered pocket.

"Let's go then," he says.

"Shouldn't we warm up first?"

Jiwon taps his foot impatiently. "I'll be good."

Immediately, Daniel recognizes that something is very wrong. Jiwon always opts for the best before-and-after exercise precautions. His eyes skip from house to house, jumping everywhere but to Daniel.

Even though Jiwon's mood reads cold, Daniel braves a probing question. "What's up?"

"It's just an ordinary Friday night."

"And what does an ordinary Friday night usually include?" he presses, disturbed that he sounds too much like Dr. Greene.

Jiwon's gaze finally locks onto Daniel. An invisible coil tightens between them, as Daniel waits for his response.

"It's nothing really," Jiwon says in a calculated tone. "I can't focus on anything but the meet. We have to do better than last week."

Before Daniel can process the information, Jiwon starts walking aimlessly down the road. Daniel matches him, shoulder-to-shoulder. "We're all putting forth our best effort," Daniel says. "We'll do well if we try our hardest."

"No." Jiwon sucks in a sharp breath, then visibly wilts. "Maybe. You know, it's all a little different when your college applications depend on it. These aren't playground games."

Like an unleashed arrow, Jiwon breaks into a sprint, too fast to maintain. Daniel chases after him until their speeds meet once more. The pounding of their feet rebounds off the metal gates and sleepy windows. Jiwon's strained breath mixes with Daniel's, swirling in their ears. The world flashes past them far too quickly, and Daniel desperately wants to slow down. This pace isn't flying but careening, tearing through the sky without oxygen to spare. Every time he tries to slow his gait, Jiwon threatens to overtake him, even though he has no clue which way to go.

Jiwon's whole attitude toward tomorrow's meet confuses Daniel. Just days before, Jiwon delivered an optimistic speech about the team's improvements. All week, each member has put in one hundred and ten percent in order to increase their endurance and speed, Daniel included.

"The team is taking this just as seriously as you," Daniel thinks aloud as he curbs his speed to a fast jog. He doesn't have to run like a madman just to prove his worth to Jiwon.

Jiwon spins abruptly, trotting backward down the straight road. "No one is making new PRs. Coach spends way too much time on strength training, but no one complains, because half the time, they just want to horse around and talk about the girls' team."

Daniel's blood throbs. Only yesterday, Jayden ran three seconds under his personal record. Kevin stayed behind after practice on Wednesday to discuss strategies with Coach Rasmussen for improving his aerobic threshold. Owen saved his girl talk for the locker room, his focus set on increasing his core strength. Everyone has their areas of growth, but each member has been taking responsibility for their shortcomings.

"You can't judge everyone like that just because you're the fastest," Daniel says, tone low to cover up his irritation.

"What do you know? You only recently joined the team. You didn't even do any summer training."

The criticism knifes Daniel's heart. Every word out of Jiwon's mouth is targeted to hurt. Jiwon, who usually high-fives each member after an especially tough practice, who double-checks the guys' sore ankles and stiff knees, who stocks extra water in his gym locker for the forgetful—a mask of bitterness eclipses the very Jiwon who messed with feather and glitter and stars.

"You don't know the first thing about me," Daniel spits.

"And you think you have me all figured out?"

Jiwon whirls around and takes off. The temptation to leave him and run back to the shelter of his bed tugs at Daniel's legs, but something in Jiwon's small frame, dashing farther and farther away, sets fire to his pride. He bursts forward, each tendon and bone advancing until he equalizes the distance.

They round a cul-de-sac, and then another, hurtling like thieves. Daniel spots an upcoming pothole and swerves, but Jiwon, blinded by agitation, trips. He might have easily reclaimed his balance if his mind were focused on the run. Instead, he smashes into the pavement with a sickening thwack.

Daniel tapers his speed to a screeching halt. Jiwon doesn't move. Panic seizes Daniel. He skids to Jiwon's side, kneeling to the ground. Jiwon's eyes blink languidly.

"Are you hurt?" Daniel exclaims, failing to keep the frenzy out of his voice. His shout snaps Jiwon out of his trance. He hauls himself up to a cross-legged position. The knee of his leggings is shredded. When Daniel touches the torn cloth, his fingers come back wet with blood.

"Enough of this. Let's walk home," Daniel pleads, standing and extending a hand in peace.

Refusing the help, Jiwon steadies himself upright. "I'm fine. We can keep going."

"You can't risk an injury."

"I just want to run."

"No."

With unexpected force, Jiwon shoves Daniel. He skitters back several steps, heart leaping to his throat. He isn't prepared to fight.

Jiwon is supposed to be his friend. Yet, when he peers into Jiwon's eyes, he doesn't see anger. Instead, he finds the burnished gleam of unshed tears.

Jiwon lunges toward Daniel, sinking a fist into his chest, then another. Daniel doesn't budge, petrified by the barrage.

Jiwon won't stop. "You don't know anything, Daniel! Other people survive cancer all the time! Why did she give up?"

Daniel's blood chills. The punches weaken as Jiwon screams. "Why couldn't she beat it? She didn't try hard enough!"

Then, just as suddenly as the attack started, Jiwon grasps Daniel's shirt and buries his face. Sobs rack his body, dragging him deeper into Daniel's racing heart. Stunned, Daniel just listens to the surge of tears, until Jiwon gradually stills. Neither moves. As the truth behind Jiwon's anger becomes clear, Daniel raises his arms and wraps them tightly around his shoulders.

Daniel wishes he could give Jiwon all the answers he needs, but he doesn't know much about mothers or what it's like to lose one. He does know a bit about death, and in that moment, that tiny shard of knowledge is all he can share.

"She didn't give up," Daniel says. "She went to Neverland."

"She's not in any kind of heaven," Jiwon shouts into his shirt. "I saw her body the day she died. She's just dead."

Daniel holds him tighter. "She's in Neverland."

A few lingering cicadas cry out to the streetlamps. Jiwon shifts his head so that his cheek rests against Daniel. "She can't really be there," he says faintly.

Daniel tilts his head forward, his mouth barely grazing Jiwon's hair. "It's better there. It's always warm and beautiful, and everything can be fun if you let it."

Locked in his arms, Jiwon's heart pulses into Daniel's chest. They are dangerously close, and the urge to press his lips against Jiwon's soft hair nearly overwhelms Daniel. His logical side tells him to let go, but his arms won't listen.

With a sniffle, Jiwon gently pushes off. He stares into the starry sky. "Neverland, huh?" He turns to Daniel, tear tracks staining his cheeks. "Let's go back. I'll walk."

The trek to Daniel's house is long and quiet. When they reach Jiwon's car, Daniel is surprised by his own disappointment. He doesn't want Jiwon to leave. Their argument still weighs heavily between them.

"You should disinfect your knee before it gets bad," he says, chalking his emotions up to concern. When Jiwon nods, he adds, "I have rubbing alcohol and Band-Aids."

Cocking his head, Jiwon considers the offer. "I don't think my dad keeps that stuff around," he replies, and a strange intuition tugs at Daniel. Jiwon probably has Band-Aids at his house, and he may just want to come inside.

Either way, he leads Jiwon through the gate. "Wait here," he says once they reach the front door. "I'll climb the tree back to my room and disable the security alarm. Nana should be asleep by now"

"You snuck out?"

Daniel shrugs. He heads to the tree, ascends carefully, and hoists himself through the window. After he creaks open the door, he confirms that Nana's door is indeed closed for the night. After plucking the first aid kit from his bathroom, he slinks down the stairs and lets Jiwon inside.

"We'll have to be quiet," he whispers and guides him to the living room couch.

Jiwon cracks open the first aid kit. After soaking a cotton ball with antiseptic, he presses it against his wound, but the fabric gets in the way.

"This is no good," he grumbles before stripping off his shorts and leggings. Heat creeps up Daniel's neck. Jiwon stretches his bare legs across the coffee table like it means nothing, because it does mean nothing. They're on the same team. Lazing around in shirts and boxers is a commonplace locker room occurrence.

"Shit, this stings," Jiwon grumbles. "Forget it. I'll just leave it."

The crusting gash glares angrily at Daniel. "No, you gotta take care of it. The meet is tomorrow. Coach will be pissed if you wind up with an infection. Let me do it."

"Whatever. If it means so much to you."

Jiwon passes Daniel the cotton ball and leans into the couch. Timidly, Daniel stoops to the floor and sweeps the antiseptic across the wound. Jiwon hisses but otherwise doesn't complain.

"I didn't mean all that stuff I said about the team," Jiwon admits apologetically.

"I kind of guessed."

"Today would have been her birthday. She'd be forty-two. You know, I could never remember her birthday when she was alive."

The cotton ball wears down, so Daniel prepares a second. Without thinking, he wraps his free hand on the underside of Jiwon's leg for leverage as he continues cleaning. He feels Jiwon's calf muscles flex, and an odd thrill fizzles through Daniel's lungs. He tries his best to ignore the sensation, focusing his attention on the task.

When the scrape is completely clean, Daniel glances up at Jiwon. A strange expression settles on Jiwon's features. His lips are slightly parted, but no breath sounds. Their eyes hold for too long, as the thrill shudders through Daniel's chest once more.

Jiwon lifts his leg out of Daniel's grasp. "Where are the Band-Aids?" he asks hurriedly, rummaging through the first aid kit. He slaps a large bandage over his knee and promptly redresses. All the while, Daniel sits frozen to the floor. He replays Jiwon's expression over and over again. Something feels different between them, something more than overcoming a fight.

"I should go," Jiwon says. "I don't want to wake your housekeeper."

When Daniel doesn't speak, he starts making his way to the door, but he pauses before entering the foyer. "Thanks for everything."

The front door opens and shuts with a click. Everything falls silent. Daniel might believe that the whole night was another of his Neverland adventures if not for the first aid supplies on the coffee table.

CHAPTER EIGHTEEN

The coach bus lurches out of the parking lot. Early morning malaise wafts from member to member, mixed with premeet jitters. Even the presence of the girls' team can't relieve the anticipation. No one wants to rank in the bottom half of the four competing schools.

To Daniel's surprise, Jiwon scuttles from his usual roost beside Kevin and nabs a seat beside him. Coach Rasmussen crosses his arms disapprovingly at the seat swap on a moving vehicle, but he seems to let it go for the sake of morale.

"How's your knee?" Daniel asks. A layer of tan adhesive tape winds around the wound.

"Looks way worse than it is. I did some stretches this morning, and nothing hurt. I doubt my run will be affected. Coach didn't want to hear it though. He really laid into me before you got here."

"What did you tell him?"

A little grin lights Jiwon's mouth. "The truth, but I left you out of it."

"Thanks."

Jiwon reclines his seat, cozying up for a short nap. "Don't mention it."

Twenty minutes later, a wilderness park comes into view, and the team shuffles off the bus. The two other private schools arrive. Daniel already knows Cambry isn't one of them. He glimpsed Coach Rasmussen's season schedule that morning. Two more weeks will pass before he races against his old team. The upcoming date seems out of reach, like a rainy forecast for tomorrow when it's still sunny today.

As they wait for the meet to begin, the guys mingle with the girls' team, who look torn between humoring them and focusing on their goals. He recognizes a few faces from Owen's party, but in uniform, the drunken craze dims to a genuine competitive spirit. All the boys stay on their best behavior.

"Anyone want to scope out the course?" Jayden asks the group.

"I'll pass," Jiwon replies, much to Daniel's disappointment. "I ran here a lot over the summer."

Although Jiwon declines the offer, Daniel decides to join Jayden, Kevin, and two girls named Jackie and Ki-Jeong. He's pretty sure Ki-Jeong was Jayden's dance partner last Saturday.

Jackie smiles brightly. "I don't think we've officially met. I think I saw you talking to Owen though."

"Owen's her boyfriend," Ki-Jeong pipes in. Her ponytail bobs with each step over the rough terrain. "Well, ex-boyfriend."

Kevin snickers. "You've broken up with him four times now. I'm not sure what you see in him."

"Aren't you his friend?" Jackie shoots back.

"Doesn't mean I'm blind."

When Jayden laughs, Ki-Jeong is quick to come to her friend's defense. "Well, I guess that's love."

"That's love, huh?" Kevin baits her, but the girls tire of the topic and steer to chatting over the day's contests.

"The course looks pretty hilly," Jackie says. "Today won't be a walk in the park."

"At least it's cloudy and not too windy, right, Daniel?" Ki-Jeong peers at him. He nods a little, not sure what to say. "You're quiet, aren't you?"

Jayden throws an arm over Daniel's shoulders, nearly knocking him over. "That's Daniel for you. He's deadly serious about his craft."

Of course, Daniel cares about the meet, but the conversation rumbles around him in a reeling storm. The gang chatters effortlessly, clearly having built friendships somewhere along the way at parties and in classes. Even Jayden, with his leave in England, seems completely included in the fold. All the while, Daniel fights just to keep his head out of the clouds.

"It's a good day for a run," Daniel manages to squeeze out.

"Lighten up, friend," Jayden says, and everyone laughs. It takes Daniel several seconds to determine that they're not quite making fun of him but just trying to include him. So, he smiles, because even if he doesn't get the joke, he doesn't want to be left out either.

Once they return to the tents, the 3K runners begin fastening their numbers to their shirts. Jiwon lines up. The starting gun sounds, and the runners quickly dissolve into the horizon. Daniel sits beside Ki-Jeong and Jayden, but he isn't really paying attention to their banter. Instead, he listens for the incoming competitors.

Although Jiwon assured him that his knee won't affect his abilities, Daniel can't help but fear the worst. The silhouettes of the runners approach the finish line. Daniel holds his breath, praying that a single fall hasn't sabotaged Jiwon's hard work. The shapes take form. Number 008 leads the pack. Jiwon crosses the white tape. Cranbrook erupts with cheers.

"What was his time?" Jayden shouts.

"I think it was 8:31!"

Daniel's jaw hurts from grinning. After Jiwon turns in his scorecard, he paces around the tents to cool down. Even though the runners haven't all completed the race, Daniel excuses himself and goes to Jiwon.

"You did it!" he congratulates.

Jiwon laughs giddily. "It's a new PR for me. One second faster."

"Let's get you some water."

Back beneath the canopy, the team surrounds Jiwon, smacking his back and bumping fists. He just beams. The praise only fades when the girls' 3K runners are called to prepare. Their race ends with Ki-Jeong in a confident third, and finally, the boys' teams are summoned for the 5K.

Jiwon squeezes Daniel's wrist. "Kill it out there."

The racers take their place behind the starting line. The pistol cracks, snapping Daniel into form. Inspired by Jiwon's success, he begins a little too fast but reclaims control and paces himself in preparation for the rugged turf. He plans to maintain a stable third until the last mile and a half, then overtake whoever tries to defend second and first.

When the time comes for him to pick up his speed, he easily dashes past 014, but 017 proves to be a challenging adversary. His lungs are bursting, but he cannot fail. He needs every ounce of strength. He needs wings. He won't let Jiwon down.

Stretching his gait to his fullest capacity, Daniel leaps through the rushing air. Just a few more surges and he'll pass 017. His spikes hit the ground, rebounding to his next step like a rubber ball on a sprung floor. Screams roar around him. The tape slaps his stomach, but he can't be sure who touched down on the finish line first.

When the place card is crammed into his hand, he blinks at the number: a solid vertical line. His team stamps their feet as his name chants into his exhausted bones. The scorekeeper announces his individual time. Five seconds short of his personal record, but his best of the season. If happy thoughts really could make people fly, Daniel would soar into the sky, but instead he opts for a cool down and a cup of cold water.

His teammates applaud him, mussing his sweaty hair and throwing out compliments like confetti. When the crowd parts, Daniel sees Jiwon. They share knowing smiles. At this rate, Cranbrook is a shoo-in for first place in the meet.

"You're amazing," Jiwon tells him.

"Look who's talking."

Jiwon shakes his head. "I wish," he says. Then, leaning in so that only Daniel can hear, he adds, "I won't be winning the 10K. It hurts."

Daniel's stomach drops. "Your knee?"

"Basic cause and effect. I pushed too hard in the 3K. I can't fake my way through the 10K, or I'll end up with a real injury."

The disclosure pins Daniel in place. Jiwon chuckles dejectedly.

"It's all right," he says. "Owen and Kevin can carry the 10K. Cranbrook'll still win. I was careless. Lesson learned."

When the boys' 10K finally commences, Daniel swallows hard as Jiwon heads out to the middle of the throng. While he should admire Jiwon for choosing safety over ego, he knows firsthand how it feels to draw a line between what's best and what could have been.

As predicted, Owen claims a strong third, with Kevin close behind in fourth. Jiwon fumbles to a frustrating sixth. No one puts him on the spot about it, choosing to celebrate the other seniors instead, but Coach Rasmussen casts Jiwon a wary glance.

By the end of the day, the boys' team earns a first place victory, and the girls land in second. With the meet officially over, the exhausted athletes collapse onto the bus, shuttering windows for late afternoon naps.

Once more, Jiwon chooses to sit beside Daniel. "Let's skip out on the party," he says, purple under his eyes. Daniel wonders how late he stayed up after their nighttime run. "How about we finally watch the rest of that play?"

"Okay." Daniel doesn't feel like enduring another round of drinking anyway.

Snores fill the bus cabin, melding with the low tones of the few who manage to stay awake. Jiwon's breath relaxes. His chin drops, as he unconsciously moves into a more comfortable position. The back of his hand presses against Daniel's thigh. His head falls to Daniel's shoulder.

Daniel stills. The heat from Jiwon's breath flutters against him. He doesn't have the heart to scoot away. No one can see them in the dark anyway, and even if they could see, all they would find are two teammates resting after giving their all in a cross-country meet.

Even though Daniel's eyes are closed, he can't sleep. Jiwon shifts again, his hand drifting to rest near Daniel's fingers. His stomach flips. He tries to focus on his breathing, but the sighs of Jiwon's soft exhalations steal all his attention.

He tells himself that he's just not used to having another person so close. There's nothing strange about enjoying a friend's company, nothing wrong with not pulling away.

❖

Jiwon cuts the engine in Daniel's driveway and pops the trunk. "I always take an extra set of clothes with me to meets," he explains. He grabs a drawstring bag from atop a pile of notebooks and binders, and they head inside.

Nana comes flying down the foyer. "You never texted! How'd you get home?" she exclaims but halts when she spots Jiwon.

"We're going to finish *Peter Pan*," Daniel says as he makes a break for the stairs. He doesn't want any probing questions about whether or not they'll be donning makeup this evening.

"Nice to see you again, Nana," Jiwon calls over his shoulder as he rushes to Daniel. They scurry to the third floor, where Jiwon asks to use the bathroom. "To change," he adds, even though they've never been too modest before.

After Jiwon shuts the door behind him, Daniel tears through his wardrobe. If Jiwon isn't going to laze around in his fusty athletic gear, then Daniel can't either. Yet, every article of clothing looks subpar. He wishes he'd caught a glimpse of whatever Jiwon has packed. Then, he could dress similarly. Sweeping through the hangers, he eventually selects a pair of gray shorts and his customary black T-shirt. At the last second, he throws on a zip-up track jacket. His mirror reveals a put together but not over-the-top reflection.

Even though the bedroom door is cracked, Jiwon knocks before entering. A sky blue hoodie falls loosely from his shoulders to just above his knees. Baggy gym shorts peek out from underneath.

"How very Wendy of you," Daniel says without thinking.

"Why, thank you, Peter," Jiwon replies sarcastically.

"We should get your acorn." Daniel teasingly opens the top dresser drawer and retrieves the antique box.

"Not happening!" Jiwon charges him, making a grab for the box. A laugh escapes Daniel as they tussle back and forth. The acorn was only a joke, but seeing Jiwon's reaction, he can't help but taunt him. Jiwon yanks a little too hard, knocking the box to the floor, scattering its contents.

"Serves you right," Jiwon says.

"You have to help me clean it all up."

Crawling on hands and knees, they collect the hodgepodge of nature objects, pixie dust, and miniature action figures. When Jiwon discovers a thimble under the bed, he slips it on his index finger, wagging it in Daniel's face.

"Peter, I'd like to give you a thimble," he says in his best British accent. His eyes glint with playfulness. His teeth flash in a mocking grin, and Daniel can't shake the terrifying realization that Jiwon isn't just a normal, good-looking high school senior. He is attracted to Jiwon.

So when Daniel kisses the thimble on Jiwon's finger, he isn't really thinking about how Jiwon will respond. His body just slants forward, and his lips press against the metal. Electricity slices through him like lightning striking a kite.

But once he sees Jiwon's shock, regret seizes him with enough overpowering nausea to send his head reeling.

Jiwon rips the thimble off, hastily tossing it into the box. "Don't do that," he snaps.

"I'm sorry," Daniel says, wanting nothing more than to rewind and erase everything. He would have never taken out the box. He would have never called him Wendy. "It was just a joke."

"Yeah, well, you took it too far." Jiwon's skin is blotchy, and Daniel can't tell if he's furious or about to cry.

"Jiwon, please, I'm sorry."

He hates the way he's begging, but he needs Jiwon to forgive him, to forget anything ever happened. They can turn on the movie and move on as friends, as teammates.

Miraculously, Jiwon answers his prayers. "Let's just get the play and go downstairs."

Without hesitation, Daniel digs the movie from the third drawer. "I think we left off when the Lost Boys shot Wendy down," he says, words tumbling out too fast.

By the time they enter the living room, the red has drained from Jiwon's face. When Nana sees them putting the movie on, she offers to make popcorn. Jiwon eagerly accepts, smiling as though whatever happened upstairs has unhappened. They sink into the sofa, eyes locked on the screen.

As Peter shoves the Lost Boys aside only to discover a presumably dead Wendy with an arrow in her chest, Jiwon mutters, "This is gonna be good."

Daniel might have relaxed if not for the obvious distance separating them—Jiwon curled up as far away as possible.

CHAPTER NINETEEN

The crocodile circles Dr. Greene's office, ticking the seconds that will eventually make an hour. As Dr. Greene deals a game of blackjack, Daniel lines up a series of safe topics in his mind: cross-country, schoolwork, his favorite dinner foods. He prepares to fill the next sixty minutes with nothing.

"How would you describe your mood today?" Dr. Greene starts. His white coat beams with the sunlight streaming from the window.

"I'm okay. The same as usual."

"Just neutral?"

"I'm feeling ready to get this session over actually," he replies. The same old bookcase, the chairs, the perfectly arranged desk—Daniel is tired of the one-dimensional space. Couldn't Dr. Greene at least hang a new piece of artwork every once in a while?

"Is there something else you'd rather be doing?" he asks calmly as he peeks at his card.

"Not really. It'd be nice to have a day off for once."

Dr. Greene nods. If he's noticed that Daniel hasn't looked at his cards, he doesn't mention it. "Have you been feeling overwhelmed by schoolwork and extracurriculars?"

"No. School is getting easier, and cross-country is the best thing I've got going right now. I won first place in the 5K yesterday."

"Congratulations. You must practice a lot." When Dr. Greene smiles, an unexpected swish of pride whirls through Daniel. Running is something he's good at.

"I practice every day, after school. Sometimes, I go for a jog on Sundays, too, but not every Sunday. Coach promotes recovery days."

"Our bodies need rest, even if we think we can keep going. The tank might run empty when we least expect it."

Daniel doesn't know how to respond, so he lets the clock do the talking and checks his card. A three of hearts. Dr. Greene seems okay with the pause, perhaps waiting for him to volunteer more information, which of course, Daniel won't do. In the end, Dr. Greene poses another question.

"How are you getting along with your teammates?"

"We get along fine. They invite me to hang out after meets. We have a good time."

"Would you call them your friends?"

Dr. Greene has a special preoccupation with the F-word. "Not all of them, but we're a team, so we do stuff together. We compare personal records, and they talk to me about their goals and their grades."

"So, you're comfortable around them?"

Daniel knocks for a third a card. "I'd say so."

"They must consider you a good addition to the team, what with you getting first place and all."

Daniel sits up a little straighter. "I'm the second fastest," he admits. "Cranbrook could really go far this season, which is a big deal for the seniors."

"Who is the fastest?"

"What?"

"You said you are second fastest. I was just wondering who is the fastest member."

An invisible clamp seals Daniel's mouth. For inexplicable reasons, Jiwon is one of his unsafe topics. Their friendship is separate from Dr. Greene—a completely unrelated subject from medicine and therapy and incessant interrogations.

But, as usual, the psychiatrist has him backed into a corner. "Jiwon is the fastest." Although he tries to keep his words even, Daniel can hear the anxiety in his tone. Dr. Greene doesn't miss it either.

"Tell me more about Jiwon," he says, and Daniel hates the open-endedness of the phrase. There is no escaping a prompt like that.

"He beat his PR at the meet in the 3K." Daniel hopes the vague response will satisfy, but Dr. Greene only blinks, waiting for more. "He's a senior, and he's trying to earn a scholarship." The clock ticks. Dr. Greene stares. "We aren't rivals or anything. We push each other to keep improving. Jiwon is nice. Sometimes we get snacks together at lunch."

"So, is he your friend then?"

Daniel sighs and takes a moment to check his third card. A ten of diamonds. "You really want me to have friends, don't you?"

"It's not up to me. I'm curious, Daniel, what you think about the distinction between a teammate and a friend."

"I don't know." Defining unclear terms isn't Daniel's favorite pastime. Whenever he thinks too hard about ambiguity, a fog swallows the thin line between reality and imagination. Friends are like the Lost Boys, but the Lost Boys are figments of make-believe. Pretend friends and real friends blur into one image, but no one seems to know the difference between the real and a dream.

"If you tell me what a friend is," Daniel says, "then I'll tell you if Jiwon is my friend or not."

Dr. Greene leans back in his chair, the card game forgotten. "For me, a friend is someone I can rely on, who shares common interests. They understand my ideas, or if they don't, they try to understand. After I spend time with a friend, I feel happy, and I'll often wonder when next I'll see them again."

"I like spending time with Jiwon."

"What do you do together?"

Daniel scratches the armchair's embroidery. He won't tell Dr. Greene about the parties, and he can't imagine admitting to watching *Peter Pan* or dressing as Peter and Wendy. The psychiatrist would probably condemn those activities as potentially unhealthy. He would never understand the importance of wearing glitter and shirts in green and blue, or crying over mothers in Neverland.

A psychiatrist in a pure white coat with an immaculate desk could never comprehend something as messy as kissing a piece of metal on another boy's finger. Dr. Greene and his ordinary friends have never tasted the frightened ache of sitting too far apart on a couch or experienced the unattainable longing to wipe the upset from Jiwon's face after his lips touched the thimble.

Pain slices through Daniel's chest and down his arm to his wrist. His thoughts tumble, burying him beneath their weight. He feels like a complete idiot for kissing Jiwon's finger. As if Jiwon could accept a gesture like that without freaking out. How did Daniel expect him to react? Take Daniel's hand and kiss him back?

Daniel's heart smashes his ribcage like a fist against a wall. His legs tense, the urge to flee taking over. He can't run, though. He's trapped in this office for another forty minutes. But he needs to run, because he can't sit in one spot for too long or he'll have to face the fact that, yes, he had wanted Jiwon to return his kiss. He wanted Jiwon to sit near him on the couch in the same way he rested against him on the bus, only they would be awake, and they would be choosing to touch.

Now, there is nothing but pain. A knife twists in his chest, so forcefully that he chokes on his own breath. A voice in his head whispers, "This is what a heart attack feels like. You're going to black out. You're going to die."

White specks swarm his vision, obscuring the cards and the office and Dr. Greene. He tries to cry for help, but the fear paralyzes his throat.

Fingers wrap around his shoulders. "Daniel, I think you're having a panic attack," says Dr. Greene, who cannot conceal his worry with his practiced, even tone. "Do you have your Lorazepam?"

Unable to speak, Daniel weakly shakes his head. He left it in the nightstand. Nana will kill him for his stupidity, if he doesn't die now.

"I'm going to make a phone call, but I'm still here. You're all right, Daniel. You're going to be all right."

Even though Daniel hears the psychiatrist's explanation, his entire body still walks on death row. He tries to tell himself to calm down, but it's like throwing a cup of water on a wildfire. He is evaporating.

A door opens. Words are exchanged, and then a pill is pressed against his mouth.

"Take this, Daniel."

He complies, but nothing changes.

"It'll take half an hour to take effect," says Dr. Greene. "Just concentrate on my voice. This is temporary. Even though this feels like it will last forever, this will subside. You will get through this."

The psychiatrist places something solid into Daniel's palm. "Try holding on to this stone. Focus on how it feels cold and smooth and heavy."

Daniel rubs his fingertips along the stone. Gradually, his vision returns, but the wild pounding in his chest continues. He sees Dr. Greene, kneeling in front of him, his reflection glinting off Dr. Greene's glasses. He takes in the office, the window, the ticking clock. He latches on to the second hand as it journeys round and round. Time slips by, minute after minute, until the pain finally ebbs and his breathing slows. All that remains is a crushing exhaustion.

"Daniel, how are you feeling right now?" Dr. Greene asks softly.

"Did I have a panic attack?"

"You did, but you're all right now."

"I want to go home." He wants his bed, to pull his comforter over his head, and to sleep forever.

"I'll call your parents to come get you."

The fatigue seals his eyes shut. "They're in Tokyo."

"Then I'll call Ms. Naff."

"Nana," Daniel whispers. That's who he wants—his Nana to tuck him in his bed and make the nightmares disappear.

Chapter Twenty

The lunch bell rings, rousing the lifeless students into action. For once, Daniel doesn't need to visit the library for the first half of his lunch. He gathers his belongings and heads to his locker. On the way, an early autumn breeze hits his back. He snags his food from his stacks of textbooks, ready to sit on the concrete and eat alone, but his phone buzzes with a text message from Jiwon.

Are you in the library?

If he were, he wouldn't be able to read the message till Mr. Bartel returned his phone. Before opening his lunchbox, he types a quick response.

Not today

Come eat with us then. We're by the laurel tree

The invitation burns into Daniel's eyes. Already a month into the school year, Daniel can't help but feel a little pathetic whenever he spends lunch alone. Still, after yesterday's panic attack, he's not sure if he's ready to see Jiwon again. He doesn't know when he'll ever be ready. His Lorazepam burns a hole in his jacket pocket.

But he's already told Jiwon that he's free this period. Although he could make up a lie about a preplanned conference with a teacher, he would risk being caught in the hallways, and there is no way he'll stoop to hiding in the restroom until his next class.

He sucks in an anxious breath and replies:

Be there in a bit

After stuffing his backpack in his locker, he sets off to the bleachers, lunchbox tucked under his arm. The laurel tree stretches its branches across a sheet of sod and benches. From a distance, Daniel sights Kevin and Ki-Jeong leaning against the trunk. Owen and Jackie seem to be on talking terms, sitting on the grass and chatting away. Jayden hovers over a bench, laughing over none other than Jiwon, who is stretched out lazily.

Ki-Jeong spots Daniel first and waves him over. "Hey, Daniel! Quick, tell Kevin I'm right."

"About what?"

She throws her hands on her hips. "That doesn't matter. Just say it."

"She's right."

Kevin rolls his eyes. "There's no way the girls' team will have a better season than us, especially after the last meet's scores."

"We placed better than you guys at our first meet," Jackie pipes in. "After this Saturday, we'll take the lead again."

Jiwon sits up. "So long as our teams stay on track, we'll both make it to district finals again." He swings his legs over the side of the bench. "Hey, Daniel," he says with a faint smile.

A blush sweeps down Daniel's neck. Jiwon is wearing a light blue polo, the same shade as the clear sky above them. The color brings out the gold streaks in his bleached hair. If any shred of doubt existed in Daniel's mind that his feelings toward Jiwon extend beyond friendship, he knows now, for sure, that he is dangerously close to desiring more than a kiss on the hand from him.

"Hi, Jiwon," he chokes out.

"You're one to talk about staying on track," Owen cuts in, pointing to Jiwon's knee. A pair of black jeans conceals the bandage. "Sixth place in the 10K? You said it was just a scratch."

"It is just a scratch," Jiwon shoots back. "I held back in the 10K just to play it safe. I'd rather fall behind in one race than blow it for the rest of the season."

"You could've just asked Coach to put in a substitute." Owen's jest starts teetering toward actual criticism.

Jiwon glares, sensing the shift in the conversation. "I didn't need a substitute. Besides, who would Coach have put in? We only brought seven runners to the meet, and all our 3K runners are also in the 10K. Was he supposed to pluck a 5K runner who hasn't fully recovered and throw him in a 10K? They would've wound up in sixth anyway."

"All I'm saying is you're thinking of yourself before the team. Am I right?" Owen looks to his audience. Everyone remains tight-lipped. No one wants to trip either Owen's or Jiwon's fuse.

Jiwon stands to his full height. "I would never do that. I made the best call I could at the time."

Owen gets off the grass, looming a few inches taller than Jiwon. "Coach is the one that makes the calls, not you. I bet you were just scared he'd replace you with Kim."

In an instant, Daniel is gone, staring down at the whole scene from the laurel tree. He watches as the helpless brown-haired boy—the one that he sees in the mirror so often—throws up his hands defensively. That Daniel opens his mouth and speaks: "Don't involve me in this."

Everyone holds their breath, eyes scurrying from Jiwon to Owen to Daniel. Jackie takes advantage of the hesitation to tug on Owen's sleeve.

"Chill out," she says. "You all still won first."

"Lucky us," he retorts but backs down, resituating himself on the grass. "No one can ever say anything bad about Golden Boy Jiwon without everyone acting like I've cut off his arm."

Nestled on a long branch, Daniel drifts further away. He glimpses the sawed-off arm of Captain Hook, the curved weapon that stands in for a hand. Daniel draws a dagger, clashing metal against metal with an ear-piercing clang. They jump from the tree, and their blades cross once more in front of a makeshift house of sticks and rope. Something is inside the house. Something Daniel must guard from the evil pirate.

Jayden nudges Jiwon toward the bench. "Let's just cool off."

"I'm cool." Jiwon throws himself on the bench and crosses his arms just as Captain Hook drives for Daniel's neck. He spins out of the way, slashing blindly so the pirate will keep his distance. Hook scowls. "Whatever is in that house was never yours to begin with," he taunts Daniel. "Give it up."

"What did you bring for lunch?" Ki-Jeong asks Daniel in a mediocre attempt to change the subject. "That lunchbox looks promising."

Jiwon perks up. He too seems willing to move on. "Daniel's housekeeper makes awesome food."

But Daniel doesn't smile or show off his homemade lunch. He's too busy defending something precious. He charges Captain Hook, dagger high above him, pointed to dive into the pirate's heart. Hook parries but loses ground, falling to his knees. Daniel's knife meets Hook's throat, presses lightly against the exposed skin.

Ki-Jeong peals with nervous laughter. "Daniel? Earth to Daniel?"

While everyone blankly stares at Daniel, a deep-seated concern writes itself into Jiwon's features. He steps toward Daniel's frozen figure. "Are you okay?"

Captain Hook surveys his surroundings, searching for a way to regain the upper hand. Defeated, he pleads for mercy. Daniel is no killer. With a threat to forgo any leniency next time, he sheaths his dagger. Hook rises and runs, but not without a final word: "Sleep with one eye open!"

Jiwon wags a hand in front of Daniel's face. "Hey! What's up?"

The sun's rays sift through Jiwon's hair. Beneath the halo, the collar of his blue shirt opens just enough to reveal a hint of collarbone.

"Everything's okay," Daniel manages to say, but whether he speaks to Jiwon or to the makeshift house he's successfully protected, he isn't sure. He climbs a rickety set of porch steps and pushes open the door.

"Wendy," he murmurs so quietly that almost no one hears. Jiwon's eyebrows shoot up, and Kevin glances sharply in Daniel's direction. Everyone else just shakes their heads, perplexed by Daniel's soundlessly moving lips.

Jiwon grasps Daniel's elbow, yanking him toward the gymnasium. "Let's get some snacks," he states sternly.

"But the bell is about to ring," Jayden shouts after them.

"Well, I'm hungry!"

Several yards away and sheltered by the vending machine, Jiwon shakes Daniel roughly. "Snap out of it!" he yells, shaking and shaking.

Daniel's breath floods his ears, and he grabs onto the exhalations. In and out, he counts each movement of his lungs. His mind and body gradually unite.

"Jiwon, I'm fine. I'm fine!"

Jiwon releases him and leans into the vending machine, gazing at Daniel like he's watching a psychological thriller. "Are you really?"

"Yeah, I just zoned out."

"You called me Wendy."

"I did?" He doesn't remember that.

Jiwon sighs. "You did, but I don't think they heard you."

The bell rings, quashing any further discussion. Jiwon reaches out a tentative hand and rests his palm on the crook of Daniel's neck.

"You kind of scared me back there. Let's go to class. We can talk after practice."

As Jiwon heads off, Daniel calls out, "I'm sorry!"

Jiwon turns. "I'm not mad."

Daniel can only pray that it's the truth.

After Coach Rasmussen dismisses practice, Daniel burrows in his usual spot. Nana is on her way. Hugging his knees into his chest, he spies Jiwon sharing parting words and handshakes with the team. Noticeably, Owen stomps past without a good-bye. Jiwon stares after him but keeps any comments to himself. At least until he perches beside Daniel.

"He's such a jerk," Jiwon says.

"Maybe he's jealous."

"We're supposed to be a team."

Daniel nods, somehow both relieved that Jiwon hasn't brought up his lunchtime blunder but also desperately wanting to get the conversation over and done with. He sips at his water bottle. Now would be a terrible time to slip away again.

Jiwon doesn't keep him waiting. "About lunch—don't sweat it. Just be more careful, okay? Calling me Wendy is only funny when it's just the two of us."

"Won't happen again." He hopes he can keep that promise.

Jiwon taps his foot angrily. "I'm so pissed at Owen. I don't even want to go home. I've got a pile of half-written college essays to work on, but I doubt I can focus tonight."

While even sitting this close to Jiwon jangles his nerves, he doesn't want to lose him either. Seeing an in, Daniel tests the fragile foundation that their friendship rests on. "You can come to my house."

Jiwon smiles widely. Daniel knows he's said the right thing. "Should we go get my car?"

"Nana's already driving here. You can ride with us."

"Yeah, I'll just jog home." He rubs his knee. "Just a light jog. No need to push it."

Jiwon laughs self-deprecatingly, so Daniel laughs too. Before long, Nana pulls up, and they scramble inside.

"Jiwon's coming over," Daniel tells her.

Nana glances at Jiwon in the back seat. "Oh, well, all right. Your parents are flying in tonight."

A knot forms in Daniel's throat. "When?"

"Sometime after ten p.m."

"I won't be staying that late," Jiwon says.

Nana presses her lips together toward the windshield, so only Daniel can see. Most likely, she disapproves of the unexpected company, especially after yesterday's episode with Dr. Greene. Even so, she cranks the ignition.

Once they arrive home, they stock up on sweet potato chips and haul up to the third floor. Jiwon shuts the bedroom door behind them and quickly sheds the polite facade he wore for Nana.

"Can you believe Owen?" he says, throwing his backpack violently on the floor. "He called me arrogant. You'd think the idiot would just be grateful to have beaten me in a 10K for the first time in his life."

Daniel pops open the chip bag, tosses a few back, and offers some to Jiwon. Jiwon pauses for long enough to chomp a handful.

"Golden Boy? What kind of backhanded compliment is that? He's acting like I lord my PRs over the team. I have never traded punches with a teammate before, but I swear I was so close to socking him in front of his girlfriend."

He collapses onto the bed. "I could really use a run right now, but I'm not about to trip over another pothole and wind up with another bloody knee. Owen would just love that."

A sudden idea sends Daniel to his feet. He flings open the closet and shoves his clothes to one side. From the corner, nestled between the wall and the shoe rack, he retrieves two full-size wooden swords. The flat blades swoop toward smooth cross guards. Years ago, his tiny hands struggled to hold the toy sword in mock pirate battles with Nana. Now, the hilt fits perfectly in his grip.

"On guard," says Daniel with a playful grin. "How about we duel? You can pretend I'm Owen."

Jiwon laughs louder than a drunk pirate. "You know, I'm no longer surprised by all the weird things you own. Most guys would just play video games."

"I'm not like most guys."

Jiwon takes hold of the second sword. "You don't say."

When Jiwon stabs at Daniel, he dodges and ends up slamming into the dresser. "Why don't we take this fight to the backyard?"

They barrel down the stairs and onto the back patio. Before Daniel can get two feet on the lawn, Jiwon dives at him with a two-handed swing. Daniel jumps just in time.

"Cheap shot."

"All's fair in love and war."

Their swords bash together with each amateur swing. Laughter bubbles out, even as they hack at one another. After a particularly close call, Jiwon falls back into the shelter of the trees deeper in the yard.

"Just you wait, Peter!" he yells from behind a tree trunk. "I'll get you when you least expect it."

"Good luck catching me off guard, Wendy."

Jiwon groans breathlessly. "Wendy again? Can't I be someone more intimidating, like Captain Hook?"

Daniel lashes out, but Jiwon whips around to the other side of the tree. "If you were Captain Hook, I wouldn't be going so easy on you."

"Don't underestimate me."

Jiwon leaps toward Daniel. Their blades cross. Both lean their full weight into the assault, straining to overtake the other. Jiwon tries to shift his grip but winds up losing his momentum. Realizing his advantage, Daniel strikes the sword out of Jiwon's hand. The impact knocks Jiwon off guard, and he falls to his back before quickly propping himself up on his elbows. He searches for his weapon, but the sword is too far to reach.

Daniel sinks to his knees, hovering over his adversary. "Any last words, Wendy?" he says before plunging his sword into the grass.

A beat passes. "Don't call me Wendy."

Jiwon blinks rapidly, but his eyes don't meet Daniel's. Instead, he gazes at Daniel's mouth, only inches from his own. Their breath matches, fluttering against their skin, and Daniel knows now what it means when his heart feathers through his veins.

But he can't touch Jiwon. The upset in Jiwon's expression replays in his mind from when he kissed the thimble. He won't ruin the only friendship he's managed to build.

So when Jiwon closes the space between them, Daniel's thoughts freeze. He feels Jiwon's mouth on his, yet he remains still. Jiwon pulls away, fear and hope radiating off him in waves. Daniel shuts off every thought, but he doesn't float away. He simply kisses Jiwon back. Their lips come together, and neither of them stop.

Daniel seeks out the small of Jiwon's back, coaxing him upward, and Jiwon weaves his hand into Daniel's hair like fingers combing through warm water. When they eventually part, neither utters a sound. Daniel peers into Jiwon's eyes and recognizes the desire and relief that he feels within himself. They both sit up, dumbfounded by everything they've discovered from a single kiss.

"Daniel!" Nana calls from the patio door, dissolving the spell. She can't see them past the shelter of the backyard trees. They pull themselves upright and drag their feet to the porch. "Is Jiwon staying for dinner?"

Jiwon nods faintly as a whisper.

"Yes," Daniel says. "He's staying."

CHAPTER TWENTY-ONE

The sun sets, casting an orange glow through the dining room window. Bowls of oxtail soup, rice, and daikon radish line the table. To Daniel's relief, Nana has set the table for two. He and Jiwon can eat alone.

When they take their seats, Nana comes to fill their glasses with bottled sparkling water. Even after she returns to the kitchen to clean, Jiwon fidgets in his chair, glancing nervously in her direction. He doesn't speak.

Daniel knows firsthand that Nana can hear them, even when the faucet runs, and every word he wants to say dies in his throat. A thousand questions bloom in his mind, but he drowns them in a spoonful of soup. Jiwon kissed him first, but the gesture had been small. Daniel was the one to take things further. He completely lost himself in their second kiss.

What if Jiwon just got carried away in their role play? He could blame everything on the intensity of the day. He could pin everything on Daniel. After all, Daniel was the one to kiss his finger only two days ago. As much as Daniel wants Jiwon to find him attractive, this isn't Neverland. Bad endings happen here. After dinner, Jiwon could still leave and never speak to Daniel again.

Several minutes into their silent dinner, Nana reenters the dining room, sparkling water in hand. Their glasses are untouched. She sets the bottle in the center of the table.

"I'll just leave this here," she says. "I need to head upstairs, to tidy your parents' rooms. Remember that Jiwon should go home after you finish eating."

Jiwon shovels a bite of soupy rice into his mouth, so Daniel does the talking. "We'll wrap things up," he says.

Once Nana exits the dining room, Jiwon stares toward the stairs. "Can she hear us?" he asks.

Daniel shakes his head. He's not sure if he's ready for whatever Jiwon wants to say.

"Do you think she saw us?"

"I doubt it. We were behind the trees and on the ground."

Jiwon sighs and leans back into his chair with closed eyes. The food is cooling, but neither touches the meal. The bubbles in their water rise to the surface.

"Have you ever done that before?" Jiwon asks.

Daniel hates Jiwon's questions. The right answers feel too far out of reach. "It wasn't my first kiss," he finally replies.

"That's not what I meant."

"No, I haven't done that before."

Jiwon rests a thumb against his mouth. "Me neither. Maybe we just overreacted, to the sword fight and everything?"

Daniel can sense that Jiwon is testing him, but he isn't sure what Jiwon wants him to say, so he opts for the truth: "It's what I wanted." The words fall like loose gravel on the table. Once voiced, they can never be unsaid.

Jiwon smiles at his soup. He picks up his spoon and mashes his rice with a trembling hand. "Me too," he whispers. "I don't know how, but it's like you could see right through me since we first met."

Daniel's heart races as Jiwon continues. "I've liked guys before. You know, I'd fall for a guy. He'd be obviously straight. I'd get over it. I thought that it would be the same story with you, so I kind of lost it when you kissed the thimble the other day. I didn't want to give away that I liked you. I've never actually imagined what could happen if my feelings were mutual." His teeth tug at his lower lip. "I guess this is what happens."

Despite his wildest hopes, Daniel never expected such a clear confession from Jiwon. Just last weekend, he was swimming in regret, terrified that he'd lost a friend. Somehow, now, Jiwon is less frightening, more safe.

When Daniel fails to respond, Jiwon adds, "Your turn to talk."

"I like you," Daniel says, and Jiwon blushes.

"I hope so." After sipping at his soup, he asks, "When did you realize you were gay?"

The three-letter word sends ripples of anxiety through Daniel. His left cheek suddenly stings, as if slapped, but his body feels numb. Quickly, he takes a gulp of water and focuses on the cold liquid washing over his tongue.

"I don't know if I'm gay," he manages to reply.

Jiwon lets go of his spoon. "Oh, well, it's not an easy thing to work out." Even though his voice remains calm, worry furrows his brows.

"Are you gay?"

Their eyes meet. "Yeah, I guess I am," Jiwon says with obvious discomfort, and Daniel wonders if he's disappointed Jiwon.

"How do you know? How long have you known?"

"Since middle school. Back when I used to dance, my cross-country teammates would tease me about my sexuality. They thought it was all in good fun, but hearing them talk about my *homo hobby* really freaked me out. I'd get so angry, but the more I insisted that I wasn't gay, the more I started noticing that I didn't want to date girls. I paid so much more attention to my friends."

After a second of stillness, Jiwon continues. "One day, I got a new dance teacher, and he was just amazing. At first, I told myself that I just wanted to be like him, but before long, I realized that I actually wanted to be with him. Which was stupid because I was thirteen and he was in his late twenties. Still, whenever he'd correct my posture, I would break out in a nervous sweat. Finally, I couldn't take it anymore, and I told my mom that I wanted to quit modern and focus on cross-country and track instead. It was a big deal. We fought a lot about how I was squandering my talent and years of lessons, but I refused to go to any dance practices. I wanted to tell her the real reason why, but I knew that would only make everything worse."

Jiwon squeezes his hand into a fist beside his untouched rice. Daniel gently touches the flexed knuckles, and Jiwon laces their fingers together.

"I've never told anyone about this before," Jiwon says. "Some days, after there was a bad meet or whenever I found myself falling for some random straight guy in class, I'd try to tell my mom, but I could never get up the courage. I'll tell her tomorrow, I'd say to myself, but then that changed to, I'll tell her next year, or I'll tell her when I go to college. Then she died, and I lost my chance."

Jiwon flushes and seems distressed. Daniel wants to trace a hand along his face, but he doesn't let go of the hand that holds his tightly.

"You can still tell her," Daniel says.

"And what? She'll hear me up in heaven? From somewhere in Neverland?"

"You could write to her." Daniel remembers how, when he was still in elementary school, he would write letters to his traveling parents. Silly messages about wishing he had a dog or poems about eating ice cream for dinner. He gave each letter to Nana, but knows she never sent them. It was the same as postmarking a Christmas list to Santa Claus. At the time though, all that mattered was the hope that, one day, he might receive a response or even a postcard.

"Hold on." Daniel grabs the bottle of sparkling water and heads to the kitchen. At the sink, he tips the bottle till it's completely empty. By the time he returns to the dining room, Jiwon has collected himself and even eaten a little.

Daniel thunks the glass bottle on the table. "You'll write it in a letter, and we can send it to her in this."

"In a bottle?" says Jiwon, clearly not following Daniel's train of thought.

"Exactly. You put the message in the bottle, and it'll get to Neverland by water."

"We're a good thirty minutes from the ocean, Daniel."

"I have a pool."

Jiwon shakes his head. "I can never tell with you, whether you actually believe in the things you say."

For some reason, that makes Daniel smile. "You'd be surprised what pretending can lead to." After all, a sword fight brought him closer to Jiwon. He summons courage from Neverland to lean forward and brush his lips on Jiwon's forehead. The simple kiss seems to do the trick. Jiwon chuckles softly.

"Let's at least eat first," he concedes.

"You have to leave after dinner, so we need to do this now and eat later."

"Okay, okay," he laughs, letting Daniel entwine their hands and guide him to the living room.

After retrieving paper and a fine-point permanent marker from the coffee table drawer, he sets the materials in front of Jiwon. Jiwon stares hesitantly at the empty lines.

"Just write exactly what you wish you could tell her when you go to college."

Jiwon picks up the marker. "Don't look," he says.

Several seconds pass before Jiwon begins the letter, but once he starts, the words flow freely. He scribbles for a few minutes, never marking out a word. Finally, he signs the message and announces that he's done. Daniel unscrews the bottle. Jiwon curls the letter and fits it inside.

Out on the back patio, the sky has dimmed to twilight. Stars expel their first evening light. They make their way to the phosphorescent pool. Built perpendicular to the house, the pool stretches halfway down the yard, beginning at fifteen feet deep and eventually ending with shallow steps.

"So now what?" Jiwon asks.

"Set the bottle in the pool."

"And then what? Pixies will come get it?"

Daniel laughs and gently pushes Jiwon toward the water's edge. "Now *that* would be weird."

Once Jiwon drops the bottle with a small splash, Daniel pulls him back to his side. "Now close your eyes."

"Daniel—"

"If we close our eyes, maybe it will float to her when we're not looking." He needs Jiwon to play along, or else his plan won't work.

Jiwon covers his eyes with his hands like a child prepping for hide-and-seek. "For how long?"

"Just long enough."

As soundlessly as possible, Daniel slips to the poolside. His muscles strain as he kneels and reaches for the bottle. The next challenge is reclaiming it from the water without stirring up a splash. After an achingly meticulous lift, he manages to pull it out. He checks to see if Jiwon has opened his eyes, but he still stands in the same position.

Holding his breath, Daniel inches to the nearest lawn chair, scoots the cushion aside, and buries the bottle beneath. Task complete, he creeps back to Jiwon.

"I think we can open our eyes now," Daniel says.

He hopes to make Jiwon smile, or even better, laugh. The game was meant to be light-hearted fun. But when Jiwon sees the empty pool, he inhales sharply. As a cool wind tousles the water into gentle waves, tears flood Jiwon's eyes. They course down his cheeks till they drip from his chin.

"Jiwon, she got it," Daniel says.

Jiwon only watches the water until Daniel pulls him into a tight hug. After Daniel leaves a tentative kiss on his lips, Jiwon finally speaks. "Maybe she did."

CHAPTER TWENTY-TWO

Before Daniel can settle down for the night, he reaches for his phone. Jiwon swims in his mind—their conversation about Jiwon's mother, the sword fight, their kiss. Even though Jiwon left over an hour ago, his fingers fumble a text message:
Are you home yet?
Before he can worry that he's texted too soon, Jiwon's reply lights up the screen.
Jiwon: *I'm home, but I wish I wasn't*
Daniel: *Where do you want to be?*
Jiwon: *Do you really have to ask?*
Daniel: *I wish my parents weren't coming home tonight*
Jiwon: *Can I see you tomorrow after practice?*
Daniel: *Probably not. My parents don't like company, and I have an appointment*
Jiwon: *What kind of appointment?*
Daniel: *Do you really have to ask?*
Jiwon: *I like you just the way you are*
Tuesday morning continues much the same. At breakfast, he can barely concentrate on his parents' tales of Tokyo business meetings and real estate. Not that they are really talking to him anyway. It takes all of Daniel's self-control to ignore his phone during their meal. He doesn't want his parents to ask who he's talking to. After all, Jiwon is not a simple breakfast conversation.

During the car ride to school, Daniel manages to keep his phone locked up in his backpack, away from Nana's prying eyes. As he dashes out of the car, he makes a mental note to powerfully avoid Jiwon's name in that evening's session with Dr. Greene. Finally, once he and Amber are sent off to the library with a math quiz, he wastes no time texting Jiwon.

I've got a test today. Will you be in the library during your free period?

No response. He needs Jiwon to reply before Mr. Bartel confiscates his phone.

Amber skips ahead of him, then flips to walking backward. "I know you're a good, straight B student now, but I would be a bad fellow-504er if I didn't at least offer what's up my sleeve." She lifts the hem of her sleeve to reveal an answer key in blue ink. "Feel free to take a quick peek."

"I'll pass."

She fake pouts. "I knew you'd say that."

Daniel's phone vibrates. He snatches it from his pocket faster than a starting pistol.

I was planning to ask for help on my English essay, but now that I think about it, there's a shelving cart with my name on it

Daniel grins as he thumbs a quick response.

What would Mr. Bartel do without you?

"Wow, Daniel!" Amber says. "You can actually smile! Who are you texting?"

He locks his phone screen. "Just a teammate."

Amber rolls her eyes. "Guys and sports. I heard from Jayden that your team destroyed at your last meet. The after party was crazy, but I didn't see you there."

"I was tired." Daniel finds it hard to believe that only a few nights ago, he was afraid he'd ruined his friendship with Jiwon—the same Jiwon who texted him until midnight last night.

"We'll have to take Jell-O shots together next time." Amber grins. She's probably aware of the low likelihood of Daniel getting that hammered.

They enter the library. The shelving cart rests unattended beside the circulation desk. After Mr. Bartel impounds their belongings, they head to the quiet rooms. Fortunately, Daniel remembered to bring a digital watch, a remnant from his middle school track days. As he slides the glass door shut, he spies Jiwon entering the library. If he ever needed a reason to focus on an exam, a simple glimpse of Jiwon met that need. Math never felt so effortless.

He scratches out formulas and graphs. Luckily, the quiz only covers the previous week's content in a mere five questions. Even so, when he double-checks his work, his shoulders sag from the obvious number of errors. After a sixty-second reboot with his watch, he begins erasing and revising. Ten minutes later, he feels satisfied with his answers, excluding the incorrigible latter half of the fourth problem.

Twelve minutes before the bell rings, Daniel exits the cubicle. Amber has already fled the scene, doubtlessly fiddling on her phone in the restroom instead of returning to math class.

When Daniel turns in the quiz to Mr. Bartel, he nods approvingly. "A new PR," he jokes. Daniel is surprised that he knows anything about cross-country at all.

"The watch helped," he half-lies.

Once he collects his things, he fakes a casual stroll to the entryway. As soon as Mr. Bartel's attention returns to his computer, Daniel ducks into the book stacks. He weaves in and out of the aisles and locates Jiwon bent over the literary criticism section.

"There you are," Daniel whispers.

Jiwon jumps. "You scared me."

Finally face-to-face again, they immediately slip into an awkward silence. A letterman jacket overwhelms Jiwon's small frame. His bleached hair has gotten messy while he worked, his bangs hooding his brown eyes. While Daniel has wanted to see him, he isn't prepared for how his heart picks up speed.

"I wish we could meet up after school," Jiwon says, tossing a book onto the cart.

"There's still lunch and practice."

"That's not the same."

Daniel agrees. "There's no way I can get out of this appointment."

"It's therapy, isn't it? How often do you go?"

"Twice a week."

Jiwon slides a hand down Daniel's arm. "That's good."

Daniel shrugs. Dr. Greene isn't his favorite talking point, but he doesn't want Jiwon to let go of his arm, so he fumbles a reply. "It's not like much goes on whenever I'm there."

"I had to see a psych a few times when I was on antidepressants. Mostly, it was just a short interrogation followed by a prescription refill. Still, the meds helped me clear my head enough to process through things."

Even though Jiwon is trying to relate, Daniel feels a rift between their mental health histories. Most likely, Jiwon's cabinets never harbored four different pill bottles with his name on them, and he probably hasn't jumped off a roof either, or been hospitalized for a full month. He wishes he could cry like Jiwon instead of withdrawing from his body like a ghost without an afterlife.

"I'm okay for the most part," Daniel says, because the truth is too much to share.

"Of course you are, Peter Pan."

Daniel can't tell if he is mocking him, but when Jiwon's hand trails from his arm to his waist, he decides it doesn't matter. In spite of his medications and his J. M. Barrie fixation, Jiwon likes him. Daniel takes a step closer.

"You can come to my house tomorrow," Jiwon offers.

As much as Daniel wants to say yes, the gravity of Sung-Min and Monica's return imprisons him. "Not this week. My parents have this weird obsession with eating dinner together. I don't think I can get around it for a few days."

"At least they want to spend time with you," Jiwon replies, and Daniel chooses to leave the misunderstanding uncorrected. There's a definite line between care and control. "My dad can get like that, too. Can you still make it to Saturday's party?"

"I'll sneak out for that."

"Perfect. We can—"

"Daniel, shouldn't you head back to class now?" says Mr. Bartel, decapitating Jiwon's sentence. Jiwon tears his hand off Daniel's waist, and Daniel jerks away from him. Daniel can feel his ears burning, and he glimpses Jiwon's red face from the corner of his eye.

Mr. Bartel eyes them curiously, but he makes no mention of their behavior, waiting for Daniel's excuses instead.

"I had a question about cross-country," he mutters. "Thanks, Jiwon. I'll get going now."

Tail tucked between his legs, Daniel scurries past Mr. Bartel. As he rounds the corner toward the exit, he hears him say, "Those books need to find their shelves, pronto."

How much did Mr. Bartel see? They were standing far too close. Jiwon's hand might have been concealed by the shelving cart. A whirlwind crashes through Daniel. He dashes to an empty bathroom, then locks a stall door. With deep inhales of the stale air, he counts his way to the end of the period.

Classes float by. Lunch with the team feels unnaturally normal. Jiwon artfully ignores Owen and pays little attention to Daniel. The act is almost too convincing, but once Jiwon sends him a covert text, Daniel can finally relax.

That was a little too close with Mr. Bartel. Let's play it safe and stick to just texting

Better safe than sorry

Jiwon waits a good four minutes before checking Daniel's response. So when Daniel's phone vibes, he also practices restraint.

We'll figure this out

Daniel loves that they're a *we* and that they're in this together. Secrets are less burdensome when shared with another person, especially when that other person finds a way to privately trace his fingers along Daniel's spine after the bell rings.

An atypical giddiness marks Daniel's steps to PE. In the locker room, he changes clothes with less apprehension. Everything feels easier. The ordinary becomes breathable.

Until Coach Rasmussen calls him to his office.

Jayden shoots Daniel a startled look. Coach Rasmussen never summons anyone to his desk unless there's trouble. Not just any kind of trouble. After all, the man saw nothing wrong with laying into a noncompliant student in front of an entire class. Daniel runs through a list of possible misdeeds. His grades are decent, his times consistent, his attitude up to expectations. He shuts the office door behind him, dreading whatever awaits.

Coach Rasmussen plunks into his mesh chair. "I don't want to make a big deal out of this, Kim," he begins, resting his chin on folded hands. "Cranbrook always makes it to district finals, but for the first time in a few years, I feel like we have a real shot at qualifying beyond regionals. I'm talking state championships here."

Daniel nods, unsure where this is leading.

"You're good, and you're getting even better. With Jiwon and Owen, we might be able to steal all three spots in the 3K and 10K. That is, if we do some rearranging. How about we shift Kevin to the 5K and put you in the 10K instead?"

At first, Daniel stays silent, assuming the question is rhetorical. After all, Coach Rasmussen is well-acquainted with each team member's times, but Coach Rasmussen stares hard, clearly expecting Daniel's opinion. A wave of emotions sweeps over him. He wants the 10K. At Cambry, he worked tirelessly to win a varsity spot in the longest race, earning the honor in his freshman year. Even in practice, Daniel's speed and endurance surpasses Kevin's.

"How would Kevin feel about this?" Daniel says.

Coach Rasmussen smiles. "I'm impressed. You're a real team player, Kim. That's another thing I like about you. You're humble. The thing is, last week's meet had me worried. Jiwon's minor injury really riled me up. We need a plan if one of our 10K runners gets hurt during a meet. We need more than one ace. Kevin is a solid runner. He shines in track and field, but he isn't a cross-country trump card. He can dominate a 5K, but you can accomplish what he can't in a longer race."

"Is the decision already made then?"

"It is, unless you refuse, of course. A lot depends on this season. I know at least one of our seniors is aiming for a sports scholarship with a handful of top colleges."

Without asking, Daniel knows he's referring to Jiwon. Kevin's ego and Jiwon's future lie on the chopping block, and Daniel has to choose where to swing the ax. Coach Rasmussen fixes him with a watchful gaze.

Tucked safely on the ceiling fan, Daniel observes as the terrified, brown-haired boy opens his mouth. From above, he hears the words: "I'll do it."

Coach Rasmussen stands. "I'll talk to Kevin before practice. Then, I'll announce the switch to the team. You may have just won us the season, Kim."

The coach dismisses him to the gym for class, and even though Daniel would rather escape than face Jayden's unavoidable inquiries, he trudges toward his classmates.

He takes an oath of silence. The whistle blows. A flurry of volleyballs hurtles over nets, and Daniel realizes with distasteful certainty that his choice will probably make his parents proud.

CHAPTER TWENTY-THREE

When Daniel overtakes Jiwon for first in the 3K, he shrouds his joy. When Kevin wins the 5K, he hangs at the back of the congratulatory crowd. When he lands a narrow third in the 10K behind Jiwon and another school's top runner, he hides behind Jiwon's shadow. Cranbrook dominates the tri-meet. Coach Rasmussen is thrilled. Yet, the bus ride back to school feels more like a three-hour standardized test than a twenty-minute celebratory procession. Kevin and Owen murmur between themselves, occasionally glancing toward Daniel and Jiwon.

"Don't even look at them," says Jiwon. "Coach made the right call."

Daniel wants to curl into a ball and disappear.

"Owen is addicted to melodrama," Jiwon continues. "Trust me. Kevin doesn't hold grudges. He isn't even applying for any scholarships. His college tuition has been fully funded for three generations."

Still, over the last three days, lunch banter has been sedate at best. No one wants to be the first to name the unfairness of the team switch. Kevin has left the topic untouched, but he hasn't really spoken to Daniel either.

Jiwon sighs tiredly. "We can't let upperclassmen favoritism determine who runs what. You're clearly more qualified."

Daniel wonders if Jiwon would be as supportive if he'd beaten him in the 10K. He knows for a fact that Jiwon held back in the

3K—probably to ensure his 10K victory—which led to Daniel's win. Even so, with a mere four seconds separating their times in the longer race, Jiwon is no doubt feeling the pressure.

"We all just need a drink," Jiwon groans. "You're still going to the party tonight, right?"

The bus flinches as a wheel strikes a pothole. "I don't know anymore."

Jiwon dares a hand on Daniel's knee. "C'mon, you have to go. Kevin's parents are out of town again. If you bail, he'll take it as a personal insult. Besides, I've been looking forward to this all week."

Jiwon attempts a sly smile. "Kevin's house is huge," he adds. "We can easily avoid any close encounters with resentful teammates."

Daniel already knows he'll say yes. He wants to find a way to be alone with Jiwon and skipping the party altogether would be social suicide. "I'm not drinking," he says.

"Then I won't either."

As the bus slows into the school lot, Jiwon squeezes Daniel's knee before releasing. "We're a shoo-in for district finals. After next Saturday's meet, everyone will be too hyped to care about petty position changes."

While Jiwon's premonition should comfort Daniel, their upcoming meet—the last of their qualifying races before finals—pits Cranbrook against Cambry. Daniel will compete against his old school, all while trying to prove his worth to his own critical teammates.

The bus staggers to a stop. "We'll have a good time tonight," Jiwon insists, and Daniel tries to focus on each word as he scuttles past Kevin and into Nana's car.

❖

Daniel showers. He doesn't feel like getting dressed but manages to piece together a decent combination of black jeans with a pinstripe tee. The smell of grilled chicken lures him downstairs. As his feet hit the marble floor, Sung-Min calls him to the table. While

Daniel dreads another round of lifeless family chitchat, his stomach begs for sustenance after the arduous cross-country exercise.

Daniel's chair squeals when he pulls it out, earning a disapproving frown from Monica. He quietly spreads his napkin across his lap. Sung-Min swirls his bourbon, the ice singing.

"How went that 10K?" his father asks.

"I got first in the 3K and third in the 10K."

The glass meets the placemat. "The other team bested you then?" he says coolly.

Daniel shakes his head. "Well, second place went to another school but one of my teammates got first. Cranbrook took first place overall."

"That's excellent," Monica says behind a wall of perfect teeth.

"You'll practice even harder this week, I'm sure," adds Sung-Min. "You always strive for first. That's been your way since middle school."

"Of course." In truth, Daniel doesn't mind letting Jiwon take the lead. He doesn't need to ruffle any more feathers on the team.

"How would you like to spend Christmas in Korea with us, Daniel?" Monica asks, her eyes drifting to the window. "There will be snow in Seoul, and you can visit your grandparents."

Daniel hasn't seen his grandparents since they ventured stateside over ten years ago. Their faces blur in his memory. "Okay," he replies, knowing that he has little say in the matter.

"If you can keep your grades up, that is," Sung-Min warns.

"I've been getting higher scores recently."

Sung-Min delicately knifes his chicken. "Once we start seeing a few As, we'll buy the tickets. Of course, your mother and I will be going regardless. There are a few business opportunities we'd like to check on at our Incheon branch."

In other words, Daniel will spend a week or two playing nice with his unfamiliar grandparents while Sung-Min and Monica work the holiday away. "Will Nana come?" Daniel asks.

Monica taps her wine glass with a pale pink nail. "Someone has to watch over the house."

"You don't need a babysitter, Daniel," Sung-Min adds.

A familiar face wouldn't hurt though. He busies himself eating, quitting the one-sided discussion. Christmas in a foreign house. He wonders how Jiwon celebrates the holidays. Will he be lonely with just his father?

The conversation redirects to a potential redesign of the Incheon staff, so Daniel lets himself wander to Mermaid's Lagoon. For a moment, he thinks he spies a glass bottle bobbing toward the shore, but the setting sun blinds his vision.

After dinner, he scans a few chapters in his English Literature homework. After a few hours, Nana's door clicks shut. The house falls quiet, except for the shuffling of papers from his parents' locked offices. He breathes for a few minutes, then grabs his sneakers and creeps out the back door and onto the street.

A brisk jog carries him to Kevin's red brick gate. Several partiers lounge around the front lawn, committing some sort of minor crime with the Art Deco fountain in the driveway. As he slips past them, one boy calls out, "Hey, Daniel!" but he doesn't recognize him.

As soon as he's inside, he whips out his phone to text Jiwon. A sea of people ebbs and flows around him. He needs to find Jiwon before Kevin or Owen see him. Before he can press send, a hand tugs at his elbow.

Just great, he thinks, but when he turns toward his assailant, he's faced with none other than a red-lipped Amber. A can of spiked cider fizzes in her hand.

"Look who I've found!" she shouts over the thrumming music. "A wild Daniel outside his natural environment. C'mon, let's get you a drink."

"I'm not drinking tonight."

"That's so you. Just walk with me, please." She gestures toward a crowd of fist-bumping jocks. "My ex is over there, and he's already made a pass at me tonight. I want to meet a friend in the backyard without him intruding."

Daniel acquiesces, mostly because he might spot Jiwon on the way, but also because he can sympathize with trying to avoid someone. They navigate around the dancers and the couch that Daniel passed out on just a few weeks ago. A silent autumn wind greets them on the patio. Amber sits on the porch steps and pats the space beside her. Daniel joins her.

"My friend will probably be here in a minute," Amber says before tipping back her can. Daniel fights the urge to finish his text to Jiwon. He doesn't want Amber to ask any more questions.

"I'll wait with you."

She watches him from the corner of her eye. "You know, Daniel, you're an actual decent person. I don't have any guy friends like you. Most boys either want sex or just flat-out ignore me. *There's Amber*, they think, *only good for a screw*. But you're not like that at all. Sure, you're too shy for your own good, but you actually look at me when I talk to you."

"Thanks, I guess."

Amber cracks up. "It's a compliment. Don't take this as me hitting on you. I have too many relationship troubles as it is. Just don't change. Don't turn out like all those other idiots."

The door opens behind them, unleashing a firestorm of hip-hop. "There you are, Amber!" shouts a tipsy girl in out-of-season flip-flops. She notices Daniel. "Who's this?"

Amber jumps to her feet and crushes her empty can. "Just some cross-country meathead," she snickers. Then, to Daniel, she adds, "Thanks for protecting me from the big, bad ex. Congrats on the meet."

The girls reenter the party, arm-in-arm, closing the door after them. The stillness of the night seeps into Daniel's bare arms. Finally alone, he informs Jiwon of his location. When the door reopens a few minutes later, Daniel's breath catches as Jiwon steps forward. A white shirt hugs his chest, tucked into a pair of ripped jeans. A beer bottle graces his hand.

"I thought you said you weren't drinking."

"Nice to see you, too," Jiwon says with a laugh. He sets the beer on a nearby table. "I only drank half. Owen got it for me. Not like I could say no."

Daniel nods, not sure why he's monitoring Jiwon's alcohol intake in the first place. After a long week, he's alone with Jiwon. Now that the moment has arrived, he isn't sure where to begin.

Jiwon seems to feel the same, approaching Daniel as hesitantly as a jittery butterfly. Finally, he catches Daniel's sleeve between his index finger and thumb.

"Let's go upstairs," he says.

"What? Here?"

Jiwon tugs gently. "It's still early. No one will be up there."

Daniel wants to feel safe with Jiwon, free of any interruptions, so he follows him back inside, past a group playing a rowdy game of king's cup, up a carpeted staircase, and into a dark hallway. Through a cracked door, he glimpses a baby's crib.

"Kevin's little sister's room. His parents always travel with her," Jiwon explains before testing a doorknob to another room. The door gives way, and they venture within. Jiwon activates the lock and flips on a lamp.

Framed sports photos and Sentinel banners line the walls. Tall shelves border a messy desk. Sweatshirts hang from the bed posts. In the corner, a black TV screen displays their distorted reflections.

Jiwon takes a casual seat on the edge of the bed. "When we were kids, Kevin used to have these cheesy wolf illustrations up instead of basketball players."

Daniel laughs and sits beside him. "You two have known each other for a long time."

"His mom went to college with mine. Apparently, they were thrilled when they realized their first kids would be born the same year." He shifts so that their knees touch. "Funny how you can know someone for your whole life, and they don't know the most important things about you."

"I don't have any friends like that."

Jiwon reaches for the base of Daniel's neck. "Are you jealous?"

Their lips meet. Their fingers trip over shoulders and arms and wrists. Jiwon tastes a little like beer and a little like mint. When he pulls at Daniel's shirt, they fall into the mattress. Daniel props himself up by an elbow but lets his free hand linger on Jiwon's hip. He wants to be as close as possible to Jiwon, but he doesn't want to hurt him.

Jiwon seems to have a different idea, curving his spine so that their bodies brush together. When Jiwon's breath hitches, Daniel's lungs go up in flames. Jiwon runs a hand underneath his shirt, and Daniel wonders if he can sense the rapid-fire of his heart, but then, he notices the way Jiwon's hand trembles against his skin. Whatever Daniel is feeling has possessed him as well.

Until a painful knot twists in Daniel's stomach. From a dark corner of his mind, another hand presses into his chest. He tries to shut out the shadowed flashback, but it persists. So when Jiwon trails to the button of Daniel's jeans, he freezes. Every muscle stiffens, but his heart smashes harder against his ribs.

Jiwon notices the change and halts. Too late. Daniel jerks away, just as his chest tightens. Not now, he thinks. Not this again. He almost wishes he *would* die, because his memory is racing, spiraling through images he never wants to remember. He has spent months locking up each picture of that floral bedspread, the long auburn hair, those blue eyes. His left cheek stings, blood pooling beneath the surface.

"Daniel, I'm sorry." Jiwon's voice calls out from miles away. "I got carried away."

He can't see Jiwon anymore. Everything is white—the same white as the pill in his pocket. Even though Jiwon watches, Daniel retrieves the Lorazepam. He dry-swallows the tablet. He has to stop the memories before they kill him.

Clutching the blanket beneath him, he tries to focus on the fabric, each soft fiber, but he can only feel the embroidery of a flower quilt. The scent of vanilla perfume overwhelms him until he gags.

"Daniel, just breathe. Please breathe." Jiwon touches his hand, but it isn't Jiwon's hand anymore. Instead, he tears away from her clasping fingers. She holds him down. She tells him, "If we try again, it will get easier."

She keeps talking. "We can fix this."

Then, just as suddenly as the blindness came on, his vision clears. Jiwon's face, panicked, emerges from the dust. The dimly lit room replaces the hot summer sun streaming through her open window. Daniel gasps for air. The pain gradually dissipates. She is gone.

"Jiwon," he whispers against the gravel in his throat.

"I'm so sorry," Jiwon pleads. "I wasn't thinking. I know you're still figuring things out. I pushed you too far. I—"

"Jiwon, no. It's not you."

"But I should have been more patient. I rushed things. You're still not even sure if you're gay."

"I am gay," Daniel responds, his voice removed. If not for the Lorazepam flooding his veins, the anxiety would probably return full force, but seeing Jiwon blame himself pushes him to speak. He can't lose the one thing he's truly wanted.

"I've known for a couple years now," he continues. "I even told other people. I already came out."

"What do you mean?"

Daniel wants to collapse on the bed, fall asleep, and wake up to a mind swept clean of all the memories, but now that he's started, he can't leave Jiwon with non-answers to well-deserved questions. Otherwise, Jiwon will go home believing he has done something wrong, but none of this is his fault.

"I realized it when I was a freshman," he begins. "I started hanging out with this girl. She was the sister of my teammate, an upperclassman named James."

Her name was Brooklyn. They met in the back seat of James's white Lexus. On a late spring Friday night, Daniel slid into the leather back seat, and she passed him a bottle of rosé. He was taller and more fit than most freshmen, but he thought he wore his age like a badge of shame. He never imagined that Brooklyn would find him attractive.

When she played video games with him in James's room, he assumed she was bored. When she started texting him about schoolwork and friend drama, he figured she wanted someone outside of her social circle to listen to her problems, but when she kissed him one day, after her brother left to grab snacks, he learned just how blind he'd been and how much he didn't like girls at all.

"She told her brother that she wanted to date me." From his perch atop Kevin's TV, Daniel listens to the words tumbling from his detached mouth. "Brothers can be brutal. James told me if I hurt Brooklyn, I'd pay for it."

He finished his freshman year with track and field ribbons, a close-knit team, and a girlfriend. By the end of June, Brooklyn started asking why they never did anything more than kiss. In the beginning, Daniel convinced himself that he was just warming up to his first girlfriend, but once he started fantasizing about other boys during their rendezvous, the real reason became clear.

"I was immature and naive," Daniel recalls, "and I really liked Brooklyn. She and I called each other every day. We played video games. She listened to me vent about my issues with my parents and pointed out all the ways they tried to care about me. We partied together and drank ourselves sick. I thought if anyone could understand that I might be gay, she was the one."

Brooklyn was pridefully pretty and relatively popular. When Daniel broke the news to her on an uneventful July afternoon, she responded with a distorted show of support and a bitter dose of truth. No one at Cambry—his classmates, his teammates—would accept a gay friend into their network. Perhaps Daniel was going through a phase. She offered to help him out. If they slept together, he might break free from his misfortune and resume life as a normal, straight student. Confused and scared, Daniel agreed.

"After the first time, I knew that sex wasn't going to change anything, but Brooklyn promised that I would get used to it. I think I wanted to get used to it. I wanted to believe that she was right. If she wasn't right, if I didn't like girls, then I would be worse off. Just like she said. No one was ever going to accept me, and not just at school. My parents have planned my future since before I was born. Me being gay would never fit into that plan, and they have this way of making everything and everyone do whatever they say. No matter what."

By the end of the summer, Daniel started telling himself stories to get through each encounter. He would fly away to a safer place, full of adventures and characters that knew nothing about his parents or his teammates or Brooklyn or sex. *Peter Pan* had been his childhood favorite, something Nana still turned on whenever he was sick or if his parents hadn't returned from an especially lengthy trip. Brooklyn's floral duvet was the forest beneath his feet as he chased the pirates away from Hangman's Tree.

He went through all the motions—his body reacting even with his brain tuned into Neverland. Still, for all his trying, Brooklyn decided that Daniel was too much effort. One week into his sophomore year, she broke up with him for a senior on the tennis team.

"I went to school every morning, afraid that she'd told everyone about me. I started avoiding James and the rest of my teammates. I couldn't concentrate in class. Every single person around me might have known the truth, but I don't know if she ever said anything. Maybe to protect her own reputation, she never told anyone."

Still, the anxiety ate him alive. Neverland became the only world where worry and fear didn't exist. His grades fell from As to Cs. One day, his parents called him into the parlor, and he feared the worst. Their questions squeezed the air out of his lungs.

"Do you need a tutor?"

"Is cross-country taking up too much of your time?"

Then, his mother finally asked, "Are you trying to get our attention? Is there something you want to tell us?"

He looked into her face, and he saw concern and maybe love—a hint of the same love that kept Mrs. Darling sleeping by an open window in the hope that her children would fly home from Neverland. So, he told them, not about his encounters with Brooklyn, but he started with them in the same way that he'd tried with her. He told them that he *might* be gay.

"My dad slapped me across the face, so hard that my ears started ringing. So, I took it all back. I even said that I had just been making a joke. They never brought up my grades after that, even when my GPA fell too low for me to run track and field."

Daniel closes his eyes, the weight of the panic attack, the Lorazepam, and the memories threatening to drag him into an immediate slumber. He can't sleep, not when Jiwon is right in front of him. Not when he's told him everything.

"It's pretty pathetic, isn't it?" he says when he finally reopens his eyes.

Jiwon shakes his head slowly, as if through water. "You are the furthest thing from pathetic."

When Jiwon pulls him into a hug, Daniel nearly pushes away, but then he remembers that this is what he wants. He has always wanted someone to listen and understand. His body gives out, collapsing into Jiwon like a box of bricks thrown from a window.

"I'm so tired," he murmurs against his shirt. "From the medicine."

"We gotta get you home," says Jiwon as he sifts his fingers through Daniel's hair, but neither gets up. Enough time passes that Daniel really thinks he might fall asleep in Kevin's bed at a party in the middle of a Saturday night. But when Jiwon speaks again, he's roused from an oncoming dream.

"Not a thing you just told me was your fault. You do know that, right? They don't deserve you."

Daniel wonders if Jiwon is referring to Brooklyn or his old friends at Cambry or his parents. Perhaps it's all of the above.

CHAPTER TWENTY-FOUR

From the hallway, Daniel can hear the shouts of drunken partiers melding with raging dance music. A noxious mix of sweat, beer, and liquor grows stronger as he and Jiwon descend the stairs. Jiwon fiddles with his keys as he pushes through the crowd. Even though he feels childish, Daniel clings to the back of Jiwon's shirt. His head splits from the cacophony.

When they reach the front door, a smothered voice hollers Jiwon's name. Too drained to look, Daniel leans into the threshold.

"Where are you off to?" Kevin asks, the consonants slurring.

Jiwon steps in front of Daniel. "Heading home."

Kevin crosses his arms. "Last week you didn't even show up. Now, you're bailing early?"

"It's not that early."

"Early for you." Kevin glances between Jiwon and Daniel, who presses into the wall with eyes fluttering beneath the weight of the Lorazepam. "What's wrong with him?"

"Nothing. He's just tired."

"I doubt that. I saw you two come down from upstairs. I'm not an idiot, Jiwon. I've watched you play this game for years."

Jiwon fists his keys. "What game?"

"You want me to spell it out for you?" Kevin steps closer. "I heard him call you Wendy."

"Daniel likes *Peter Pan*. Everyone knows that," Jiwon sputters, visibly blanching. He turns to the door, but Kevin yanks him back.

"Don't mess with Daniel," he warns. "Just because he's a freak doesn't mean he's like you. You're going to single-handedly rip apart the team."

"Not everything's about sports, Kevin." Jiwon grabs Daniel's elbow and drags him out the door and onto the lawn.

Daniel's tank nears empty, but Kevin's threats rattle through his hollowed mind. "He knows," he mumbles.

"He doesn't know anything."

They squeeze past the brick gate and stumble a block to Jiwon's car. Daniel all but keels over onto the passenger seat. Instead of starting the engine, Jiwon slams his hands against the steering wheel. His breath pumps hot and fast.

"He doesn't know anything," he repeats. "At this point, it's all speculation. Coach won't stand for shit like rumor-spreading or drama. And Kevin, well, he isn't one to spread rumors."

Then, to Daniel, he says, "Let's get you home. Don't worry about Kevin. Nothing's gonna happen, and if it does, I'll take care of it."

Daniel nods, too fatigued to form a sentence. Jiwon steers onto the street. At a stop sign, he laces Daniel's fingers into his own. With Jiwon's thumb tracing his knuckles, Daniel gradually relaxes. The next time he opens his eyes, they're already parked a few yards from his house.

The clock on the dashboard reads 12:47. Daniel's neck aches. Although Jiwon appears to be napping beside him, their hands are still intertwined. When Daniel rolls his stiff shoulders, Jiwon jumps to attention—not sleeping after all.

"I didn't want to wake you," he says gently.

Every muscle in Daniel's body still begs for rest. "I should probably go to bed."

"Please tell me you didn't climb down that tree when you snuck out."

"I used the back door."

Jiwon squeezes his hand. "Good night then."

They stare at each other. Daniel doesn't want to be the first to let go. So he tips forward, and their lips meet softly. When they separate, Jiwon is smiling.

"Don't fall into the pool on your way in."

"I'll do my best." Daniel cranks the car handle and finally releases their hands. Despite the roller coaster of the night, a part of him wishes it would never end, but he closes the car door behind him and watches from the gate as Jiwon drives away.

❖

A series of short vibrations coaxes Daniel out of dreamless unconsciousness. He pats his bedside table but comes up empty. Sitting up, he finds his phone underneath the comforter. The screen refuses to light. It buzzed itself to death.

Abruptly, he realizes he's naked except for his underwear. Last night's clothes lie strewn on the floor. The door stands ajar. Had he slept with it wide open?

As though answering the silent question, Nana appears in the hallway. She walks in uninvited and takes a saucer and glass off his dresser.

"I see you're finally up," she says before sitting on the rumpled bed.

"What time is it?"

"Half past noon." She presents him the water, and he gulps down the three pills. His parched throat soaks up half the glass. "I told your parents you weren't feeling well, that you'd taken your sleep medicine and wouldn't make it to breakfast."

Roused by the water, his stomach lets out a vicious growl. "I'm starving," he admits.

Nana nods. "Lunch is almost ready." She scans the room, probably not for the first time that day, taking in the crumpled clothes and tossed-aside sneakers. "Where were you last night?" she asks.

"Here," he lies. "Where else would I be?"

"Daniel—"

A gray cloudy light illuminates the murky room, highlighting the wrinkles that web through Nana's forehead. A deep-rooted distress spiders across her features. This expression harkens back to another day, nearly a year ago.

After Sung-Min slapped him and the excuses poured from Daniel, his parents angrily dismissed him from the parlor. In the foyer, he stumbled across Nana, arranging blue flowers in a vase. She peered straight into Daniel's bloodshot eyes, her brow furrowed. Of course, she had overheard everything. Daniel pushed past her, retreating to the third floor. Minutes later, Nana entered his room. She pressed an ice pack to his swollen left cheek. He longed for her to hold him, to whisper fake promises that his parents would come around. Instead, she straightened her composure in the same way she straightened her apron. Sung-Min and Monica didn't pay her to talk.

"Were you with Jiwon?" she asks.

"It's like you said. I couldn't sleep. I took my medicine."

With a deep sigh, she collects the dishes. "Come down and eat. Remember, you have an appointment with Dr. Greene in a few hours."

Once she leaves, he plugs in his phone and chucks his clothes in the laundry hamper. A hot shower loosens his throbbing limbs. After throwing on a pair of sweatpants, shirt, and sports jacket, he lumbers to the dining table. To his relief, a single placemat sits on the mahogany.

Nana sets a simple sandwich and fruit in front of him. "Your parents are running errands," she explains, and Daniel couldn't care less. He eats with the Lost Boys.

As Daniel settles into the embroidered armchair, Dr. Greene retrieves his trusty card stack.

"No thanks," he says.

"Would you like to play something else?" the psychiatrist offers as he slides the deck back into his pocket.

"Not really." He doesn't feel like games, or talking for that matter. After last night, he plans to opt for silence. He's done enough talking for a whole month. Dr. Greene can ask his questions. Daniel prepares an onslaught of one-word answers.

"Is there something on your mind?"

"No."

"Have you had another cross-country meet?"

"Yes."

"How did that turn out?"

"Good."

Dr. Greene fiddles with his glasses. The crocodile stomps about the office, circling their chairs. The muted sun glints off the frames that harbor the psychiatrist's diplomas and accolades. For someone so invested in friendship, his desk shows little evidence of a life outside his practice. Maybe he's married to his work, like his parents.

"Do you have any kids?" Daniel wonders aloud, breaking his own rule.

"I have three actually. Two girls and a boy."

Daniel has only ever imagined the man alone. "What are they like?"

"My son and eldest daughter are in college. My little girl is in the fourth grade."

"Are you proud of them?" Daniel doesn't know why he asks. The question just tumbles out.

Dr. Greene crosses his ankles. "I am," he says. "I'd like to have your family come for a visit here someday."

"Good luck. Maybe you can come by for dinner some time."

The sarcasm bounces off the psychiatrist like rubber. "What's dinner like at your house?"

"Nothing really happens."

Daniel glances out the window to the overcast field, the distant hedge of trees. Only ten minutes into the session and he's ready to go. Shackled, he conjures up the Neverland forest. Who can he adventure with today?

"Are your parents proud of you?" Dr. Greene inquires, shredding Daniel's faint image of Neverland.

"Why don't you ask them?"

"I'm asking you."

Daniel takes out his phone. "Here. I'll give you their number. You can call them right now if they're not too busy."

"I don't want to contact your parents," he replies evenly.

"Then call Nana. I'm sure she can give you a good assessment of my parents' feelings toward me."

"I won't be calling Ms. Naff."

"Why not? You called her last week."

Dr. Greene takes a deep breath. "That was for you."

"And I'm sure you gave her and my parents an in-depth report on the whole panic attack." A well of anger spills over his words. Unsure of the spite's source, Daniel can do little to plug it.

"I would never do that, Daniel."

"Sure you would."

Dr. Greene shakes his head. "Our conversations are confidential. Unless you seek to hurt yourself or others, everything you tell me is private. There are a few matters, such as your medications and diagnoses that I share with your family, because you are a minor and under their care."

"What if I told you I was cheating on all my exams?"

"I wouldn't tell your parents," he replies easily. "Are you cheating on all your exams?"

"No." Daniel pauses, considering. "What if I told you I went to a party last night and got drunk?"

Dr. Greene smiles. "I wouldn't tell your parents."

"I didn't get drunk by the way."

"But you went to a party?"

Daniel rolls his eyes. "Maybe," he says, because he doesn't want to talk about the party. "What if I told you that I'm quitting cross-country. Would you tell my parents that?"

"No, Daniel."

"Would you tell them if I were having sex?"

"No."

"Would you tell them if I had a boyfriend?" As soon as he says it, he tries to cram the question back into his mouth, but the words hang in the air, unchained.

Dr. Greene blinks. "I wouldn't tell them," he says slowly. Daniel fidgets nervously, out of hypotheticals. "Do you have a boyfriend, Daniel?"

"What if I did?" he tests carefully. "Would you spend the next thirty minutes telling me why it's a terrible choice to date another guy?" A part of him—small and lonely—wants to tell Dr. Greene the truth. His brain is overflowing with secrets, pinning him down each morning when he has to wake again just to spend another day staying silent.

Dr. Greene folds his hands. "Not at all. I would probably ask his name, how you met him, what you like about him, how long you've been—"

"It's Jiwon." Daniel's fingers are shaking, but when he finally speaks the unthinkable into existence, the world doesn't crash down around him. The bookshelf holds strong. The chairs stay steady. The wind taps gently at the window.

"You can't tell anyone," Daniel says.

"I won't." Dr. Greene smiles again, a real smile that reaches his eyes. "I'm glad you confided in me."

"Why?"

"Because I'd like to get to know you, Daniel."

"There's a lot you don't know about me."

"So, tell me."

Daniel sifts through pictures of Monica and Sung-Min and Brooklyn, each of them fighting for territory in his mind, warring and warring, drowning him in the bloodshed. The carnage suffocates him every day, until only a flicker of his soul escapes, flying off the roof to another world.

"It's hard to put it into words."

"I'd like it if you tried."

Daniel draws his knees into his chest. He opens his mouth, and his soul almost slips out, feeling for the bookcase or the window, but he grips his sleeves. He counts the ticking crocodile.

When he speaks, he can't re-create the security that he felt when he shared his past with Jiwon. He sticks to the facts, dropping them like nails on concrete.

"I had a girlfriend. She wanted to fix me, to make me like her, and I went along with it. When it didn't work, she broke up with me.

I told my parents that I liked guys, and now they'll never be proud of me. We'll never be like you and your family. And I…"

His voice falters, but then he remembers that Dr. Greene already knows the rest of the story—the really pitiful part where the stupid kid couldn't even jump off a roof right.

"Daniel?"

"And I just want to play cards now," he says after a moment. "Please."

"Of course." He retrieves the deck and drags the accent table between them. As he deals out a game of gin rummy, he adds, "You've shared a lot today, and I'm thankful that you trusted me and told me more about your life."

Daniel nods, unwilling or unable to say more.

"It's good to take a break," Dr. Greene continues, fanning out his cards. "Let's play."

CHAPTER TWENTY-FIVE

Daniel stares at the group of people around him, all eating lunch with carefree smiles. Owen chats away with Jackie. Jayden arm wrestles Kevin, while Ki-Jeong pokes him teasingly in the side. Jiwon flits between each of them, laughing and sharing pretzels. Everyone seems either oblivious or dedicated to avoiding hard feelings or rivalries or bad blood. They walk a tightrope, pretending to teeter only two feet instead of two hundred above the ground.

Despite winning the arm wrestling, Jayden throws his hands in exasperation. "I don't want to be thinking about Chemistry. We've gotta go up against Cambry this weekend!"

Ki-Jeong pats him on the shoulder. "At least you all have a fighting chance. Cambry completely destroyed us last year. We were so close to qualifying for district finals, too."

"I doubt we'll make it this year," Jackie pouts. "We got torn to pieces at the girls' meet on Saturday."

No one brings up Jackie and Ki-Jeong's big talk about overtaking the boys this season. Owen slides a comforting arm around his girlfriend's shoulders.

"It's my senior year, too," she continues.

Daniel, Jayden, and Ki-Jeong—the only juniors in the crew—nod solemnly. "It's not fair," Jayden adds. "Cambry's teams have four coaches to share between themselves. They even have summer training retreats."

"What were those like?" Kevin asks Daniel. Even though he addresses him with a calm demeanor, Daniel can still hear the word *freak* in between the lines. "That's your old school, right?"

Ki-Jeong and Jackie gasp playfully, stunned to learn that their comrade once ran for their rival. Jiwon laughs at their dramatics.

"They were pretty intense," Daniel recalls. The summer retreats were pure torture by day, but after dinner, they would sleep only a few hours and then stay up late, talking in low tones about anything except the day's drills. No one dared drink alcohol, knowing they'd pay for it the following morning, but on those nights, alcohol wasn't needed. James opened up about wanting to leave California and study filmmaking at an East Coast school. Francisco shared that he hid his insecurity by playing the class clown. Even Karter confessed that he felt like he was hitting a plateau in his running times.

"The term retreat was used pretty loosely," Daniel continues vaguely. "Mostly, we holed up in the mountains and ran inclines until we felt sick."

"I guess that's how they win every year," says Owen. "So that means you've made it to state championships before. You probably weren't even their fastest runner, huh?"

"I held up in the top two when I ran the 5K, but in the 10K, I was their third fastest."

Jayden sighs. "It's gonna be like racing against ten Jiwons."

"Is that a compliment?" Jiwon asks, and everyone laughs, except Owen.

The bell rings. Jayden tells Daniel to head to the locker room without him, then bolts to grab his gym bag from his locker. Overhearing, Jiwon accompanies Daniel to PE, even though his next class is on the opposite side of campus.

"I told you Kevin wouldn't give us any trouble," he says once they're alone. "He came up to me after second period and apologized for being a jerk. Blamed it on too much alcohol. He even asked if you got home okay."

"That's all good, but he's obviously putting two-and-two together about us."

"Kevin isn't questioning you. It's all me. He's been teasing me about dance and my lack of girlfriends for years. We just have to play it cool." He pulls Daniel to the side of the locker room entrance. "Anyway, all of Jayden's griping about tests got me thinking. Maybe we should work on our group project after school."

Jiwon and Daniel don't share a single class. "What group project?"

"The one that requires you to come to my house after practice." A mischievous grin curls Jiwon's mouth. "Your parents can't say no to that, right?"

The alibi lights a wick in Daniel's heart. "I'll call Nana before practice."

"Exactly." The warning bell sounds. "I'll see you later."

Daniel's day just got a bit more worthwhile.

Once classes finish, Daniel wastes no time dialing Nana. He has only a few minutes before practice begins, so he hopes the conversation will be brief.

Her greeting scratches at his ear, the timbre a little lower through the phone. He sucks in a breath, ready to lie.

"Nana, I've got to get some group work done after practice today. No need to pick me up."

An uncomfortable pause precedes her response. "Where should I come get you when you're done?"

"That's okay. He'll drop me off."

"Who?"

Daniel weighs his options. While he could dig himself deeper into dishonesty, he worries that a complex lie will be harder to maintain. At least Nana already knows Jiwon, so she can vouch for him when she informs Sung-Min and Monica.

"Just Jiwon," he says.

"How long will you be out?"

"I'll be home after dinner."

Nana tsks. "Perhaps you should ask your parents' permission."

That is not part of Daniel's plan. "I would, but they're busy, aren't they?"

"Your father is on the phone," Nana admits. "But your mother is out on errands. You can always call her."

"I don't want to bother her if she's in the middle of something." Nerves jangling, he switches tactics. "I really need to get a good grade on this project, Nana. I can't flunk out of cross-country."

"I'll talk to your parents about you missing dinner," she surrenders. "But let's not do this at the last minute again."

"Thank you."

Daniel darts into the locker room to dress down. Most of the team, including Jiwon, are already waiting for Coach Rasmussen in the gym. He slips on his running gear and hurries to Jiwon's side.

Once Kevin starts chatting with another teammate, Daniel whispers to Jiwon, "We're in the clear."

Jiwon smiles. "I'm a genius."

"You're the best." He can't help but touch Jiwon's elbow. No one would suspect them from something so trivial anyway.

A whistle tears through the team's chatter. Coach Rasmussen calls them to start their walk to the park, reminding them sternly of their upcoming contest against Cambry. Competitiveness saturates his tone, foretelling a ruthless hour. Sure enough, after a quick warm-up and three four-hundred-meter dashes, he sends them on a forty-five-minute, nonstop distance run. A breathless cooldown concludes the arduous exercise. Everyone groans on their way to the parking lot.

Jiwon and Daniel drag their feet to the nearby neighborhood. "If this is what the rest of the week will be like," Jiwon complains, "then I'm driving to school from now on."

Daniel tries to laugh, but his ribs are too sore. He can't wait to shed his backpack and sit down, but then he wonders where he'll be sitting in Jiwon's house. What will the inside look like? What will he find on Jiwon's walls?

They trudge past Jiwon's car in the driveway, curving toward a Dutch Colonial much like Owen's. A wraparound porch leads to a red door.

"My dad will be home in an hour or so," Jiwon says as he turns his key and lets them inside.

"What's his job?"

"He's a doctor. Pediatrics."

Daniel forgets to reply because he's finally in Jiwon's house. Warmth flows from every crevice. Brown leather furniture and rustic iron sculptures surround a gray brick fireplace. Although well-decorated, the living room speaks of actual living. Where spotless upholstery and sparkling floors define his parents' home, Jiwon's sofa bears a few cracks. Pillows lie askew. Jackets, cups, and medical magazines clutter the tabletops.

Jiwon heads toward the kitchen, snagging crumpled take-out bags as he goes. "Our housekeeper comes on Wednesdays," he explains sheepishly. "Do you want something to eat? I'm famished."

He opens the refrigerator and takes out a carton of orange juice. Regular orange juice. No pulp. No organic label. There's even a cheesy smiling orange on the front. He fills two stemless glasses, then raids the freezer for microwaveable pot stickers. Entranced, Daniel watches as Jiwon grabs a plastic plate from a stack of mismatched dishware, dumps the entire package on top, and pops it in the microwave for six minutes. There are coffee rings on the counter. A few bowls fill the sink.

"I love your house," Daniel says after draining his juice.

Jiwon lifts an eyebrow. "Sarcasm?"

"No," he says, leaning his tired lower back against the counter. "I want to live in a place like this."

"Sorry to break it to you, but your house was probably featured in last year's top fifty mansions of Orange County. Well, maybe it didn't make the cut since you don't have a private golf course."

"Sometimes it feels too big and empty."

Jiwon shakes his head, chuckling. "Well, at least you don't mind slumming it." He rests his palm on the edge of the counter beside Daniel, closing the proximity between them. "You're always welcome."

The microwave beeps. Jiwon retrieves the steaming plate, unleashing the irresistible smell of cheap pork and cabbage. "Hot!" he shouts and grabs a tea towel. "Let's go to my room."

Anticipation licks at Daniel's heels. They climb a staircase and pass an array of family photos. Daniel wants to pause and admire pictures of baby Jiwon, but Jiwon has already disappeared into his room. He catches a glimpse of a portrait of two people. A woman poses with her hands on a preteen edition of Jiwon, minus the bleached hair but still the same cheeky expression. The woman's eyes and mouth match his features.

Before Daniel can get a closer look, Jiwon calls out, "It's a little messy in here, too."

While the disarray could be worse, T-shirts, shoes, textbooks, and electronics litter Jiwon's floor. Wadded paper balls spill from an overflowing waste basket underneath a desk with no workspace available on its crammed surface. A rumpled dark blue comforter—the same hue as the walls—dangles off the side of the bed. Posters of Los Angeles graffiti and a handwritten account of his personal records hang on frames or on tacks. Ribbons, medals, and awards sit on full display in a glass case, atop which rests a game system and TV.

Jiwon gathers his dirty clothes and tosses them in a wicker basket in the closet. Daniel peeks at his wardrobe. Between sports gear and jeans, a variety of shirts and hoodies drape in reds, yellow, and a multitude of light blues.

Daniel pulls out the sky-blue hoodie from the day he kissed the thimble on Jiwon's finger. "I guess you never outgrew your Wendy playdays."

"If I'm being honest, I went shopping a couple of weeks ago and bought a few too many shirts in that color. You like light blue, don't you?"

Daniel smiles. "So, you bought the color I like?"

Pink dusts Jiwon's nose and cheeks. "I wanted to get your attention."

Daniel rehangs the hoodie and turns to Jiwon. "You got it."

"I noticed."

Jiwon busies himself on the floor, unzipping his backpack. Daniel takes a seat beside him, but Jiwon artfully avoids eye contact, fussing with binders and pencils. Finally, Daniel reaches for his chin and tilts Jiwon's face toward his own. The minutes fly by, unchecked, as they lose the time in each other. When they finally part, lying adjacent on a dark blue rug, they take turns closing their eyes and gazing into each other. For a moment, Daniel feels the pull to leave his body, but he breathes deeply. He doesn't want to go anywhere, not without Jiwon.

"When did you figure out you liked me?" Jiwon asks quietly.

Daniel thinks back over the parties and moments spent on the couch watching *Peter Pan*. "Probably when we went for that night run."

Jiwon nods. "When I saw you that first day in the library, I thought, oh no, who is this hot new kid?" He chuckles nervously. "But when we took those pictures after we dressed up, you did this thing where you—I don't know—it's like you were smelling my hair. I couldn't stop replaying it over and over in my mind. I would look at that photo of us way too often."

Daniel's skin flushes. He feels busted, caught doing something he tried to keep hidden. "Maybe I already liked you back then. It's hard to tell."

Jiwon rolls onto his back. "You have to get a car," he says. "So you can visit me when I go to college. I'm only applying to California schools."

Daniel's throat catches, throbbing with the realization that Jiwon is leaving at the end of the school year, but also pulsing fast because Jiwon imagines them together for that long.

"I don't actually have a license," he confesses.

"No way! I'll teach you then. Over winter break."

Daniel groans. "I'm supposed to go to Korea for Christmas."

"Lucky," says Jiwon, and Daniel doesn't protest. "Thanksgiving break then. All of my family is in LA, so I'll be around."

Jiwon hops up suddenly and grabs the plate of pot stickers off the piles of junk on his desk. "I'm starved. I could eat all these and more."

Daniel snags a quick bite before Jiwon can Hoover the whole snack.

"I actually have some homework I need to get done," Jiwon adds with a full mouth. "We should get started on that *group project.*" They haul out their books and get to studying. The plate empties, and Daniel nearly finishes an outline for a persuasive essay when the snarl of the garage door hums through the room.

"Dad's home," Jiwon mumbles absent-mindedly as he pencils out a calculus formula. He snaps his textbook shut and heads toward the hall. Daniel tentatively follows. His only conception of fathers are people who ask to be left alone, except for at the dinner table. He tries to envision Jiwon's dad but comes up with empty air.

Back in the living room, they find a man in a button-down shirt, holding a leather briefcase in one hand, a plastic bag in another. He's about the same height as Daniel's father, but his hair thins at the temples. Kind brown eyes embrace them in a way that somehow reminds Daniel of Nana.

"Hey, Dad," Jiwon says casually. "This is my friend Daniel Kim, the one on—"

"On the cross-country team," the man replies with a tired smile.

"Nice to meet you, Mr. Yoon."

He shifts the plastic bag to his hand holding the briefcase, and they shake. "Jiwon's told me about Cranbrook's new fast rabbit."

Jiwon rolls his eyes. "I didn't say it like that."

"I have take-out if you kids are hungry," he continues, ignoring Jiwon's wisecrack. "Jiwon, how about you set the table while I wash up."

Just like that, Daniel winds up in the dining room, eating sweet-and-sour chicken and eggs rolls. Jiwon's father makes light-hearted conversation about sick toddlers and district finals. He laughs with Jiwon over a comedy film they watched together on Sunday. Soon, Daniel feels full from more than the meal.

After dinner, Daniel and Jiwon rinse the dishes in the sink.

"Your dad seems nice," Daniel says.

"He's not so bad."

Mr. Yoon strolls into the kitchen and takes three bowls from a cabinet. "You guys want dessert? There's some ice cream left in the freezer."

They spoon Neapolitan into their mouths on the living room couch. The ice cream melts on Daniel's tongue, somehow sweeter than any of the cobblers or chocolate ganache that Nana whips up on special occasions.

Mr. Yoon asks Daniel about his transfer from Cambry to Cranbrook, his classes, his transition to a new cross-country team. He answers honestly, amazed that someone else's father would take so much interest in the mundane aspects of his life.

"Well, you seem like a fine addition to the team," he says with another grin. The man smiles just like Jiwon, with genuine sincerity.

"Thank you," Daniel replies. He takes small bites of the tiny lump of half-melted ice cream in his bowl. The clock on the wall reads five past seven. Once the dessert ends, he'll have to return home, but sitting on the warm leather sofa beside Jiwon and across from his father, he wishes the second hand would slow down for once. If only the crocodile would stop chasing after him, maybe he could stay forever.

CHAPTER TWENTY-SIX

When Saturday breaks over the horizon, Daniel immediately feels that something is very wrong. The day begins like any other cross-country weekend. He takes his meds, showers, and dons Cranbrook's royal blue uniform. The forecast predicts low clouds, which means no blinding sunlight, but the wind blasts at a fierce fifteen miles per hour. Still, that's nothing he hasn't overcome before. A different villain rears its hooves into his gut.

Cambry Preparatory High School will take position at the starting line today.

At least Brooklyn and James have graduated. Still, when Daniel glimpses himself in the mirror, he sees crimson and black. He remembers the sophomore who started the season with a 10K PR of 15:47 but ended a whole minute slower. He began the year with the nickname trump card, only to hear the searing sting of Karter calling him a letdown in front of the whole team on a bus ride home. Even his old coach, the same man who declared him their most-promising runner, took him aside to scold him about his disappointing performance. All the while, Daniel just prayed that no one would whisper the word gay behind his back.

His hands tremble. Premeet jitters are atypical for him. He needs to control his breathing, but all movement burns too fast or pins him down. Glass walls separate him from the mirror, the banister, the kitchen. He approaches Nana from behind the barrier.

"You have everything you need?" she inquires before handing him a peanut butter and honey sandwich.

Without being asked, he reaches into the medicine cabinet and pockets a Lorazepam. Nana nods slowly but appraises him with slight concern.

"Are you all right?"

Daniel's head splits, nerves frayed and spraying electricity. "Just thinking about the meet," he mumbles. Nana doesn't know who he's up against. She doesn't need to know.

At the dining table, Daniel chews and swallows. The honey gunks his teeth, but he mechanically forces down the sandwich. Sawdust coats his stomach, the mandatory calories sticking to his intestines. He won't throw up, not now. He has to keep everything down. He has to bury the anxiety for the team's sake.

Nana decides to drive in silence. The houses and landscape speed past the window, branches shuddering in the gale. Daniel counts the passing cars, hitting twenty-three before the parking lot comes into view.

"Good luck today," Nana calls as he steps out.

"Thanks." He'll need all the luck she can wish him.

Daniel joins the other early risers. Jayden greets him with a handshake, but chitchat is at an all-time low, even with the added presence of the girls' team. Everyone feels the pressure in their own way. Five minutes later, Jiwon and the rest of the team arrive and load the bus.

Once they're settled in, the girls' coach addresses the two teams. "Listen up! Obviously, we're all focused on Cambry, but remember, there are two other schools that we're up against. All of you have practiced hard for this. We can make district finals if we keep our heads on our own skills."

"I'm proud of each of you," Coach Rasmussen adds. "Now, let's do our best. Also, let's show Cambry what we're made of."

Applause rings out, diffusing some of the tension. Even with Jiwon beside him, Daniel can't relax. His foot taps an unsteady beat. His spine stiffens no matter how many times he cracks his neck.

"We're gonna do well," Jiwon says, sensing Daniel's stress. "I've done all the math. We'd have to come dead last to lose our spot in district finals. That'll never happen, even if Cambry kills us in every race."

His attempts at comfort barely pierce through Daniel's walls. He wants to grasp Jiwon's hand, but the risk is too great. He prays that, somehow, Jiwon can shatter the glass box encasing him, pull him out, and stop the racing thoughts, but Jiwon is fighting his own jitters. No one can unravel the rope around his neck.

By the time they arrive on location, Daniel has sucked down the majority of his water bottle. They're running at a park that neighbors Cambry's grounds. Acres of familiar grassland spread flatly before them. Neither trees nor hills will protect them from the howling wind.

All the schools have arrived, except the home team. Since the park houses gazebos, they've only brought water jugs and snacks. Before they can head to their assigned spot, Cambry's bus enters the lot. Even though Daniel tries to keep his head down, his eyes disobey, glued to the bus's door. Crimson-clad runners leap down the steps, carefree and light on their feet. Daniel recognizes a few faces but no names. At least until the upperclassmen emerge. Khalil tumbles forth, lugging a water jug with Cameron. Francisco follows, a jubilant smile softening his hard features. Finally, Karter skips down. He's grown taller and stronger, but the same serious expression darkens his fair hair and blue eyes.

Jiwon tugs at Daniel's arm. "Let's go," he urges. As they walk to their gazebo, he adds, "Do you know any of them?"

"A bit."

"Is—?" Jiwon pauses, but Daniel can hear the unspoken question. Is Brooklyn's brother here?

"He already graduated. Both of them, last May. They were really close in age."

"That's a relief."

Daniel doesn't mention that they could have told the entire school body about him after he left. By the time Daniel's shoes hit the paved floor of the gazebo, he's gone. The team scurries around him, suddenly animated now that they've arrived onsite. Laughter swirls like underwater echoes, but he's on the outside looking in, and he doesn't want to come back.

The 3K will start soon. He can't hide under the blanket of escape. Dazed, he pours himself a cup of water, drains it, fills another. He sits against a pillar, shielding most of his body from Cambry's line of sight. Jiwon is chatting with the coach. Owen, Kevin, and Jackie share jokes. Jayden and Ki-Jeong invite Daniel to stake out the course, but he shakes his heavy head.

"I've been here a lot," he says. "I used to practice here every day."

They leave him alone. For countless minutes, he calls to Neverland, but the Lost Boys don't answer him. Tinker Bell never comes. For a moment, he hears the rustle of stealthy pirates, but then nothing. Just oppressive silence.

A hand stirs him roughly. "Get yourself to the starting line," Ki-Jeong scolds, long since returned from her walk with Jayden.

Daniel hadn't heard the call for the racers. He hurries over and pins a number to his shirt. Jiwon stares straight ahead, no doubt planning his strategy. Daniel should do the same, but his brittle thoughts snap before he can sweep them into a decent pattern. From the corners of his eyes, he spots Karter, Francisco, and Khalil. They probably see him, too.

The starting pistol cracks before he can align his body into a running posture. His legs tumble forward, rigid and resistant. He hasn't warmed up. He's skipped every necessary step.

Orange flags define the course. Even as he throws himself toward each marker, he can't gain traction. A strong headwind strips his skin, shoving him down with each disciplinary gust. Against the odds, his practiced limbs maintain a mediocre sixth place.

Then, a shrieking pain rips through his abdomen. At first, Daniel fears that his appendix is bursting, but wisdom overrides agony to meet a horrifying conclusion: a water cramp. An amateur mistake. His go-to mindfulness technique will be his downfall.

Two runners take advantage of his failing speed and pass him. The numbers on their backs mock him with each excruciating meter. When he finally crosses the finish line, Daniel can hardly believe the place card in his hand. Eighth. Owen and Jiwon are cooling down near the gazebo. He finished last on his team, surely behind each racer from Cambry.

Shame floods his veins. If he could, he would run to the bus and hide from every critical stare, but with no real options, he trudges into a slow jog. Jiwon joins him, casting a wary look his way.

"What happened?"

"I just..." His throat constricts. "I don't know if I can do this."

Before Jiwon can speak, Coach Rasmussen interrupts their jog. "Get over here, Kim," he growls and leads them to a secluded spot behind the rest of the team. Everyone pretends to look the other way. "What the hell was that?" he shouts. "I've never seen such a poor performance from you, and in a 3K!"

Daniel shrinks beneath his anger, but the coach continues, "Are you out of your mind? Do you have an injury?" When Daniel fails to respond, he raises his voice louder. "Say something, Kim!"

"I drank too much water," he mumbles to his feet.

"Are you kidding me?"

"No, sir."

Coach Rasmussen crosses his arms as if to contain his fury. "Of all the sorry excuses. That had better be it, Kim. If I see you get more than a single cup before the 10K, you'll be walking home. Finish your cool down."

When Coach Rasmussen storms off, Daniel resumes his jog alone, then returns to the gazebo with humiliation at his heels. Kevin shoots him a scathing glare. Legs shaking, Daniel folds into a defeated slump on the concrete. A pair of light blue spikes pause in front of him.

"How'd you do?" Daniel asks Jiwon's shoes.

Jiwon takes a seat. "Third, behind two of Cambry's guys. Owen placed sixth."

"Not too bad."

"Daniel, what happened out there?"

He shrugs. "Water cramp."

"Is that all?" Jiwon asks quietly, worry lacing each word. "What did you mean by what you said earlier, that you couldn't do this?"

Daniel dares a glance at Cambry's gazebo. Karter and Francisco are talking head-to-head. To his horror, Francisco points in his direction.

"They're making fun of me, aren't they?" he says.

"Forget about them. They're just a bunch of show-offs with bad sportsmanship."

"I want to," Daniel whispers. "I want to forget everything about them."

"You can do this. You're an amazing runner. Just pretend like they're not even here. Just run like it's only Cranbrook out there. Make-believe it."

Daniel watches Jiwon through the glass wall. He's faked his way through the school year so far, but he doesn't know how to erase Cambry from his world. He can only retreat to another dimension, constellations away.

"C'mon, Daniel." Jiwon traces circles into Daniel's shoulder, and even though he worries he shouldn't, Daniel accepts the touch. His brain zeroes in on the pressure from Jiwon's fingertips, grasping to his only lifeline in the turmoil.

"Hey there, Kim," calls a voice from the past. Daniel and Jiwon turn to Karter. The rest of Cranbrook's team size him up as well but keep their distance.

"Long time, no see," he says. "I wondered where you ran off to when you didn't show up on the first day of school. Some people said you transferred to public school."

"I'm at Cranbrook now."

Karter nods at the obvious. "I wasn't sure if you'd still be competing. After you quit during track season, I mean. That caused quite the commotion, since it was such a big deal to have such a high-performing runner on the varsity team during his sophomore year."

Daniel deflates beneath Karter's composure and looming stature. Karter is clearly enjoying the pretense of small talk, now that his times are finally superior.

"If you were in the 3K, does that mean we'll be up against each other in the 10K? I hope you do better. Maybe you were just conserving your energy back there."

Jiwon leaps to his feet, still several inches shorter than Karter. "Look, why don't you just go back to your team if you don't have anything important to say."

"I was just catching up," Karter replies with a smirk. "See you on the course, Kim."

As he lopes away, he passes Daniel's open side. With the wind and the ruckus of the 5K runners' return, Daniel barely hears Karter muttering a final parting word: "Faggot."

Panic seizes Daniel's chest. His breath stops, cold seeping through the cracks of his eyes and ears. Another round of applause erupts, but the cheers might as well be miles away.

"What an asshole," Jiwon hisses.

"Did you hear it?"

"Hear what?"

"When he called me a faggot."

Jiwon sucks in a breath. "He didn't say that. I didn't hear it."

An uncontrollable tremor possesses Daniel's hands. "I think he did."

"Are you sure?"

"I'm not sure, but I think—I don't know."

"He didn't say it," Jiwon insists with unexpected vehemence.

Daniel's vision feathers. The panic overwhelms his chest. He grasps desperately at his inhales and exhales trying to stop time, to earn enough seconds to freeze the attack before it boils over.

Jiwon notices the shift in Daniel's demeanor. "I'm gonna get you some water."

"I can't."

"You can have a little."

Daniel tries to beg him to stay, but his voice dies before it reaches his tongue. At this point, he knows he should take the Lorazepam, but then he'll be too exhausted to run the 10K. He reaches into his jacket pocket and hopes to find something to reground him. All he comes up with is his phone. He turns on a stopwatch app and counts the seconds. In the back of his mind, an imaginary metronome ticks. The pirates stir in the forest, then pounce.

"Find that crocodile!" Hook cries out before aiming his sharpened blade at Daniel's neck. Daniel strains against the pirate, quickly losing strength. There are no happy thoughts to lift him into the sky.

Jiwon reappears, pressing a plastic cup in his hand. Daniel obediently takes a sip. The fuzz begins to clear. By the time he finishes the water, he can feel the ground beneath him once more.

Right then, the 10K runners are called to the starting line. Jiwon helps Daniel stand.

"Should you tell Coach that you can't run?" he asks.

Cambry's runners are already double-checking the pins on their numbers. "No," Daniel states. "I'll do it."

Jiwon nods. "We got this. It's just Cranbrook out there, remember? No one else."

Daniel takes position, as far from Karter as possible. After a few stretches, he pulls himself into flawless form. He tries to heed Jiwon's advice, to treat the race as just another practice, but in truth, he wants to throttle Karter, to leave him coughing in his wake.

But his resentment can't beat out the fear. The gun sounds. He lunges forward. With each pounding footfall, he hears it again and again. *Faggot.* His form slips beneath the weight of the slur. His lungs hurt. His legs burn. The wind screeches like scraping metal. Blindly, he runs, trying to fly but never lifting off. A rope straps his wings to his shoulder blades. Daniel runs on feet alone.

The roaring crowd welcomes him to the finish line. Another place card falls into his hand, but he doesn't need to see the number to know the outcome. Karter, Khalil, and Francisco exchange high fives with their team. Jiwon cools down to the chants of Cranbrook's racers.

The card glares an unsatisfying 7, but it might as well read Failure. Loser. *Faggot.*

CHAPTER TWENTY-SEVEN

S hould we skip the party?"
Daniel busies himself by feigning sleep for most of the
bus ride back to Cranbrook. With his eyes closed, he doesn't have
to look at the judgment written into his teammates' faces. After the
meet, Coach Rasmussen's disappointment manifested as silence.
He high-fived each team member as they boarded the bus, proud to
have pulled in at second place even if they lost to Cambry. But when
Daniel approached the coach, he received a limp slap on the hand
with no smile or spoken affirmation. After all, perhaps they could
have made first if he hadn't choked.

Jiwon nudges Daniel, not buying his sleeping facade. "I don't
feel like hanging out with a bunch of drunk idiots tonight."

For the first time in a year, Daniel longs for a drink. The
promise of uninhibited forgetfulness lures him, but he can't imagine
downing shots with a team that abhors his pathetic performance. He
cracks open his eyelids, peeking at Jiwon—the only safe face in a
sea of disparagement.

"Let's ditch the party," he agrees, "but I could use a drink."

Jiwon squeezes his knee. "I'll bring something. We'll go
somewhere, just the two of us."

He nods, not ready to leave the security of fake slumber. Jiwon
leaves him be. They'll talk later, free of Kevin and Owen and anyone
else who eagerly waits for an opportunity to stab Daniel with an
accusatory critique.

The bus parks outside of Cranbrook's campus gates. Daniel waits till the other members depart before making his exit. He has never longed for the four doors of a car so much. Jiwon gives his shoulder one last reassuring pat, then heads to his Acura. He'll go home and recount his decent times to a complimentary father. Daniel dreads his own impending dinnertime conversation.

Coach Rasmussen grunts his farewell as Daniel lumbers off the bus and slides into the car. Nana is all sweet smiles and warm welcomes. Daniel hides behind a mask of fatigue. He can't talk, won't confess his shortcomings. In self-inflicted muteness, he bleeds defeat onto the leather passenger seat.

But he can't avoid the nightly dinner interrogation. Plates of squid fried rice nauseate him. Monica and Sung-Min babble about an ongoing advertising campaign for a Japanese company.

"They'll have to choose between the three templates we've drawn up," says Sung-Min before turning his attention to Daniel. "How about that meet, Daniel. How'd you do?"

"Cranbrook ranked second," he deflects, then spoons a fried sea creature into his mouth.

"Second isn't first. How about your personal times? It's a shame you run for a team that ranks lower than Cambry."

Daniel frowns. "I could've done better."

"What does that mean?"

"It means I placed eighth in the 3K and seventh in the 10K," he admits, knowing that if caught in a lie, the repercussions would be twice as explosive.

Sung-Min takes a long draft of his bourbon. "That's less than exemplary. We don't need a repeat of last year."

"I'm sorry," Daniel says to his plate.

"Sorry doesn't win."

Monica clears her throat. "You must have had some steep competition. Who were you racing against?"

"Cambry," he says as neutrally as possible.

Sung-Min clenches his jaw. "You could have done better."

"I know."

"If you know it, then do it."

Monica touches her husband's arm. "We know you care so much about cross-country. I'm sure you'll try harder next time." Daniel drops his spoon with a harsh clank. "May I be excused?" The dead squid writhe in his stomach.

"No, you may not," Sung-Min retorts. Even so, the discussion is clearly over. His parents return to their business affairs. Daniel shovels another spoonful of rice, despite the unbearable queasiness. The food sloshes with his evening medicine.

Sung-Min and Monica take agonizingly slow bites, but eventually finish their plates. When Nana collects the dishes, Sung-Min notes Daniel's half-eaten meal.

"Is Nana's cooking not good enough for you?"

Daniel turns to his nanny. "It was delicious, Nana. I ate a few too many snacks at today's meet."

She smiles sympathetically and quickly withdraws into the kitchen. She has long since learned not to interfere with family matters. Daniel envies her the privilege of hiding behind her work. He has nowhere to retreat until his parents grant their permission.

When Sung-Min and Monica finally leave the table for the parlor, Daniel flees up the stairs. With each step, his stomach roils. Instead of heading to the bedroom, he collapses before the toilet. Chunks of undigested rice and seafood burn his esophagus. His eyes sting with each retch. Rancid toilet water splashes onto his cheeks. Once his stomach empties, he flushes and falls into the wall. He wonders if he's hurled his medication, too, but doesn't feel like taking any more.

After brushing the taste of bile from his teeth, he crawls into bed. For hours, he tosses and turns. Sleep would be too sweet of a release, so naturally his brain refuses to quiet. Karter, Coach Rasmussen, his parents—each demon claws at him mercilessly.

Eventually, Nana locks herself in her quarters. By now, Monica and Sung-Min will be savoring a nightcap in their separate bedrooms. Daniel texts Jiwon. He is almost free.

Fifteen minutes later, he receives a response.

I'm here

I'm coming down

A single text from Jiwon untangles the knots in his gut, replaced by eager anticipation. Daniel throws a windbreaker over his T-shirt and gray sweats. He glides to the first floor and out the back door and gate.

Jiwon's car sits patiently down the street. The screen light of his phone haloes his face. A light blue sweater protects his shoulders from the night chill. When Daniel taps the window, Jiwon startles, then smiles. He exits the car, wine bottle in hand.

"My dad hates Zinfandel," he says. "He won't even notice it's gone."

"Where should we go?"

"It's your neighborhood," he laughs.

Daniel shoves his chilly hands in his pockets. "Well, you have a car."

Jiwon wags the bottle. "If we're drinking this, I'm not driving."

The nearest park is a three-mile walk and is more suited for toddlers than teenagers. "There's a house under construction a few blocks away."

"Are you suggesting we break in?"

"Maybe there's a back porch."

"Sounds good." Jiwon locks his car, then thinks better of it. He reaches inside and grabs a wine bottle opener, which he stuffs in Daniel's jacket pocket.

Despite the thick sweater, Jiwon shivers on the walk to the abandoned house. Daniel places an arm over his shoulders, earning him a smile in return. Once they arrive at the taped-off adobe mansion, they easily jump the wrought-iron gate. Sure enough, they find a half-constructed sandstone patio in the backyard. An empty pool yawns toward a moonless sky.

Daniel passes Jiwon the corkscrew, and they take turns sipping the bittersweet liquid. Daniel's chest burns with each gulp.

"Take it slow," Jiwon teases. "I don't think I could carry you all the way home."

Before long, their bodies take on the wine's artificial heat. For the first time that day, Daniel feels light. Jiwon plays soft music from his phone, and Daniel hops to uncertain feet, swaying to the rhythm.

Jiwon laughs. "What's that supposed to be?"

"You can't recognize dancing?"

Jiwon joins him, locking an arm around his waist. Daniel hugs Jiwon closer, nestling his nose in his blue sweater. He breathes in the ocean, and he knows that Jiwon is the one person who can chase his past away. If he has Jiwon, maybe he can keep on waking each morning—to real life, not to Neverland.

"Are you feeling any better?" Jiwon asks.

"A little," he says into his sweater.

"You really scared me at the meet. I didn't know what to do."

"I'm sorry. I let everyone down."

Jiwon pulls back slightly. "You didn't let me down, and the others have no idea what you were up against. We got second. Everything's fine."

"It doesn't feel fine."

"What do you mean?"

Daniel sighs and heads back to the wine bottle. "I mean, I need another drink."

"Watch out or you'll end up sick like last time."

Daniel doesn't think there's anything left in his stomach to throw up. He takes a long swig. Jiwon does the same, then sets the wine as far from Daniel as he can reach. Daniel fakes a grab for the bottle, only for Jiwon to playfully push him away. Daniel's vision swims, but he doesn't mind. He's in his body for once, feeling every emotion, even if the intensity is blunted by the alcohol.

Lying on his back, he relishes the warmth of the wine, like a blanket against the cold sandstone. "I really wanted to beat him," he says.

Jiwon reclines onto his side. "That guy who came up to you after the 3K?"

"Yeah, Karter. I wanted to take him down, but I wasn't fast enough. I made a complete fool of myself."

"Daniel, you almost had a panic attack and still took seventh in a 10K. No one on the team could manage that."

"But I still let them all take me down."

Jiwon rests his head on his shoulder. "Well, Karter beat me in both races, too."

"And that pisses me off even more."

Jiwon laughs. "Don't go getting angry at Karter for my sake."

"And he called me a faggot." He finally says it—the real piece of the story that chews his insides like termites on wood. "That means everyone at Cambry knows that I'm gay."

Jiwon sighs. "You don't go there anymore."

"I hate them." Daniel blinks into the starry sky, looking for a road map that can lead him far from his body—the skin and bones of a freak, someone to be laughed at. "And I hate myself for being the insect under their shoes."

Daniel doesn't realize he's crying until Jiwon wipes the tears away with the hem of his sleeve. Water leaks from his eyes, but the tears might as well pour from a stranger. As he watches Jiwon console him, a stream of sadness spills through him, but not for himself. There is Jiwon, doing his best to comfort someone who can't even feel his own tears.

The well dries.

"I hate them, too," Jiwon says before getting to his feet and helping Daniel up. "That's why we'll practice twice as hard this week and crush them at district finals."

"Do you think we can?"

"We will. Now we know what we're up against. They know you're gay. So what? They've got nothing else to hurt you with. All that's left is the race."

Daniel nods slowly. He's not sure, but he'll try.

"It's getting late," Jiwon says. "Let's head back before someone hears us and calls the cops."

A part of Daniel aches for another sip of alcohol, but his dizzied balance warns him against it. Leaving the bottle behind, they head to the gate and stumble over with considerably less grace than on the way in. Jiwon links their arms as they flounder down the street.

"I'm so glad we didn't go to that party," Jiwon singsongs. "Jayden will be bummed we missed his first time playing host, though."

"He's probably wasted."

"And dancing awfully with Ki-Jeong."

"While someone films it."

Jiwon cackles drunkenly. "Yeah, this is so much better."

They near Daniel's house. "What? Listening to me vent?"

"No." Jiwon spins to face him. "Getting to spend time with you."

Daniel almost kisses him but then remembers where they are. "You can't drive home," he says instead. "You've had way too much to drink."

"I'll just walk."

"Drunk and alone?"

"Last I checked, we don't live in a high crime area."

Daniel takes Jiwon's wrist. "You can come inside for a little bit."

"No offense, but your parents kind of terrify me."

Daniel laughs. "They're fast asleep on the second floor. They won't hear us."

"Isn't Nana's room right next to yours?"

"Her room is like a whole house. She won't hear us if we're quiet."

Jiwon cocks his head, considering the offer. "Just for a bit," he gives in.

After speeding across the yard, they tiptoe through the back door. As Daniel slips off his trainers, one skitters across the marble floor, landing inches away from a glass floor vase. Jiwon bites his own hand to keep back a fit of nervous laughter, which almost makes Daniel burst out as well. Recollecting themselves, they slink up the staircase, sneakers in hand. The bedroom lamp remains off, the only light cast from the distant streetlamps through the window. Daniel shuts the door with painstaking care, then turns toward his accomplice with a triumphant grin.

"This has to be the craziest thing I've ever done," Jiwon whispers, an excited smile brightening his eyes.

Daniel leads him to the bed, heart racing in a way that feels nothing like panic. "It'll be easier when you go to college. I can just come see you in the dorms."

Jiwon winds their fingers together. "You'll come visit me?"

"Of course."

Out of words, they stare at each other, and Daniel wonders what's next. "Come here," Jiwon murmurs, and Daniel wastes no time capturing Jiwon's lips with his own.

They trade kisses in the dark. Jiwon's hands brush lightly against Daniel's arms, revealing his hesitancy. Emboldened by the night's drinking, Daniel pulls him closer. Encouraged, Jiwon wraps his arms around his neck. Daniel lowers him onto the comforter, legs overlapping.

Everything flows differently than the time at Kevin's party. Daniel wants to keep going, to touch and be touched. He gazes down at Jiwon, drawn to him like flame to paper, and presses a kiss into his neck. As Jiwon's breath grows heavy, Daniel kisses him harder. He glides a hand up Jiwon's sweater, much like Jiwon tried in Kevin's room. Only this time, Daniel is in control.

Drawing back slightly, Daniel lifts the hem of Jiwon's sweater. Without question, he raises his arms, letting Daniel toss it aside.

"You too," Jiwon murmurs.

As soon as Daniel removes his jacket and tee, Jiwon slides his hands along his spine. Their kiss deepens, and when Jiwon's fingers dig into his shoulder blades, Daniel's hips press hard against Jiwon.

But then, Jiwon pushes Daniel back with a careful gentleness. "We should stop."

"Is it too much?" Daniel asks, a little confused.

"No, I just—I don't want to make you uncomfortable."

Of course, Jiwon is afraid he'll have another panic attack. "I'll be all right," Daniel says, "if it's just you."

"Just me?" After a moment, he asks, "Should I keep my hands to myself?"

"I can just touch you."

Once Jiwon nods, Daniel eases him into the bed and leans in for another kiss. His fingers fumble with Jiwon's jeans. As he unfastens the button, Jiwon's breath picks up again. He buries his face in Daniel's neck, trying to keep as quiet as possible. Daniel's pulse quickens, and Jiwon raises his hips into Daniel as they finish.

They hold each other tightly for several minutes until their breathing slows. Daniel isn't scared or numb. He hasn't run away to another world. He feels Jiwon against him, and he wants to stay. The day wears heavily upon them. Daniel can already feel sleep tugging at each muscle, but when Jiwon shifts off the bed, Daniel sits up. Jiwon slips on his boxers and sweater.

Daniel catches his hand. "Don't go yet."

"I don't want to go," Jiwon whispers, sitting on the edge of the mattress. "But your parents...And my dad..."

He leans back into the bed, laying his head against Daniel's chest. "I'll stay until you fall asleep," he decides.

They curl into each other, and Daniel pulls Jiwon close enough to feel his heartbeat. His breath slows. His vision blurs at the edges, but he tries to fight the drowsiness. He doesn't want to wake to an empty bed.

Chapter Twenty-eight

In between a dream and waking, Daniel perceives the click of his door opening. He squeezes his eyelids shut, not willing to watch Jiwon leave. He tells his brain to turn back off.

But then, a sharp slam knocks him to full attention. The first thing he realizes is the sun streaming hotly through the window. He's warm. Too warm. Because he's not alone. Nestled beneath the comforter, Jiwon twitches in his sleep.

Which means someone else opened the door.

Daniel sits up, revealing his bare chest. Jiwon's jeans still lie crumpled on the floor.

"It's time for Jiwon to go home," Nana says sternly. "Now."

At the mention of his name, Jiwon stirs. Unaware of Nana's presence, he places an incriminating hand on Daniel's thigh.

"Jiwon, get up," Daniel breathes, still caught in Nana's harsh glare. "It's morning."

Jiwon languidly stretches. "I fell asleep."

"Jiwon—" Daniel warns him.

This time, Jiwon hears the alarm in Daniel's tone. He looks to the door and visibly freezes.

When Nana speaks again, she avoids Jiwon's terrified eyes. "Your parents are in the living room, waiting for breakfast. I suggest Jiwon finds a different way out than the back door. Like the tree you used a few weeks ago."

She places his daily medicine and water roughly on the dresser. The water sloshes, splattering on the floor. With subdued anger, she exits the room.

The gravity of Nana's parting words crashes through Daniel's skull. How often has she observed him sneaking out, only to keep the knowledge a secret? Now, she's discovered his relationship with Jiwon, too. Yet, she orchestrated an escape. For how much longer can Daniel bet on her silence? In her own taciturn way, she insists on protecting him. Daniel can't help but wonder if she would have swept his suicide attempt under the rug had the outcome been less destructive.

Is sheltering secrets for the sake of peace the same as love?

"I've messed up everything," says Jiwon, still under the blanket.

For now, Daniel needs to focus on the most pressing issue. Jiwon has to make his getaway unnoticed, or else worse consequences will fall on the both of them.

"It'll all work out," Daniel says, shocked to be the voice of reason for once. "You can climb down the tree, like she said. No one will know."

"She's going to tell your parents."

"I don't think she will."

Jiwon pulls himself from the bed, throwing on his jeans with trembling hands. "That doesn't make any sense."

Absentmindedly, Daniel tongues his pills, gulping them down with the water. For good measure, he drains the entire glass. He needs to stay solid.

The expression on Jiwon's features reads perplexed and almost disturbed. For a moment, Daniel tries to see what he sees. An intrusive housekeeper with unknown motives. A father and mother who slap their child when he attempts to come out. A freakish boy compulsively downing medication in the middle of a crisis. Jiwon doesn't fit into this equation. With inevitable anxiety, Daniel realizes that he could lose Jiwon—his only refuge—to the very instability in his life that he's been desperately trying to escape.

"I'm so sorry that I fell asleep," Jiwon says.

"Don't be. I wanted you to stay. It's my fault, too." Daniel opens the window. "It's an easy climb. Just watch out for weak branches." Jiwon finishes lacing his sneakers, then hauls himself onto the roof. He turns back, reaching for Daniel's hand. "Text me or call me. Just tell me how things turn out."

"I will."

Even though they need to part, Jiwon clings to Daniel's hand. "You gotta get out of this place," he says. "This house isn't—it's not right here."

If he could, Daniel would crawl out the window after Jiwon. He would run out the gate and never look back, but he has nowhere else to go.

"This is all I have."

Jiwon squeezes Daniel's hand tightly, his lips parting with what seems like unspoken words. Finally, he lets go, casting a longing look over his shoulder before disappearing into the sweetgum leaves. Daniel lingers by the window. He should dress and go down for breakfast, but the mid-morning sun warms his skin. He would spread his wings and fly, if not for the shackles around his ankles. With his eyes closed, he can almost taste the cloudless sky. But there's no pixie dust that can lift him into the air.

So, he shuts the window and secures the lock.

Sunday chugs along with painful normalcy. With no other means to quiet his racing thoughts, Daniel retreats into a Peter Pan rendition. From the couch, he glimpses his parents conversing on the back patio near the pool. Sung-Min's cigarette smoke floats above their heads. Yesterday's clouds are a figment of the past. The autumn sun roars with California's perpetual summer.

As Peter Pan and company battle the pirates at Skull Rock, Daniel wonders how he'll spend his appointment with Dr. Greene. Having finally confessed his connection with Jiwon last Sunday, they'd spent Tuesday's session mostly chatting about Jiwon. It seemed unreal that another person would listen to the details of his new relationship. Compared to his parents' hostility and Nana's restraint, Dr. Greene has somehow managed to become a trusted confidante. For once, Daniel looks forward to the armchair in the immutable office.

A few minutes before the movie credits roll, Nana approaches the sofa. She towers over him—her once-comforting height suddenly intimidating.

"We'll head to your appointment in ten minutes. Be sure you're ready." While she says nothing wrong, every syllable sounds threatening.

"I'm ready," Daniel replies to her retreating back.

As Daniel ejects the movie disc, Sung-Min and Monica reenter the living room. Monica passes Nana an empty sparkling water bottle. "Throw this out for me," she says. Without a glance in Daniel's direction, his parents disappear into the parlor.

Daniel snaps the disc into its case. A cloud shadows the sun. The clink of glass resonates from the kitchen.

Then, his name echoes down the hall. "Come sit with me and your mother," Sung-Min calls.

Daniel feigns deaf ears, but his father won't let up. "Daniel, now!"

On his way to the parlor, Daniel dares a peek into the kitchen. Nana meets his eyes. Her brow furrows. She seems just as confused, which could mean good or bad news depending on whatever happens once he seals the parlor door.

The spacious room is furnished to elicit a serene atmosphere. Even so, the white walls and muted greens do little to calm Daniel's twisted nerves. An elaborate case spans an entire wall. Inside, various business placards and celadon pottery accompany Daniel's sports awards. The gleaming medals and trophies wink menacingly beneath the spotlight chandelier.

Sung-Min and Monica rest in separate accent chairs, so Daniel takes the whole sofa for himself. It doesn't take long for the cross-examination to begin.

"Who is Jiwon?" Sung-Min asks with too much composure.

Daniel's stomach drops to the floor. "I've mentioned him before," he stammers. "He's on the cross-country team."

"The fast one?"

Daniel nods. Nana must have given the game up. He sits on his hands to hide the tremors.

"I have to go see Dr. Greene," he mentions desperately.

"This is more important than therapy," Sung-Min retorts.

"Weren't you at Jiwon's house on Monday to work on an assignment," Monica questions coolly.

"Yes."

Monica narrows her eyes. "Is there anything else you'd like to tell us about him?"

"Nothing is coming to mind."

After an excruciating pause, Sung-Min clears his throat. "Is Jiwon gay?"

"I'm not sure," Daniel says, begging his voice to stop quaking.

Monica pulls a folded sheet of paper from her blazer pocket. "I found this tucked in a bottle under the cushion of my patio chair." She waves the weathered letter between herself and Daniel. "Would you like to see it?"

Daniel accepts the paper. In the intensity of that night at the pool, Daniel forgot all about the bottle he'd hidden from Jiwon. He had foolishly left it behind.

When neither of his parents speak, he realizes they expect him to read the note that Jiwon wrote for his mother alone. Daniel unfolds the paper with shaky fingers. Jiwon's handwriting fills the lines from top to bottom.

Hi Mom,

It's strange writing to someone who has no address. Wherever you are, I hope it's someplace better than underground, a place like heaven or Neverland. I hope you're not in pain anymore. I miss you, especially in the mornings when Dad's already left for work. That used to be our time, just you and me. Now, it's only me.

Can you see me, Mom? Do you already know why I'm writing to you? I never told you when you were alive, because I was too scared. The truth is, I'm gay. I wish I had told you on one of our

*mornings and given you a real chance at understanding me. Please
don't be sad for me. It's not all that bad, being gay. I even kissed a
boy for the first time today.*

*I wonder if you ever suspected that I'm gay, if you somehow
knew it the whole time but just never said anything about it. For
some reason, I really hope that you figured it out. Maybe you were
always waiting for me to tell you. Better late than never, I guess. But
I have to ask, do you still love me?*

I still love you,

Jiwon

Daniel doesn't move. He reads and rereads. More than ever, he
wishes Jiwon were beside him now. But not in the parlor. Somewhere
far away, galaxies away.

Monica takes the letter out of his hands.

"It's just a story," Daniel mumbles, but the excuse sounds
unconvincing, even to him.

Sung-Min frowns. "I'm disturbed that I even have to ask you
this, but are you involved with him?"

Without raising a fist, his father's words strike him against the
cheek. "No, no way. I didn't know he was gay. He didn't even let
me see the letter."

"His mother passed away?" Monica says quietly, peering at the
paper once more with an indiscernible expression.

"Earlier this year."

Sung-Min drums his fingers on his chair's armrest. "It sounds
like he has a lot he's working through. As do you. From now on, you
won't be going anywhere near him."

A knife plunges straight through Daniel's sternum. "But we
run cross-country together!" he protests, grasping at his only weak
advantage. He can't lose Jiwon—the brightest glimmer of good
amid all the uncertainty.

"Running doesn't require talking or studying together. Or even
looking at each other. I'll be making sure that you two never see
each other again."

"He's my only friend," Daniel admits feebly, but he knows he
lost this argument before he stepped into the parlor.

"That's the problem, Daniel."

Daniel turns desperately to Monica, but she averts her gaze. One letter, he thinks. One letter has stolen everything from him.

"You're dismissed. I suggest you go to your room."

His legs carry him out, but he can't feel the footsteps that lead him into the empty parlor. His heart bursts, shooting shards of glass through every limb. Worms of white burrow through his vision. Senselessly, he stumbles into the kitchen and tears open the medicine cabinet. His convulsing fingers trip over the Lorazepam bottle. Before he can twist off the lid, he hears the parlor door reopen. Panicked, he shoves both the Lorazepam and Triazolam into his pockets. He'll sleep. He'll black it all out.

Even though Sung-Min and Monica can see him dash up the stairs, neither tries to stop him.

In his room, he pops open the bottles. He doesn't need any water to force down one of each, but nothing improves. The pain slices through him with rabid ferocity. With nowhere to run, he swallows two more tablets. Still, no change.

Curling into a ball on his bed, Daniel tries to scream, but he can't breathe. He needs Jiwon. Jiwon would bring him water. Jiwon would pull him close. Jiwon always knows what to say to fend off the storm.

The only awareness he has is his ragged gasps for air. Until even that fades to darkness.

CHAPTER TWENTY-NINE

Holed up in the bathroom, Daniel dares a peek at his text messages from Jiwon. He spent the previous night in a tangled mess of unconsciousness and fatigue. Jiwon never received his promised update.

Sure enough, several messages fill the screen.

How did it go?

Did Nana tell them?

Daniel, what's happened?

Please, just tell me if you're okay?

Unsure of where to begin, Daniel sets the phone on the sink top. He washes his tired face. Monday means school and classes and cross-country practice. It means sticking to the status quo. Counting clocks and sipping water. Amber will offer him gum. Teachers will assign homework. Coach Rasmussen will push them onward to district finals. In the kitchen, Nana is no doubt preparing a balanced breakfast and lunch, but where will Daniel sit, come lunch period? He doesn't want to sit alone at his locker anymore.

When he takes up his phone again, he decides to start small. He can't imagine pouring out his parents' threats via text message.

I'm still alive

Before he can lock his screen, Jiwon responds.

Jiwon: *I have to see you. Can you come to school early?*

Daniel: *I can try*

Jiwon: *It's important*

Daniel wonders if Jiwon realizes just how important their conversation will be. Will he be angry that Daniel forgot the bottle? He doesn't know if he can withstand Jiwon being upset with him, too.

I miss you

As soon as he sends the message, a venomous paranoia sinks its teeth into his veins. His phone is password-protected, but that doesn't feel like enough. Abruptly, he deletes all of their messages. Then, he opens Jiwon's contact information. He tries to come up with a safer name. On a whim, he types, "Wendy."

Bearing the new name, Jiwon responds.

Jiwon: *I miss you, too. We're going to be okay*

Jiwon: *Meet me in one of the library quiet rooms. No one will bother us there*

Daniel: *I'll see you soon*

After deleting the new messages, Daniel tries to carry on with his regular routine. He slips on a T-shirt, flannel, and jeans, then packs his backpack and gym bag. Downstairs, he stomachs Nana's smoothie and toast at a solitary table. Sung-Min and Monica either already ate or are effectively ignoring him.

Daniel wishes he could drive himself to school, but he helplessly slides into the passenger seat beside Nana. The keys sway in the ignition, rocked by the speeding vehicle's momentum.

"I didn't tell your parents," Nana says.

"I know."

A red light halts the car. "Where are your pill bottles?" she asks. "For your Lorazepam and Triazolam."

Daniel sighs. Why talk about the big things when they can focus on minor details like missing medications. "They're in my room, in case I need them at night."

The car lurches forward. Cranbrook peers over the school gates ahead. Nana stalls alongside the horde of students shutting car doors and waving good-byes.

"I'm not sure if—" she starts, but Daniel already has one foot on the pavement.

"I have to hand in an assignment to a teacher," he lies. "See you later."

He turns his back on her concern and rushes into the crowded halls. A few minutes later, he ducks into the library.

"Good morning, Daniel," says Mr. Bartel. In front of his glowing smile, he nurses a hot cup of coffee. The mug reads, *There's a book for that.*

"I'm just here to see Jiwon," he replies. "I have a homework question for him."

Mr. Bartel blows on the steam. "And apparently he has the binder he borrowed from you. He's in one of the cubicles."

Daniel makes a mental note to work on their alibis and attempts a casual stride to the quiet room before shutting the glass door tightly behind him.

Jiwon looks tired. Dark circles mar his eyes, and a few strands of hair stick out from an unbrushed mop. Gently, Daniel fixes the inside-out hood of his white jacket.

"Nana ratted us out," Jiwon states hoarsely.

Daniel takes the chair across from him. "No, she actually didn't."

"But your parents found out about us. Did they see me sneak out?"

"No."

Jiwon presses his lips together. "Then, what happened? Daniel…" He trails off for a moment, as if revisiting a memory. "Your parents called my dad last night."

Every thought in Daniel's mind withers. He reaches for Jiwon's hand, but Jiwon shuffles away.

"Mr. Bartel can see us," he warns him, gazing past Daniel's shoulder toward the circulation desk.

When he meets Daniel's eyes once more, he continues. "At first, I figured it was my uncle calling, because my dad was speaking Korean, but then the tone was too formal, so I thought it was a random patient with a sick kid. Then, I heard him say your last name. I tried to tell myself that there are so many Kims. It wasn't until he started talking about me that I accepted the worst."

"I can't believe my parents would go that far," Daniel says, but in fact, he can picture it clearly. Sung-Min and Monica knew Jiwon's name, his connection to cross-country and to Cranbrook. It wouldn't take too much effort to dredge up a phone number.

"The next thing I knew, my dad was sitting me at the table, asking all these questions. Daniel, your parents outed me."

The earth shifts beneath Daniel's feet. So, that was what Sung-Min meant by ensuring a complete severance from Jiwon.

"They found your letter to your mom," he explains. "I stupidly left it on the back patio."

In spite of the seriousness of their situation, Jiwon smiles teasingly. "And here I thought it made it to Neverland." He runs a hand through his disheveled hair. "That makes a lot of sense. My dad kept bringing up my mom. I thought he was trying to blame my sexuality on her death, so I told him how I'd been keeping it a secret for a while. He actually listened to me. I expected him to get mad or demand I get a girlfriend or something, but he just said, *I won't lose you like I lost your mother.*"

An uninvited pang of jealousy whips through Daniel. "He doesn't care that you're gay?"

"He definitely cares. He stammered every time he said the word gay, but I'm not grounded or anything. I doubt he'll start asking about my love life at dinnertime." Jiwon exhales. "That's the weird thing though. He barely mentioned you."

"I told my parents we weren't together."

Jiwon nods slowly. "So, they know I'm gay, but they still think you're straight?"

Daniel can't help but feel like he's betrayed Jiwon somehow. "I didn't want to make things worse. They told me to stay away from you."

"My dad said the same thing."

"Are we breaking up then?" Daniel chokes out, bringing to life his greatest fear. The bell rings, but neither moves.

Jiwon watches him closely. "Is that what you want?"

Every fiber in his body begs for Jiwon to stay with him. "No, that's not what I want."

"Me neither."

Relief doesn't come close to the wave of emotions that both quiets and quickens Daniel's pulse. Even if he teeters on the edge of the steepest cliff, he'll hang on if Jiwon endures alongside him.

"What are we going to do?" Daniel asks, but then, Mr. Bartel slides open the glass door.

"I'm sorry, boys," he says, "but I have to ask you to go to class now."

Jiwon shoulders his book bag. "Thanks for lending me your notes, Daniel."

"Anytime. Thanks for the homework help."

On their way out, Jiwon whispers, "We do what we've always done. We pretend to be what they want us to be and do what we want whenever they're not looking."

CHAPTER THIRTY

Make-believe is one of Daniel's better talents. Whether withdrawing into Neverland or scripting conversations, he is well-practiced in daily charades. He make-believes his way through classes, taking notes and counting clocks. He make-believes through lunchtime, eating half his lunch outside his locker until he can brave the team for a few minutes. He playacts laughter and no hard feelings, as Jiwon smiles through it all, as though the weekend never happened. He make-believes in practice that if he runs at full strength for long enough then he can actually fly into district finals with enough speed to chase down his ghosts.

He retreats into fantasy at the dinner table, feasting among the Lost Boys instead of dining with an affected family. The sleep medicine lulls him into a mirage of peace found in complete stillness.

Then, he wakes to another day of playacting. He pretends that he doesn't mind the extra-long breakfast spent with his parents, robbing him of a few minutes with Jiwon before the school bell rings. He texts a counterfeit Wendy and make-believes that those few exchanges are enough before he deletes each message.

He rehearses his steps to math class and make-believes his way through a tedious lecture. During independent work time, Amber asks to borrow a pencil, so he puts on the show of helpful classmate and hands her an extra from his case. Then, as he gears up to playact through his assignment, Amber reaches out and touches his disembodied hand. The look on her face tells him the game is over.

"Are you okay?" she says, yanking him out of Neverland. "I've sat next to you for half a semester, and I think I've learned the difference between normal, antisocial Daniel and zonked-out, zombie Daniel."

Daniel blinks, hoping she'll turn around and get to work.

"For real though," she persists. "Are you stoned? Your eyes are glazed over."

Daniel doesn't point out that every time she's seen him, he's been hopped up on numerous medications. "I'm fine," he says.

She huffs, flaring her pink cheeks. "Here I thought we were friends. Tell me what's wrong."

Despite Dr. Greene's fairy-tale explanation, experience has taught Daniel that friendship is about walls and fake smiles. Otherwise, friends laugh at each other behind their backs, or sometimes to each other's faces.

"I've got some stuff going on at home," he replies. Perhaps the morsel of truth will satisfy her.

"Divorce?" she questions, and for a moment, Daniel wonders about her home situation, but he won't ask, and he certainly won't confess that Monica and Sung-Min prefer separate bedrooms to dividing their business investments.

"I'll tell you once I get an A on a test," he deflects.

"Was that a joke? Because if you're attempting humor, then you really must be losing your mind."

To his surprise, she doesn't pry into his home life anymore. Instead, she offers him gum, which he accepts. Maybe now they'll return to their individual assignments.

But Amber isn't interested in math. "Is cross-country going okay?"

Daniel is shocked that she has managed to hit so close to the heart of the matter. "I didn't do so well at the last meet, but I'm pretty sure we'll still qualify for this weekend's district finals. We'll hear from Coach today."

"If you guys get it, I'll come cheer you on."

He imagines Amber jumping like a rabbit on the sidelines and smiles. Maybe Dr. Greene is right. Friends try to help you feel better even when they can never understand.

❖

Coach Rasmussen gathers the team in the gym. "As I'm sure most of you already tallied on your own, we received notice this morning that we are indeed going to district finals this weekend."

Applause breaks out with more than a few whoops. Coach Rasmussen waits for the celebration to die down before continuing. "Each of you has worked hard up to this moment. I want to remind you that district finals aren't the be-all and end-all. If we remain dedicated, we can be one of the three teams selected for regionals. I believe we can qualify. The question is, do you have the discipline to grow in these next four days?"

He cracks his knuckles. "I'm going to push you, but I also need you to be cautious. The moment you feel a twinge in a knee or ankle, ice it. No injuries. Any questions before we start practice?"

Jayden raises a tentative hand. "Where are district finals being held this year?"

Coach considers his response carefully. "I don't want any of you running outside of practice, especially not on-site. If you head over there, you may wind up disqualified. District finals will be held at Huxley Nature Reserve, about thirty minutes east."

"There are a lot of hills over there," Owen chimes in.

"Exactly. So today, we'll be running incline fartleks."

Everyone restrains their groans. A few members already start stretching their calves. With no further questions, they head to the park. Once they warm up and begin the exercise, Daniel throws himself into each hill. His legs burst forward, urging him up each slope at full speed before recovering with a slower descent. He repeats each fartlek, focusing on his breathing and posture. He can't make-believe a win against Cambry. He has to earn it.

None of the runners complain about the strenuous practice. Each chases their own goal: a new PR, a chance at state championships, a scholarship. Sweat drenches Jiwon's T-shirt. His hair sticks to the sunscreen on his forehead. Even so, his endurance transcends the rest of the team. When Jayden's breath becomes coughing, when Owen and Kevin begin to slouch, when Daniel's legs beg for rest, Jiwon keeps soaring at the same relentless pace.

Daniel won't quit either.

Once the whistle finally blows, they all nearly crumble, but each runner starts a cooldown lap around the park. Jiwon matches Daniel, and the momentary contact reminds Daniel just how much he misses being alone with him.

"We're gonna take down Cambry," Jiwon declares, determination overriding his exhaustion.

"I'll just be happy to outrun Karter."

"Well, he's their fastest runner, so you'll be taking them all out when you beat him."

Much too quickly, their cooldown ends. When Coach Rasmussen initiates a round of strengthening drills, Daniel feels the distance between himself and Jiwon. He wants more time with him, but he has no idea how to make this happen, especially since Dr. Greene expects him after practice. He hasn't seen the psychiatrist for a full week since his parents held him at home last Sunday.

"This is more important than therapy," his father had said.

Daniel glances to Jiwon as they complete a set of sit-ups. There are things that are more important than his appointments with Dr. Greene, and Daniel is sure that Jiwon matters more.

After practice, he tells Jiwon his plan. "Let's go somewhere."

"What?" he replies incredulously. "Last I checked, you're on lockdown."

Daniel smiles. "I have an appointment today. I'll skip it. We'll have a whole hour and a half to ourselves."

Jiwon shakes his head. "That's too risky, and it's not like we could go to my house. My dad will be home, and I'm not allowed near you, remember?"

"So, we'll go somewhere else. Somewhere no one will recognize us."

Jiwon bites his lips, but Daniel can tell he's warming up to the scheme. "Isn't Nana on the way?"

"I haven't texted her yet. I'll tell her that practice ended late and a teammate is giving me a ride."

"She won't fall for that."

"No, but she'll cover for us."

Jiwon sighs. "I don't know, Daniel."

With the other teammates long since gone, Daniel places a coaxing hand on Jiwon's lower back. "We said we wouldn't break up, but we never see each other."

Jiwon smiles a little sadly. "I even drove to school this morning," he says, "just in case I'd get to spend an extra minute with you."

"Then, let's make up for that now."

Jiwon fiddles with his car keys. "Are you sure Nana will cover for us?"

"She's the most conflict-avoidant person I know."

"Okay," Jiwon caves. "But just this once."

Daniel could kiss him. "I'll text her now."

As they head to Jiwon's car, Daniel thumbs his excuse to Nana. He doesn't care to see her response. With a quick button press, he shuts off his phone. They sidle into the car, and Jiwon cranks the engine.

"Where are we going?" Daniel asks.

"You said we have an hour and a half, right?" When Daniel nods, Jiwon smiles. "Let's go to the ocean. I know a quiet residential spot near Huntington Beach."

The promise of sand and waves and shells fills Daniel with excitement. He hasn't traveled the thirty minutes to the beach since his old days with his teammates at Cambry. Jiwon turns on a music playlist and takes Daniel's hand. Their familiar surroundings fade away down stretches of highway. They stall in a few spots of traffic, but it doesn't bother them at all.

Jiwon starts singing off-key and slaps Daniel's arm whenever he laughs. They purchase sodas at a truck stop, and Jiwon rests his head on Daniel's shoulder while they wait in line to pay. For once, no one knows them. They're just two boys in a state that couldn't care less if they were together.

Once they parallel park near the boardwalk, they untie their trainers and run barefoot into the sand. With the scalding heat of summer long past, the sand cools their feet. Only a few passersby linger at the shore, waiting for the sunset.

"I want to touch the water," Jiwon says, tugging Daniel along.

"It'll be cold."

"Who cares?"

The receding tide reveals countless broken shells and briny kelp. Daniel breathes in the sea spray as the foaming waves engulf their toes, sinking their feet into the wet sand. Jiwon shouts at the chill, and they both run away, laughing.

Eventually, they find a spot against the boardwalk wall that shields them from the ocean breeze. Daniel wraps an arm around Jiwon's shoulder, and Jiwon leans into his chest. The sun cracks an orange yolk along the horizon.

"We'll both graduate soon," Jiwon says, "and then it'll be like this. No hiding. Your parents can't lock you up if you move to the dorms."

Daniel's graduation feels ages away, but he lets Jiwon's daydream pull him in. Even if he has to conceal their relationship from Sung-Min and Monica, there could be a day when he no longer has to follow their restrictions. He hopes Jiwon is still around when that day finally arrives.

When Daniel nestles a cheek against his hair, they both close their eyes. "If only we could come out now," Jiwon says.

"It's not possible. My parents aren't like your dad. They'd probably throw me back in Mercy again."

Jiwon turns to face him. "Mercy? Like the hospital?"

Daniel regrets the accidental confession. "Yeah, I was there last summer."

"That's intense," Jiwon replies softly. "So that's why you skipped summer training."

Long before his stay at Mercy, Daniel had all but quit running. When his sophomore year ended, he gave up nightly sprints for adventures with the Lost Boys. At that time, the only salve for the pain he was feeling could be found in Neverland. Captain Hook was an easy adversary compared to flashbacks of his discomfort with Brooklyn and his father's reverberating slap.

But he doesn't want to remember all that now. He hugs Jiwon closer. Only a few more minutes remain before their time is up and they head back home. Quietly, they watch as the last of the sun dissolves into the waves. In the dark, Jiwon kisses Daniel deeply.

When they separate, they know without speaking that they need to leave. Hands locked, they return to the car. The ride home is less jubilant. Neither wants to drive back to reality.

"I'm glad we did this," Jiwon says.

"Me too."

They arrive at Vandever Acres right on time. Parked several blocks away, they dare one more quick kiss. When Jiwon drives off, Daniel can't help but feel that his freedom goes with him.

He unlocks the front door and steps inside. Directly into his father's fury.

"Where were you?"

Daniel nearly falls back onto the porch. He spies Nana and Monica down the foyer.

"I was at Dr. Greene's."

Sung-Min raises his open hand, but instead of slapping Daniel he spits out more poison. "I've had enough. Dr. Greene called, asking if you would be attending your appointment or if we might consider a reschedule."

Before the world can come crashing at his feet, Daniel flees from his body and into the ceiling. He can't run, but he can hide.

Monica joins Sung-Min. "You told Nana that a teammate took you to Mercy. Were you with Jiwon?"

"No, I just went for a walk," Daniel watches himself lie.

"With Jiwon," Sung-Min states.

"No!" Daniel pushes past his parents, but he doesn't get far with Nana blocking the stairs.

"You won't be seeing him again," Sung-Min adds.

"I'm not!" Daniel rifles through scenes of Neverland. The Lost Boys splashing alongside the mermaids. Early morning hunts in the forest. Sword fights with Captain Hook. Nothing sticks.

With three pairs of eyes boring into him, his disconnected mouth mumbles, "Some things are more important than therapy."

This time, Sung-Min's flat palm meets Daniel's cheek, but he barely feels the flare of pain. "We're involving your coach." He hears his father's threat, but by then, he's long gone, tucked in his hammock in Hangman's Tree.

❖

There's no make believing his way out of Coach Rasmussen's office before the next day's practice. Even with Jiwon beside him, he can't pretend away the coach's words.

"I don't know what kind of trouble you two are wreaking outside of practice, but I won't be putting up with your behavior, and I won't be getting any more phone calls from anyone's parents. You come to practice. You run. You stay away from each other. This team doesn't need any of your bad choices ruining an entire season of hard work."

So, Daniel runs alone. After practice, he sits alone. His phone buzzes uncontrollably, notifications from Wendy piling up, but he can't look. Nana's car pulls into the parking lot, wheels rolling toward the solitary boy with nowhere else to go.

CHAPTER THIRTY-ONE

Thursday comes and goes—a blur of lunch alone and avoiding Jiwon at practice. They text all day, but neither has a single idea of how to proceed.

Jiwon: *We can't just let your parents do this*

Daniel: *What choice do we have?*

Daniel: *I don't know what to do.*

Daniel: *This is my problem, and I've dragged you into it*

Jiwon: *This is our problem. We'll come up with something*

Daniel: *I don't know if I can do this*

Jiwon: *Be together?*

Daniel: *Be apart*

As he waits for Nana, Daniel watches Jiwon send the messages from his car. He's only meters away, but the distance is unconquerable. Jiwon drives off as soon as Nana arrives. The ride home is unbearable. Nana says nothing after a curt hello, and Daniel wants to roll down the windows and fly away. The fantasy lasts until they reach the driveway.

"Dinner will be ready soon," she announces as they enter the house through the garage. Sung-Min and Monica's voices drift through the halls, but Daniel blocks out the sound. He shucks his sweaty running gear and showers.

In his bedroom, he pulls out the antique box that he and Jiwon wrestled with almost a full month ago. The thimble fits easily onto his index finger. Daniel has never felt more desolate.

When his parents call him down to dinner, he pockets the thimble in his sweatpants like a security blanket. Steaming plates of shrimp fettuccine alfredo cloud his vision. He doesn't know how he's supposed to eat with a stomach as tight as a fist, but ignoring the food will only invite his parents' criticism, so he chews slowly on a mouth full of slippery noodles.

"They're still complaining about the templates," Monica laments. "Every draft lacks innovation or doesn't fit their brand. I can't understand what a massage chair company expects."

"If they want more designs, they'll have to pay the price for the labor," Sung-Min replies. "We never work for free. They're just lucky that the new Tokyo branch depends on this venture, otherwise we'd drop the contract."

Sung-Min tilts his glass toward Daniel. "If we want satisfactory results, we have to play by the rules. Isn't that right?"

Daniel has no idea what his father means. "Yes, sir," he says, hoping it's the right answer.

"So, of course, you can't leave Cranbrook mid-season."

A trickle of dread slides down with the fettuccine. "Of course not," he replies carefully, not liking where the conversation is going.

"But after a good turnout at district finals and hopefully regionals, you can reset in Korea for the winter vacation and then transfer."

Daniel sets down his fork and spoon. "Transfer?"

"After all these unexpected complications at Cranbrook, don't you think it's best?" Monica says. Her wineglass swirls in her palm. "Your father and I have been discussing your options. Reenrolling you at Cambry might be for the best. After all, their track and field record surpasses Cranbrook's."

Sung-Min nods. "And you had more success there when it comes to making higher-caliber friends."

It takes all of Daniel's self-control to stay rooted to his chair. So that would be the end—his parents' master plan for undercutting any chance at happiness. How can he tell them that everyone at Cambry already knows the one thing they've worked tirelessly to bury? They might as well sign his death certificate.

"I can't go back to Cambry." Daniel's voice cracks, but he manages to force out the words.

Sung-Min's Adam's apple bobs as he swallows his bourbon. "I don't see why not. We sent you to Cranbrook so that you might improve your grades and extracurriculars. Now that you've made gains, there's nothing keeping you there. Cambry is clearly the finer school."

Karter's taunts rattle in Daniel's ears. "I just can't. Please." He hates that he's begging, but what else can he do? If he returns to Cambry, he'll lose more than Jiwon. While Daniel can't completely grasp the consequences, he can already imagine the hazing. Forget track and field. He could never call Karter a teammate.

"Your behavior hasn't really left us with any other option."

Monica stares at her son's panic-stricken eyes. "Why should we keep you at Cranbrook?" she asks.

Backed into a corner, Daniel struggles to share the truth. He's wrestled with his parents over his sexuality for over a year. They would never understand how the experience with Brooklyn would follow him around Cambry. They would never comprehend his complete helplessness beneath the suffocating weight of Karter's and the others' accusations.

At Cambry, he's nothing more than a faggot to be trampled.

"I like Cranbrook," Daniel mumbles. "Please don't make me go back to Cambry."

Sensing his upper hand, Sung-Min appraises Daniel closely. "Then you'll need to reform your behavior. As your parents, we have your best interests in mind. It's up to you to improve."

In short, no more Jiwon.

"Finish your dinner," Sung-Min adds, capping the discussion. Then to Monica, he says, "We'll need to make a final decision on how to navigate the deal."

Leave it to his father to dole out discipline and business in the same breath. Daniel forces down each bite, chunks of shrimp curdling in his stomach juices. His phone vibrates in his pocket, but he ignores the message. Instead, he thumbs the thimble, tracing the etches in the metal.

This is it. His parents have found the means to shackle him without reprieve. There's nothing left for him, except Neverland.

When Nana clears the table, Daniel escapes to the third floor, but his room offers little comfort. The sterile walls, the bare nightstand—every piece of him is locked inside dresser drawers.

Finally, he looks at his phone.

No one can force us to break up

With his loving father and perfect running times and tight-knit group of friends, Jiwon could never comprehend the unyielding grip tightening around Daniel's neck.

Daniel: *It's over, Jiwon.*

Daniel: *All I have is Neverland.*

The reply arrives faster than a whistle's call.

Jiwon: *What are you talking about?*

Daniel: *They're sending me back to Cambry*

Daniel throws his phone onto the bed. He has to fly away somehow, but all he can do is curl up beneath the blanket. The phone buzzes and buzzes, but he can't bring himself to look. Jiwon's words, once his only lifeline, have lost all meaning. Neither of them can stop the crushing weight of his parents' despotic authority.

The only control Daniel has over his life is whether or not to end it.

He hears an echo of Dr. Greene's constant concluding question, phrased in many different ways, but always carrying the same meaning: "Are you going to kill yourself?"

Why not? All the mindfulness techniques in the world won't change his circumstances.

The realization somehow calms him. He'll wait till everyone is asleep, and he won't make the same mistake as before. He won't be falling into a pool. He'll really fly this time.

The hours tick by until night hushes the house. Nana closes her door. His parents' work calls and incessant keyboard clacks finally cease. He can wait a few minutes more. There is no hurry after dark.

He sees the Lost Boys around the campfire. "I'll be with you all forever soon," he tells Slightly and Tootles and the Twins. "No more going back and forth. I choose Neverland."

A gentle tap at his window draws him from the reverie. For a moment, Daniel thinks the sweetgum tree is scratching out its farewell, but the tree has never reached that far over the roof to meet the glass. The tapping doesn't stop, clicking at a steady rhythm. Daniel unfolds and steps to the shadowed figure in the window, like Wendy greeting Peter Pan at midnight. Only the places are reversed. Wendy is on the outside looking in.

Daniel unlatches the window, and Jiwon climbs inside.

"You can't go back to Cambry," Jiwon whispers, eyes frightened. "We can't let this happen."

Daniel sits on the bed, unsure if Jiwon has really appeared in his room or if he's fallen asleep. "It's either that or never see you again."

"How will we see each other if you transfer? We lose either way."

The rivulets of the green and brown comforter glide against Daniel's fingertips—a dotted line leading him elsewhere. "Exactly," he whispers.

Jiwon paces between the bed and the dresser before reaching out to grasp Daniel's shoulders. His hands are solid and real.

"If you wind up at Cambry…" His words trail into an unvoiced nightmare. "You have to get out of here. You have to run away."

"There's nowhere to go."

Jiwon finally settles beside him. "I am not giving in to your parents," he says, and Daniel is shocked by the terror written into his features. "I'm not breaking up with you."

Their fingers wind together. "Then we can both run away," Daniel says.

"You just said there's nowhere to go.

"There's one place. The best place."

Jiwon gazes knowingly into Daniel's eyes. "You mean Neverland, don't you?" When Daniel only stares in response, Jiwon keeps talking. "It's not real, Daniel. Neverland is just a story."

Daniel opens his nightstand drawer and retrieves his medicine bottles. "It doesn't have to hurt. If we take these, it won't hurt at all."

Jiwon faintly shakes his head as if lost in a fog. "You're not talking about Neverland anymore, are you?"

"Let's go to the roof."

"Why?"

Daniel isn't quite ready to share his plan with Jiwon, or more likely, Jiwon isn't ready yet to hear it. "No one will bother us up there," he replies cryptically.

They creep into the hallway and beneath the attic door. Daniel stretches a hand to the door string and tugs the hidden stairway to the floor with a nearly imperceptible creak. He soundlessly ascends the ladder-like passage, Jiwon tracking close behind.

A skylight illuminates the abstract shapes of long-forgotten paintings and storage boxes. Dust particles shimmer in the starlight. Daniel hauls a set of boxes beneath the skylight and clambers up top. The window yields, swinging open with a downward snap.

After Daniel hoists himself up onto the shingles, Jiwon quietly follows.

The insects of summer have long since departed. Silence and soft wind wrap around them like a sheet of gauze. A waxing moon peers down from above, while the phosphorescent pool glowers four stories below. Daniel leads them to the left side of the roof, away from the pool. They sit cross-legged near the edge.

"Nice view," Jiwon comments too casually.

Daniel sets the pill bottles between them. "They can't stop us," he says. "It's easy, like Peter Pan. You just jump off and fly."

Jiwon shivers. "You say that like you've done it before."

"I have." He points to the scar on his cheekbone.

"It sounds painful," Jiwon replies carefully. He watches Daniel, unblinking.

"It'll be all right if we take the pills."

"What are those?"

Daniel twists off the lid to the Lorazepam. "This one is for panic attacks. The other one helps me sleep. If we take these, getting to Neverland will be easy."

"Neverland isn't real, Daniel."

"We won't know unless we try."

Jiwon stares hard at the Lorazepam bottle, then opens his palm. "I'll take one if you take one."

They both swallow a single white tablet. "We'll have to take more than one," Daniel says.

"Just wait," Jiwon replies delicately. "Talk to me. Tell me about Neverland. What's it like?"

Daniel's lashes flutter shut. "Everything's beautiful. There's a lagoon the same color as the sky where mermaids swim all day and night. We'll live in the middle of a forest with all the other Lost Boys in a place called Hangman's Tree. Sometimes there are fights with the pirates, but it all gets resolved in the end. No one tells you what to do or where to go or who to love."

When Daniel pulls himself to standing, Jiwon tries to grab his hand, but Daniel stretches his arms wide like the wings he usually only feels when he runs. "Jiwon, it's perfect in Neverland. I bet your mom is there, too."

The quiet night presses into them. Jiwon rises to his feet, a little uncertain on the slight slope of the shingles. His legs quaver, but when he speaks, there is no tremble.

"I'm not ready to see her yet," he says, the words spilling like rain. "I don't think she'd be happy to see me. I want to graduate and study sports medicine, and on Saturday, I want to go up against Cambry, and I want you there, too. I want you to beat Karter, and I want you to come out to your parents. I want you to get out of here someday—not to Neverland but to real life."

Jiwon takes another step toward Daniel, his foot slipping for a moment, but he rights himself, legs no longer shaking. "If we do this, they'll blame it on us. They'll say they were right, that being gay is wrong. I don't want to die when I'm with you. When we're together, I like being alive."

Daniel lowers his arms, but his eyes remain on the waxing moon. "I'm not like you, Jiwon. I don't matter anywhere outside of Neverland."

Jiwon's fingers wind around Daniel's elbow. "Don't say that. Because of you I'm running faster than ever. I'm not missing my mom as much. I even got to come out to my dad. I'm not scared of myself anymore."

Daniel has seen Jiwon scared before. When he panicked at the meet with Cambry, Jiwon feared for him. After Nana caught them in his bedroom, Jiwon was terrified. But he had never considered that Jiwon could be afraid of himself, frightened that he existed in a world that might never accept him. Yet, Jiwon went to school every day and laughed with his friends. He spent time with his dad, hoping for acceptance.

The patio spreads out four stories beneath him. Daniel shudders. He can almost hear the sickening impact of his fall.

"Don't do this," Jiwon whispers.

Maybe it's the Lorazepam taking effect, or Jiwon's mollifying plea, but suddenly the drop petrifies Daniel. He steps backward, brushing against Jiwon's frame. Jiwon clings tightly to his arm.

"I don't want to die," Daniel says. "I just don't know how to live like this."

"Come back inside, and we'll figure it out together."

When Jiwon takes his hand, Daniel lets him lead them to the skylight. At Jiwon's insistence, he leaps into the attic first. Jiwon follows, sealing the window behind them. They jump down from the boxes, their footfalls reverberating through the wood floor. For a moment, Daniel fears that Jiwon might break things off between them now. A night like this is more than enough to ruin a relationship.

But Jiwon only pulls Daniel into a warm embrace. "Please don't do something like that ever again," he mumbles into his shoulder.

They go back down the attic stairs, where Nana stands, ghostly white in the hall. Her eyes pour over Daniel, then skip to Jiwon.

"Not both of you," she breathes.

Compared to the taste of death Daniel encountered on the rooftop, Nana's unexpected appearance barely alarms him. "We're okay. We just needed some fresh air."

In a flash, she pulls Daniel into her arms, then drags Jiwon into the hug. After several long seconds, she lets them go. Daniel hands her the pill bottles. With a deep exhale, she looks to the attic steps.

"I think it's about time I put a lock on the attic door," she says. Recomposing herself, she turns to the two of them. "It's late. Go ahead and say good night to Jiwon." Then, she returns to her quarters, leaving the door wide open.

Daniel walks Jiwon to the bedroom window.

Jiwon hesitates. "I'll see you tomorrow?" His question carries a promise of survival.

Daniel reaches into his pocket, takes out the thimble, and presses it into Jiwon's hand. "Meet me in the library before school."

"I'll be there," Jiwon says before kissing him softly.

Daniel stares after the rustling sweetgum tree and tells himself it's better to be alive.

CHAPTER THIRTY-TWO

The next morning, Daniel dashes into the library with fifteen minutes to spare before the first bell. Mr. Bartel is slouched in his usual chair behind the circulation desk, looking tired or distracted, but when he spots Daniel, he sits up a little straighter.

Daniel waves awkwardly, really wanting to rush past Mr. Bartel and straight to the quiet rooms. Jiwon waits for him behind the glass wall.

"Good morning," Mr. Bartel says. "I take it you're here to ask your friend some homework questions."

"Yeah, so I'll just head over there."

He gives Daniel a gentle smile. "You two have been coming here a lot recently."

"It's quiet here."

Mr. Bartel takes a sip of his coffee from the same *There's a book for that* mug. "I'm happy that you like it here. I can tell that you feel like this is a good place to talk. Maybe something is going on? I just want you to know that I'm always available if you need someone to talk to."

"Thanks," Daniel replies matter-of-factly. Each minute he spends chatting with the Mr. Bartel subtracts precious time from his meetup with Jiwon.

Mr. Bartel presses on. "What I'm trying to say is, there may be people who understand what you're going through. I may seem like just another adult with no grasp on what you're experiencing, but I've had my own tough times that led me to where I am today. Whatever it is that you may think you have to face alone, I probably won't be surprised. I'm pretty open-minded."

"Good to know."

After another sip of coffee, Mr. Bartel feigns interest in a book on his desk. "Besides," he adds with downcast eyes, "my husband says I'm a good listener."

The simple statement ripples through the empty library. Daniel stares blankly at the librarian, well-dressed and perfectly composed, the same man he's encountered so often throughout these past two months at Cranbrook. Suddenly, he seems completely different from the hokey librarian he always assumed him to be.

But then, maybe he heard him wrong.

Mr. Bartel peers into Daniel's eyes with another smile. "Your friend is waiting."

Daniel backs up slowly before turning. His head is swimming with too many thoughts, from last night to Jiwon to the impending school bell. He doesn't have time to wonder about Mr. Bartel, so he hurries to the quiet room. As soon as he closes the sliding door, Jiwon wraps his arms around him.

"I know this sounds paranoid," he says, "but part of me was scared you wouldn't come."

"I'm sorry. I'm here. Mr. Bartel was extra chatty."

They settle at the table. A history textbook lies open, Jiwon's unfinished homework easily forgotten now that they're together.

"He was the same with me too," Jiwon says.

"Did he mention anything weird?"

Jiwon raises an eyebrow. "No. What do you mean?"

"I don't know. He said something about having a husband. I think he said that his husband calls him a good listener."

"I've gone to Cranbrook since the ninth grade. Mr. Bartel has never mentioned having a husband."

Daniel shrugs. "I was probably just hearing things."

"Tomorrow you'll be telling me that Coach Rasmussen is dating the principal."

Daniel tries to laugh, but he's not willing to pretend like last night didn't happen. He and Jiwon aren't meeting before school to gossip about the faculty. Only a few hours ago, they were on a rooftop. Daniel had nearly attempted suicide and tried to drag Jiwon into it. He can't brush those facts aside.

"Jiwon, about last night—"

He shakes his head. "I understand why you did what you did, but that doesn't make it okay. I'm glad I stopped texting and just came over."

"Me too. Sorry doesn't cut it for what I did."

Using his backpack as a shield, Jiwon captures Daniel's hand in his own. "Never again. No more skipping therapy appointments either."

"I promise."

"You better keep that promise." Jiwon sighs. "But that doesn't solve the problem."

"You mean Cambry."

He squeezes Daniel's hand. "Yeah, you have to stay here, so we can at least see each other like this, and so Karter doesn't stick his nose into your business."

"I feel like the decision might already be made," Daniel admits, the fear resettling.

"You have to talk to your parents."

Despite his jean jacket, goose bumps break out across Daniel's arms. "I already tried. They're a brick wall. All they ever talk about is work or my shortcomings."

"I mean really talk to them, Daniel." The gleam in Jiwon's eyes is stern, too serious to ignore. "You need to come out to them and explain about Cambry, about Karter."

"I can't."

"At this point, you've got nothing to lose."

For a moment, Daniel considers whether the four-story drop from the roof would be more manageable than his parents' outrage. But as much as he tries to believe in Neverland, he knows that the only thing that waits after liftoff is a crash landing. He wants to be more like Jiwon, to pull through the darkness into dawn.

"How would I even start?" he asks. "What would I say?"

"Just tell them the truth, and don't stop telling them until they listen."

A gentle knock on the glass door interrupts them. Mr. Bartel enters, even though the school bell has yet to sound. A manila folder is tucked under his arm. Jiwon surreptitiously releases Daniel's hand. Even so, Mr. Bartel glances at the backpack that may or may not have fully concealed them.

"Hey there," he says. "I'm sure you're busy talking about your homework assignments, but I printed some resources for the both of you. I've been wanting to give this to you for a while now."

He places the manila folder on the table. Daniel and Jiwon exchange wary glances. Mr. Bartel waits expectantly, so Daniel opens the folder and Jiwon looks over his shoulder. Dozens of listed online resources fill two paper copies. The second one catches Daniel's attention: "The Trevor Project—the leading national organization providing crisis and suicide prevention resources to LGBTQ and questioning youth."

Daniel turns to Jiwon, unsure of the appropriate response to Mr. Bartel's suggestion. But he takes the lead, sucking in a shaky inhale.

"Thank you," he says, but unlike before, he means it.

"You can always come to me if you have any questions or just need a safe space to unwind. So long as it's from seven to four, the library is always open. Well, I'll leave you two to yourselves then."

When Mr. Bartel makes to open the door, Jiwon calls out, "Wait! You turned out all right? You're happy?"

"I've been happily married for five years now," he tells them. The grin on his face speaks more than his words.

Jiwon nods, and Mr. Bartel steps out. For several seconds, Daniel and Jiwon sit in silent astonishment. Then, Jiwon takes his copy of the resource list and pores over it with wide eyes.

"There's one here for Asian American teens."

The school bell rings. Even though it's time to leave, Jiwon smiles. "I knew Mr. Bartel was gay," he says. "No straight man dresses that well just to go work in a high school library."

Despite it all, Daniel laughs.

❖

Throughout classes and practice, Jiwon's advice scratches at the back of Daniel's mind. He has nothing to lose. He should tell his parents the truth. The worst that awaits him is another stinging slap to the face.

On his ride home, Daniel wishes he could ask Nana her opinion, but even though she discovered him and Jiwon last night, he can't be sure how she really feels about their relationship. He has to make the decision on his own. He won't be as lucky as Jiwon. No one is going to call Sung-Min and Monica one evening and do all the telling for him.

He runs through the possible ways to bring up the subject, but he doubts that his parents will offer a clear entryway. Short of asking him point-blank, their family has expertly managed to tiptoe around his sexuality, and Daniel knows he's played his own part in covering all the tracks.

After washing up, he puts on his camouflage green shirt—the same one he wore on the day Jiwon dressed him like Peter Pan. As Peter, he might be more courageous, or at least he can pretend to have half the audacity as the boy who never grew up.

Suppressing jitters, he makes his way down to dinner uncalled. He quietly passes by Nana in the kitchen and takes a Lorazepam from the medicine cabinet. He refuses to look at her as he pockets the tablet. If she asks him if something is wrong, he might shatter, so he hastily retreats to the dining table.

When his parents enter the dining room, they nod approvingly at his promptness. For a sick moment, he realizes that they take his punctuality as a sign of improved behavior.

Nana serves up plates of beef fried rice and salad. As she pours water, wine, and bourbon, Sung-Min turns to Daniel.

"Aren't district finals tomorrow?" He doesn't wait for a reply. "How was practice?"

Daniel places his napkin in his lap. His hands are shaking even though he hasn't quite resolved to heed Jiwon's advice. "Coach focused on recovery runs so we can perform in top form tomorrow."

"That's one way to strategize," Sung-Min replies.

Monica nurses her wine disinterestedly. "They're still asking for additional designs," she tells Sung-Min. Daniel feels transparent, and Neverland comes calling. Swilling his water, he resists the pull to his fantasyland.

Sung-Min agitatedly twirls a forkful of salad. "That's exactly why we'll be meeting them in person to sort this out face-to-face."

Daniel fills his lungs with cold air. "Mom, Dad," he starts.

Sung-Min holds up a silencing finger. "They're hiding behind email and phone calls. Just wait. They'll be all bows and pretensions when we walk into the CEO's office."

After languidly chewing his salad, Sung-Min absentmindedly addresses Daniel. "What is it you wanted to say?"

Daniel straightens his spine. A perilous wave of anxiety threatens to drown him into silence, but he imagines Peter Pan opposing Hook. Dagger drawn, he strikes.

"I won't go back to Cambry."

As Monica tips her wineglass, Sung-Min narrows his eyes. "That's yet to be determined."

Daniel grips his napkin, pulling the fibers taut. "Everyone there already knows about me. I won't go to a school where everyone makes fun of me."

"And what exactly makes you think they're making fun of you?"

Sung-Min's annoyance is barely veiled. The furrow of his bows, the twitch of his wrist—these small hints usually tear Daniel to pieces, but Daniel sees the four-story fall to pavement. Jiwon's voice plays in his heart, *never again*.

"They all know I'm gay."

The wine in Monica's glass stirs. Beside her, Sung-Min balls a fist.

"Excuse me?"

"Daniel—" his mother whispers.

"I'm gay," he strains against their appalled faces. "And everyone at Cambry knows. Their whole cross-country team knows."

"You're still hanging around Yoon's son, aren't you?" Sung-Min says.

"This all happened before Jiwon."

An enraged stillness envelops the table. The whole house holds its breath. An invisible hand covers the usual sound of running water in the kitchen. Through the set of his clenched jaw, Sung-Min reveals his ill-preparedness for Daniel's sudden disclosure. In his father's immobility, Daniel seizes his advantage.

"I've already told Dr. Greene," he says. "He was glad I told him, that I trusted him. He thinks it's a sign of recovery."

Sung-Min hides a frown behind a gulp of bourbon. Monica pulls nervously at her perfect hair. The tension finally breaks under Sung-Min's scowl.

"This discussion will have to wait. I know you think the world revolves around you, Daniel, but your mother and I have serious matters to tend to in Japan this weekend. We're not carefree high school students. In spite of what you may think, we have to prioritize."

A fire blazes in Daniel's skull, kindled from a lifetime waiting, of dismissal, of sitting forgotten on the third floor. "That's all right," he says. "I'm already used to being a low priority."

No one raises a fist or voice. Neither Sung-Min nor Monica denies the painful truth. They aren't like Jiwon's father. The only thing they hold close is their pride.

With lowered eyes, Monica attempts to reclaim the conversation. "You said that you told Dr. Greene that you think you're gay. He believes this has something to do with your actions last summer?"

Daniel nods slowly. For a moment he wonders if his parents will start taking things away again, starting with Dr. Greene. But then, Monica looks to Sung-Min, an unmistakably frightened gleam in her eyes.

"Maybe when we return from Tokyo, we can consider Dr. Greene's suggestion about family therapy?"

When Sung-Min doesn't respond, Daniel whispers, "That would be nice."

"I can't believe I have to make time for this nonsense," Sung-Min mutters before taking a bite of rice.

Monica looks at Daniel as if seeing him anew. "We'll see," she says, but then she swirls her wine and takes a long drink.

For once, his parents forgo their business chatter. Clinks of silverware fill the dining room. Daniel stares at his full plate. While he knows future battles await, he can't shake the feeling that he has claimed a small victory.

"Daniel, are you finished eating?" Monica asks, even though he hasn't tasted a single sliver of rice.

When he nods, she adds, "You may be excused."

The chair whines as he exits the table, yet no one complains. With each step toward his room, Daniel waffles between dread and hope. He slips into his bed, scanning his body for any signs of panic. His heart beats steadily, protected behind the cage of his ribs.

He's not sure how much time passes before Nana enters the room. She carries a plate of leftovers to his nightstand, then sits beside him.

"What you did there was very brave," she tells him.

He drapes his arms around his bent legs. "Nana," he says. "I'm gay."

"I know." She lifts the hair off his forehead and presses a cooling kiss against his skin. "And I love you."

The tears finally break through, flooding his cheeks, and Nana circles him in the same strong arms that rescued him from the pool. This time, Daniel can feel each tear, the heaving of his chest, the snot dripping from his nose, and the pain twisting in each sob. Still, Nana holds him close, so he cries into her shoulder. As he shudders against her, she soaks up each tear without pulling away.

CHAPTER THIRTY-THREE

By the time the cross-country team reaches Huxley Nature Center, the parking lot is teeming with several participating schools. Runners in yellows, greens, and orange lug water jugs and canopy tents off buses. Several cars clog the usually vacant parking spots. District finals draws a larger crowd of supportive family and friends.

Daniel involuntarily seeks out Cambry's scarlet bus. The red beacon sits mere yards away, empty. No doubt, the team has already set up near the starting line.

As Jiwon passes his seat, he takes note of Daniel's long stare out the window. "Cambry won't have the upper hand," he says behind Coach Rasmussen's back. "We're not competing on their stomping grounds, and no one's allowed to walk the course."

Daniel hopes that will be enough. Of course, his biggest opponent is his own anxiety. It won't matter if Karter sprains his ankle in the first race, if Daniel flails beneath another panic attack.

District requirements allow for only four to seven runners per team, so everyone pitches in with hauling the tent and refreshments to their assigned spot. A warm sun beats down their necks as they erect the poles and canopy. After a good ten minutes of teamwork, they take shelter beneath the shade. The sunscreen breaks out, and each member slathers on a second coat.

When Coach Rasmussen is summoned to the announcer's booth, he calls out, "Kim! Lee! Set up the water and snacks."

Daniel and Kevin meet in the corner of the tent. Without a word, they assemble a plastic table. The water jug is too heavy for one person, so they both grasp a handle and lug it to the tabletop.

As Daniel tears open a bag of plastic cups, Kevin handles the packets of granola bars, pretzels, and trail mix. They move rhythmically, and Daniel wonders if his teammate still harbors any resentment over their assignment switch. He's not about to ask though.

"I've got the 5K covered," Kevin suddenly speaks up. "It's up to you and Jiwon to decimate the 3K and 10K."

"No sweat," Daniel replies, hoping it's true.

Kevin finishes stacking the snacks, but instead of walking off to Owen, he regards Daniel with a loaded gaze. "It's a good thing you joined the team," he says. "Because of you, we might make regionals or even championships in my senior year."

The praise punctures Daniel like a vaccination shot. He waits for a bitter follow-up, but Kevin only grins approvingly.

"Thanks," Daniel replies. A warm sensation fans his chest.

Kevin nods. "For what it's worth, you're good for Jiwon. I'm not just talking about some healthy competition. I was really worried about him last year, when his mom passed away, but now he's back to his old self again."

The vague comment implies that Kevin suspects more than friendship between them, but the look on his face swears off any judgment. Whether Daniel is reading too much into Kevin's words, he realizes that in the world of sports, a relationship between two boys might not really matter to some. Common goals and camaraderie could trump minor differences.

But coming out to Kevin is Jiwon's battle, so Daniel just smiles as they leave the refreshment table with their unspoken questions left unanswered.

Jiwon and most of the team have kickstarted a series of warm-up exercises. Even though Daniel should join them, he can't help but do another sweep of the six qualifying teams. His eyes settle on the crimson and black Cambry uniforms. In their midst, Francisco, Khalil, and Karter rush through a flurry of static high-knees. As much as Daniel wishes he didn't care, his adrenaline picks up, spurred by a deep-seated desire to beat them.

He fills his lungs, counting seven-second inhales and ten-second exhales. His heart pounds, but he won't be risking another water cramp. Deep breathing will have to get him through the meet.

Not far from Cambry's tent, a congregation of supporters steadily gathers on the grass. He spies a girl with gold hair and sunglasses who shares a striking resemblance to Amber. She chatters away with a friend. While Daniel is curious, he's not about to leave the team when the 3K could kick off at any minute. Then, the girl turns toward him and waves—a flash of amity upon a sea of nerves.

He wonders what Amber would say if he told her about Jiwon. He smiles. She would probably shrug, hand him a piece of gum, and say that Jiwon is a pretty good catch. Then, she'd offer him a cheat sheet. At least, Daniel hopes that's how she'd react.

"Finish your warm-up!" Coach Rasmussen shouts as he returns from the announcer's booth. Daniel hurries to Jiwon's side and launches into side shuffles.

"How are you feeling?" Jiwon asks.

"Honestly? A little sick."

The team switches to basic quad stretches. "You took on your parents," Jiwon says with a hint of the same grin that lit his face when he read Daniel's texts on the bus. "You can do anything."

While he appreciates Jiwon's encouragement, he can't swallow it. He wants to be as gutsy as Peter Pan, to be fearless and fly, but his legs feel leaden, despite the warm-up.

When the 3K runners are called to the starting line, Daniel channels all his focus into pinning his number to his shirt. He can't look at Karter now. One sly sneer might shatter him. Instead, he focuses on his strategy. Given that he has never run at Huxley before, the 3K will mostly serve as a course introduction. He won't push it. Given the number of top-tier runners, he'll aim for somewhere between fifth and seventh.

Readying for the starting gun, he settles into a solid alignment and measures his breath. The blank shot fires. The runners dive forward, chasing the dream of regionals. Only three teams will make the cut.

As predicted, the average pace is much slower than a typical 3K. A few overeager racers blitz ahead, but a series of hills dampens their ambitions. Daniel snags a sustainable sixth and plans to funnel his efforts into maintaining it.

He tries to concentrate on his own run, on the orange cones and rough terrain. A few hidden ponds glisten like fairies dancing in the white sun. He wants to focus on these small details, but his brain rebels, zeroing in on the runners ahead of him. The unmistakable figures of Francisco and Khalil steamroll onward. Karter dashes on and on, the number 014 swaying on his back. An unfamiliar competitor races among them, and Jiwon—016 blazing on. From his vantage point, each runner seems neck-and-neck.

The canopy tents come into view, and the crowd roars louder than at their previous meets. Mere seconds separating one runner from the next, they cross the finish line. The place card in Daniel's hand doesn't surprise him. Sixth of twenty-one is a welcome score, even if Cambry outdid him. Now he knows the course and can run harder in the 10K. If he keeps his cool, maybe he stands a chance in the top three.

The announcer bellows numbers and school names as the remaining runners complete the lap. Daniel tunes him out. He searches for Jiwon, wanting to learn how he fared.

As expected, Jiwon is jogging around Cranbrook's tent. With Coach Rasmussen scouting the finish line, Daniel eases into his cool down beside him. Before he can ask, Jiwon gives him an update.

"Third. Behind Karter and another one of Cambry's. 012."

"Probably Francisco," Daniel guesses. "I got sixth."

"Perfect. We performed well enough to stand a chance at first and didn't spend up all our energy. We're saving it for the 10K. We're gonna thrash them."

Jiwon's blinding optimism overflows into Daniel's wavering hopes. Even so, taking out Cambry's top three seems like a matter of luck more than speed.

They nab two cups of water and take a seat beneath the tent. Owen arrives a minute later, announcing his ninth-place spot. Coach Rasmussen is so satisfied with the results that he doesn't notice Daniel and Jiwon's proximity.

There's little time to celebrate before the announcer summons the 5K runners. Jayden and Kevin bury their jitters and set off at the sound of the pistol. Once the racers speed out of sight, Jiwon presses his outstretched leg against Daniel. The light touch grounds him, keeping Neverland at bay.

"There will be a big party tonight," Jiwon says.

Daniel sips his water. "Do you want to go? I could also ask Nana if you can come over. My parents are out of town, remember?"

"You think Nana would be okay with that?"

"I do," he says honestly, "but I'll text her first."

Jiwon taps his foot against Daniel's spikes. "Let's do both. I'll come over, and then we can go to the party later."

Depending on how the 10K turns out, Daniel's response could go either way. "I could do that," he says, clinging to confidence.

"Will Nana be okay with that?" A mischievous grin curls Jiwon's lips.

Daniel laughs. "I won't be texting her about the party."

When the 5K runners appear around the bend, Daniel and Jiwon hop to their feet. Crimson colors the first two racers, but Kevin follows in third. Jiwon paces excitedly, shouting Kevin's name. Not long after, Jayden darts across the finish line.

"Seventh, Cranbrook, number 031," the announcer cries out. Cranbrook is either holding second or third, but Daniel and Jiwon are too amped by the results to do the math.

From the corner of his eye, Daniel spots Amber among the crowd. She and her friend are jumping for joy. Not far off, Francisco, Khalil, and Karter are warming up again. Daniel's throat runs dry. At least Karter is too focused on the upcoming contest to saunter over and spew taunts.

With no time to mull over possible altercations, Daniel falls into last-minute stretches with Owen and Jiwon. The race starter calls them to line up, and to Daniel's dismay, his hands are shaking.

Jiwon and Owen stand beside him. Their eyes stare straight ahead. He tries to see what they see, the goals they strive to accomplish. For Owen, the race represents a new PR or perhaps a chance to prove his worth to Coach Rasmussen. Jiwon aims for championships, for a scholarship, for proof that he made the right choice when he gave up dance for sports.

Why does Daniel run?

The starting gun splits his thoughts. He throws himself forward, posture perfect, breath even. The initial swarm of runners thins as talent and strategy divide them. The 10K will take them through two laps on the 5K course. The first round will be easy. The second will separate the great from the good.

The screams of the crowd and shouts of the announcer greet them at the end of the first five kilometers. Their excitement melds into one explosive rumble and mixes with Daniel's hastened heartbeat and labored breath. He dashes forward, legs pumping over hills. A twig snaps at his heels. It's just him, racing in his own body, against all that has tried to stop him.

Daniel loves running, but he doesn't want to run from Sung-Min and Monica, or from himself, anymore. He wants to win for his team. *For himself.*

A ray of sunlight pierces a nearby pond, spraying prisms of light. A single swan floats on the surface. The bird watches him. Daniel knows that he and the swan are nothing alike. One can fly. The other is just a boy on two legs, doing what he loves most.

Daniel spreads his wings, but he isn't flying into the sun. He shakes off Neverland's pixie dust. He soars with his feet on the ground, and he doesn't want to reach the sky. He wants to stay in his own skin.

The final kilometer of the course opens up before him. He glides toward the opposing racers. His stride increases. His chest catches on brilliant fire. It takes only a moment to pass Khalil, then Francisco.

Ahead, the crowd chants. Karter is ahead and Daniel knows he can't overtake him in the few remaining meters, but suddenly that seems unimportant. All that matters is his legs moving like magic, his arms pumping at his sides, and the breath flowing through his lungs.

He sees Jiwon in the distance, the unstoppable number 016. Jiwon, meters ahead of Karter, and the white tape a hand's breadth away.

It's like Karter isn't even there. It's just the two of them, pressing on to the finish line.

The End

About the Author

Lauren Melissa Ellzey—known as @autienelle on Instagram—is a Black multiracial, queer, and autistic activist and advice columnist. Her work has crossed paths with *NeuroClastic*, *Cripple Media*, *BBC Minute*, *Healthline*, and *AbleZine*. She completed her BA at Scripps College, where she won the Crombie Allen Award for creative writing, and her MS LIS at Syracuse University. Lauren Melissa resides and works in New York City.

Books Available from Bold Strokes Books

Boy at the Window by Lauren Melissa Ellzey. Daniel Kim struggles to hold onto reality while haunted by both his very-present past and his never-present parents. Jiwon Yoon may be the only one who can break Daniel free. (978-1-63679-092-3)

Deadly Secrets by VK Powell. Corporate criminals want whistleblower Jana Elliott permanently silenced, but Rafe Silva will risk everything to keep the woman she loves safe. (978-1-63679-087-9)

Enchanted Autumn by Ursula Klein. When Elizabeth comes to Salem, Massachusetts, to study the witch trials, she never expects to find love—or an actual witch…and Hazel might just turn out to be both. (978-1-63679-104-3)

Escorted by Renee Roman. When fantasy meets reality, will escort Ryan Lewis be able to walk away from a chance at forever with her new client Dani? (978-1-63679-039-8)

Her Heart's Desire by Anne Shade. Two women. One choice. Will Eve and Lynette be able to overcome their doubts and fears to embrace their deepest desire? (978-1-63679-102-9)

My Secret Valentine by Julie Cannon, Erin Dutton, & Anne Shade. Winning the heart of your secret Valentine? These award-winning authors agree, there is no better way to fall in love. (978-1-63679-071-8)

Perilous Obsession by Carsen Taite. When reporter Macy Moran becomes consumed with solving a cold case, will her quest for the truth bring her closer to Detective Beck Ramsey or will her obsession with finding a murderer rob her of a chance at true love? (978-1-63679-009-1)

Reading Her by Amanda Radley. Lauren and Allegra learn love and happiness are right where they least expect it. There's just one problem: Lauren has a secret she cannot tell anyone, and Allegra knows she's hiding something. (978-1-63679-075-6)

The Willing by Lyn Hemphill. Kitty Wilson doesn't know how, but she can bring people back from the dead as long as someone is willing to take their place and keep the universe in balance. (978-1-63679-083-1)

Three Left Turns to Nowhere by Nathan Burgoine, J. Marshall Freeman, & Jeffrey Ricker. Three strangers heading to a convention in Toronto are stranded in rural Ontario, where a small town with a subtle kind of magic leads each to discover what he's been searching for. (978-1-63679-050-3)

Watching Over Her by Ronica Black. As they face the snowstorm of the century, and the looming threat of a stalker, Riley and Zoey just might find love in the most unexpected of places. (978-1-63679-100-5)

#shedeservedit by Greg Herren. When his gay best friend, and high school football star, is murdered, Alex Wheeler is a suspect and must find the truth to clear himself. (978-1-63555-996-5)

Always by Kris Bryant. When a pushy American private investigator shows up demanding to meet the woman in Camila's artwork, instead of introducing her to her great-grandmother, Camila decides to lead her on a wild goose chase all over Italy. (978-1-63679-027-5)

Exes and O's by Joy Argento. Ali and Madison really only have one thing in common. The girl who broke their heart may be the only one who can put it back together. (978-1-63679-017-6)

One Verse Multi by Sander Santiago. Life was good: promotion, friends, falling in love, discovering that the multi-verse is on a fast track to collision—wait, what? Good thing Martin King works for a company that can fix the problem, right...um...right? (978-1-63679-069-5)

Paris Rules by Jaime Maddox. Carly Becker has been searching for the perfect woman all her life, but no one ever seems to be just right until Paige Waterford checks all her boxes, except the most important one—she's married. (978-1-63679-077-0)

Shadow Dancers by Suzie Clarke. In this third and final book in the Moon Shadow series, Rachel must find a way to become the hunter and not the hunted, and this time she will meet Ehsee Yumiko head-on. (978-1-63555-829-6)

The Kiss by C.A. Popovich. When her wife refuses their divorce and begins to stalk her, threatening her life, Kate realizes to protect her new love, Leslie, she has to let her go, even if it breaks her heart. (978-1-63679-079-4)

The Wedding Setup by Charlotte Greene. When Ryann, a big-time New York executive, goes to Colorado to help out with her best friend's wedding, she never expects to fall for the maid of honor. (978-1-63679-033-6)

Velocity by Gun Brooke. Holly and Claire work toward an uncertain future preparing for an alien space mission, and only one thing is for certain, they will have to risk their lives, and their hearts, to discover the truth. (978-1-63555-983-5)

Wildflower Words by Sam Ledel. Lida Jones treks West with her father in search of a better life on the rapidly developing American frontier, but finds home when she meets Hazel Thompson. (978-1-63679-055-8)

A Fairer Tomorrow by Kathleen Knowles. For Maddie Weeks and Gerry Stern, the Second World War brought them together, but the end of the war might rip them apart. (978-1-63555-874-6)

Holiday Hearts by Diana Day-Admire and Lyn Cole. Opposites attract during Christmastime chaos in Kansas City. (978-1-63679-128-9)

Changing Majors by Ana Hartnett Reichardt. Beyond a love, beyond a coming-out, Bailey Sullivan discovers what lies beyond the shame and self-doubt imposed on her by traditional Southern ideals. (978-1-63679-081-7)

Fresh Grave in Grand Canyon by Lee Patton. The age-old Grand Canyon becomes more and more ominous as a group of volunteers fight to survive alone in nature and uncover a murderer among them. (978-1-63679-047-3)

Highland Whirl by Anna Larner. Opposites attract in the Scottish Highlands, when feisty Alice Campbell falls for city-girl-about-town Roxanne Barns. (978-1-63555-892-0)

Humbug by Amanda Radley. With the corporate Christmas party in jeopardy, CEO Rosalind Caldwell hires Christmas Girl Ellie Pearce as her personal assistant. The only problem is, Ellie isn't a PA, has never planned a party, and develops a ridiculous crush on her totally intimidating new boss. (978-1-63555-965-1)

On the Rocks by Georgia Beers. Schoolteacher Vanessa Martini makes no apologies for her dating checklist, and newly single mom Grace Chapman ticks all Vanessa's Do Not Date boxes. Of course, they're never going to fall in love. (978-1-63555-989-7)

Song of Serenity by Brey Willows. Arguing with the Muse of music and justice is complicated, falling in love with her even more so. (978-1-63679-015-2)

The Christmas Proposal by Lisa Moreau. Stranded together in a Christmas village on a snowy mountain, Grace and Bridget face their past and question their dreams for the future. (978-1-63555-648-3)

The Infinite Summer by Morgan Lee Miller. While spending the summer with her dad in a small beach town, Remi Brenner falls for Harper Hebert and accidentally finds herself tangled up in an intense restaurant rivalry between her famous stepmom and her first love. (978-1-63555-969-9)

Wisdom by Jesse J. Thoma. When Sophia and Reggie are chosen for the governor's new community design team and tasked with tackling substance abuse and mental health issues, battle lines are drawn even as sparks fly. (978-1-63555-886-9)

A Convenient Arrangement by Aurora Rey and Jaime Clevenger. Cuffing season has come for lesbians, and for Jess Archer and Cody Dawson, their convenient arrangement becomes anything but. (978-1-63555-818-0)

An Alaskan Wedding by Nance Sparks. The last thing either Andrea or Riley expects is to bump into the one who broke her heart fifteen years ago, but when they meet at the welcome party, their feelings come rushing back. (978-1-63679-053-4)

Beulah Lodge by Cathy Dunnell. It's 1874, and newly engaged Ruth Mallowes is set on marriage and life as a missionary...until she falls in love with the housemaid at Beulah Lodge. (978-1-63679-007-7)

Gia's Gems by Toni Logan. When Lindsey Speyer discovers that popular travel columnist Gia Williams is a complete fake and threatens to expose her, blackmail has never been so sexy. (978-1-63555-917-0)

Holiday Wishes & Mistletoe Kisses by M. Ullrich. Four holidays, four couples, four chances to make their wishes come true. (978-1-63555-760-2)

Love By Proxy by Dena Blake. Tess has a secret crush on her best friend, Sophie, so the last thing she wants is to help Sophie fall in love with someone else, but how can she stand in the way of her happiness? (978-1-63555-973-6)

Loyalty, Love, & Vermouth by Eric Peterson. A comic valentine to a gay man's family of choice, including the ones with cold noses and four paws. (978-1-63555-997-2)

Marry Me by Melissa Brayden. Allison Hale attempts to plan the wedding of the century to a man who could save her family's business, if only she wasn't falling for her wedding planner, Megan Kinkaid. (978-1-63555-932-3)

Pathway to Love by Radclyffe. Courtney Valentine is looking for a woman exactly like Ben—smart, sexy, and not in the market for anything serious. All she has to do is convince Ben that sex-without-strings is the perfect pathway to pleasure. (978-1-63679-110-4)

Sweet Surprise by Jenny Frame. Flora and Mac never thought they'd ever see each other again, but when Mac opens up her barber shop right next to Flora's sweet shop, their connection comes roaring back. (978-1-63679-001-5)

The Edge of Yesterday by CJ Birch. Easton Gray is sent from the future to save humanity from technological disaster. When she's forced to target the woman she's falling in love with, can Easton do what's needed to save humanity? (978-1-63679-025-1)

The Scout and the Scoundrel by Barbara Ann Wright. With unexpected danger surrounding them, Zara and Roni are stuck between duty and survival, with little room for exploring their feelings, especially love. (978-1-63555-978-1)

Bury Me in Shadows by Greg Herren. College student Jake Chapman is forced to spend the summer at his dying grandmother's home and soon finds danger from long-buried family secrets. (978-1-63555-993-4)

Can't Leave Love by Kimberly Cooper Griffin. Sophia and Pru have no intention of falling in love, but sometimes love happens when and where you least expect it. (978-1-636790041-1)

Free Fall at Angel Creek by Julie Tizard. Detective Dee Rawlings and aircraft accident investigator Dr. River Dawson use conflicting methods to find answers when a plane goes missing, while overcoming surprising threats, and discovering an unlikely chance at love. (978-1-63555-884-5)

Love's Compromise by Cass Sellars. For Piper Holthaus and Brook Myers, will professional dreams and past baggage stop two hearts from realizing they are meant for each other? (978-1-63555-942-2)

Not All a Dream by Sophia Kell Hagin. Hester has lost the woman she loved and the world has descended into relentless dark and cold. But giving up will have to wait when she stumbles upon people who help her survive. (978-1-63679-067-1)

Protecting the Lady by Amanda Radley. If Eve Webb had known she'd be protecting royalty, she'd never have taken the job as bodyguard, but as the threat to Lady Katherine's life draws closer, she'll do whatever it takes to save her, and may just lose her heart in the process. (978-1-63679-003-9)

The Secrets of Willowra by Kadyan. A family saga of three women, their homestead called Willowra in the Australian outback, and the secrets that link them all. (978-1-63679-064-0)

Trial by Fire by Carsen Taite. When prosecutor Lennox Roy and public defender Wren Bishop become fierce adversaries in a headline-grabbing arson case, their attraction ignites a passion that leads them both to question their assumptions about the law, the truth, and each other. (978-1-63555-860-9)

Turbulent Waves by Ali Vali. Kai Merlin and Vivien Palmer plan their future together as hostile forces make their own plans to destroy what they have, as well as all those they love. (978-1-63679-011-4)

Unbreakable by Cari Hunter. When Dr. Grace Kendal is forced at gunpoint to help an injured woman, she is dragged into a nightmare where nothing is quite as it seems, and their lives aren't the only ones on the line. (978-1-63555-961-3)

Veterinary Surgeon by Nancy Wheelton. When dangerous drugs are stolen from the veterinary clinic, Mitch investigates and Kay becomes a suspect. As pride and professions clash, love seems impossible. (978-1-63679-043-5)